"Lark Chadwick is my hero! A true investigative reporter in every sense of the word, Lark reminds me of me in the early days of my career: driven by curiosity and the need to unravel true and compelling stories. It's no surprise that veteran journalist John DeDakis so accurately depicts the life and work of a reporter and how a complicated mystery gets solved. But how DeDakis can so accurately write from a woman's point of view – with all the intrinsic curiosity, emotion and passion – is nothing short of astounding. The public rarely gets a glimpse of what an investigative reporter's life is like: the curiosity-propelled pursuit of a story, the loneliness and the inherent danger in many assignments. That's the real untold tale of how meaningful journalism gets to the public. I want more Lark Chadwick adventures!"
—*Diane Dimond / Author and Investigative Journalist*

"I raced right through it. Definitely hard to put down! John DeDakis is a masterful storyteller who has adroitly woven several story lines into this fast-paced page-turner. With true-to-life characters and an insider's knowledge of the world of journalism, the second of DeDakis' Lark Chadwick mysteries will not disappoint fans of *Fast Track*."
—*Charlene Fu*
Former Veteran Foreign Correspondent for the Associated Press

"Lark is like an old friend. I'm glad she's back and as fierce as ever. *Bluff* is a good, fast read. I can't wait until the next adventure."
—*Carol Costello*
Former CNN Anchor / Journalism Lecturer, Loyola Marymount Univ.

"In his first novel, *Fast Track,* John DeDakis introduced his readers to the impulsive 25-year-old Lark Chadwick as she investigated the mysterious death of her aunt. Now, in *Bluff*, he continues to unveil the hidden truths in Lark's past and the hair-raising dangers she once again encounters in her new role as an investigative reporter. Using his own forty-five years of experience as a broadcast journalist, of which the past twenty-five years have been as a Copy Editor at CNN, John reveals the sinister twists in Lark's life as she desperately searches for the truth under the watchful eye of retired *New York Times* editor Lionel Stone. The outcome is unpredictable; the story, unforgettable. A great read!"
Barbara Casey / Author and Literary Agent

Praise for *Fast Track:*

"*Fast Track* is one of those rare novels that you simply can't put down. I was hooked on page one and it was non-stop until the very end—an emotional roller coaster."
Wolf Blitzer / CNN Anchor, "The Situation Room"

"From a heart-breaking opening to a heart-stopping finale, this story kept me turning pages. A well-crafted and exciting novel."
Patricia Sprinkle
Former National President, Sisters in Crime

"Another Hemingway, but better. John DeDakis writes with clarity, sensitivity, and passion."
Patricia Daley-Lipe, Ph.D. / National League of American Pen Women

"It kept me on the edge of my seat until the very last page. John DeDakis is a skilled writer."
Jennifer Sparks / Barnes & Noble

"*Fast Track* sucked me in and kept me up half the night."
Judy Boysha / AP Radio

"DeDakis crawls inside the mind of a twenty-something female, authentically capturing her character, curiosity and self-expression in this can't-put-down thriller."
Kris Kosach / ABC Radio

Praise for *Troubled Water:*

"As a young female journalist, I spent most of this novel wondering how John DeDakis got into my head. *Troubled Water* is sharp, suspenseful and – most importantly – utterly believable."
Jenna Bourne / Investigative Reporter
10 Tampa Bay, WTSP-TV (CBS)

"What happens when you pair a cub reporter with murder, mayhem, and a handsome bad boy? A great read. Once again, John DeDakis proves he knows how to write a gripping thriller. I loved it."
Jillian Harding / Former Producer CNBC, CBS

Books by John DeDakis

Lark Chadwick mysteries
Fast Track
Bluff
Troubled Water
Bullet in the Chamber
Fake

Bluff

A Lark Chadwick Mystery

SPEAKING VOLUMES, LLC
NAPLES, FLORIDA
2021

Bluff

ISBN 978-1-64540-413-2

To Darlene

Bluff

A Lark Chadwick Mystery

John DeDakis

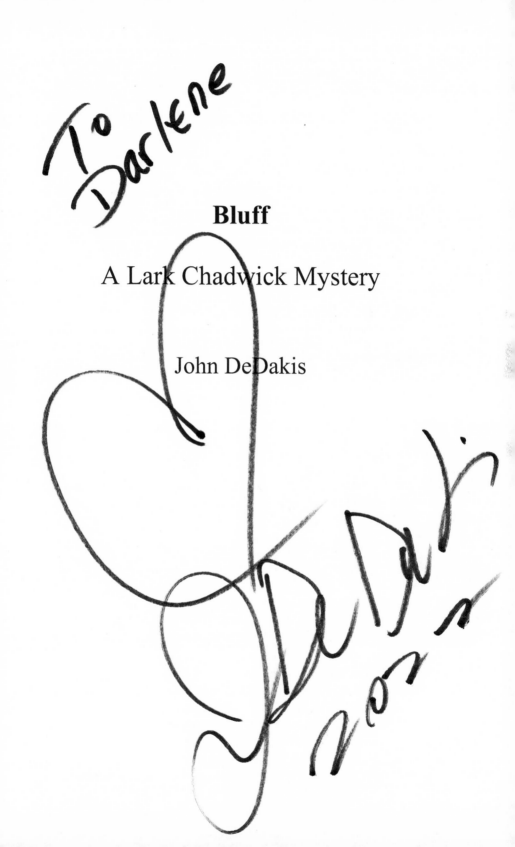

To the memory of:
Myles Allen
Beth Pollard Hancock
Peter Dean Lakin
Marsh Shapiro

Acknowledgments

Writing is a solitary endeavor, but it should also make a connection with others. In the more than fifteen years since the debut of my first novel, *Fast Track*, in 2005, I've been amazed and blessed to have connected with so many new people – not only all around the United States, but in many other countries, as well. Through conversations at speaking events, book signings, writing workshops, on Facebook, in emails, over a glass of wine, or walking the D.C. Mall, these new friends have added so much joy, fulfillment, and meaning to my life. To you, and to my future friends, a special thank you.

Many people helped bring this book to fruition. First, and foremost, an author needs people who will generously give of their time to read the manuscript and then give honest feedback about what needs improving. The following people told me what I needed to hear: Alan Audet, Hugh Brown, Bernadette Watts, Lilia Trujillo Bullock, Mandy Carranza, Barbara Casey, Susan Fitzgerald Carter, Caroline Comport, Cynthia DeDakis, Emily DeDakis, James DeDakis, Sarah Gerdes, Karen Hallacy, Carolyn Presutti, and Lisa Sileo.

I'm also indebted to Justin Tuttle, Erin Klingele, and Nathan Leedy of the Visalia, California Public Defenders' Office. I met them while doing research for this book in Peru when we were there to hike the Inca Trail to Machu Picchu. Their visit to the morgue in Cusco added details that supplemented my own observations of the place.

For insights into how next-of-kin notifications are handled for Americans who die abroad, I received help from my friend and D.C. neighbor, former U.S. Ambassador Mike Senko, and his contacts at the U.S. State Department—Greg Morrison and Jeffrey Vick.

For historical insights into Peru, I learned much from the book *The Last Days of the Incas* by Kim MacQuarrie. It's a vivid account of what amounts to the rape of a civilization.

Thanks also to my friend Lowell Mays of Madison, Wisconsin for his wise counsel. Lowell has been a long-time sounding board for me, dating back to at least 1980 when I consulted with him on a documentary on grief I produced when I was a reporter at WMTV (NBC-15). Lowell was one of the officials on the scene the day my sister took her life. As a blurb for the paperback edition of *Fast Track,* Lowell wrote, "This is vintage DeDakis. I first knew him in the midst of tragedy. Hope followed." It certainly did, my friend – and you helped.

I'm indebted to D.C. District Judge Russell F. Canan for suggestions that make this 2021 edition of *Bluff* more legally accurate than the earlier version.

Garry Dinnerman, of Beverly Grant & Associates (BGA) in Atlanta, worked passionately and diligently for many years to bring the exploits of my heroine Lark Chadwick to the attention of Hollywood. Thank you, Garry, for all your efforts.

And then there are the people behind the scenes who brought *Bluff* into being:

Barbara Casey has been my agent and champion since 2004 when we met at the Harriette Austin Writers' Conference at the University of Georgia in Athens. She put the *Fast Track* and *Bluff* manuscripts in front of Robert Gelinas, publisher of ArcheBooks. Thanks, Bob, for taking a risk on this unknown writer.

Thank you to Kurt Mueller of Speaking Volumes. Kurt resurrected and re-issued *Fast Track* and *Bluff* when they went out of print at the beginning of 2020.

I'm humbled by the support and encouragement you all have given to me.

Finally, a big hug and kiss for my wife Cindy who has graciously made room in our forty-two year marriage for Lark and Lionel.

For all of the above reasons, I continue to be blessed.

John DeDakis
November 2010
Washington, DC
Revised December 2020
Baltimore, Maryland

Chapter One

My hand trembled as I gripped the shiny-smooth ebony fountain pen. I took a deep breath. It's not easy signing over a treasured place I've known and loved all my life. But putting my signature on the document transferring ownership of Grampa's farm to realtor Shane L. Duran became easier when I remembered how rich I was about to become. Until now, life had been pretty much hand-to-mouth for me.

Lark Chadwick, I wrote neatly. So neatly, in fact, the name printed below my signature was unnecessary.

Shane sat across from me, dwarfed by his massive mahogany desk.

"You've just become very wealthy, Wonder Woman."

"Why do you keep calling me that?" I put the cap back on the pen and slid it across the desk to Shane.

"Haven't I ever told you? You look just like Lynda Carter."

"Who?"

"The babe who plays Wonder Woman on the Sci-Fi channel."

"You watch the Sci-Fi Channel?"

"But she shows more cleavage than you," he grinned.

"You're disgusting."

"You hide the goods under those baggy sweaters."

I grimaced.

"Keep those tight jeans, though," he smirked.

"Stop it, Shane. Your sexism is showing." I would've stood to leave, but he still had to write me a check. A big check.

"You know me all too well, Lark."

"Actually, I don't, and I'd sort of like to keep it that way."

"Ah, Lark, Lark," he chuckled, "you really should go out with me. You don't know what you're missing."

"If I asked your first two wives, I bet I'd get a thorough update."

He sighed. "They never understood me."

"Or maybe they understood you all too well."

His leering had become obnoxious long before, but at least he was up front about it. We'd met a few months earlier when he approached me to see if I'd sell Grampa's property. At first Shane was just flirty, but when I'd made it clear I wasn't the least bit interested in him, he settled into being his normal, loutish self, instead of pretending to be the charming gentleman we both knew he wasn't. To me, the relationship was purely business—and most importantly, he was willing to pay me way more than anyone else.

He opened the top drawer of his desk and brought out two cigars the size of calves' legs. "Join me for a celebratory stogie?"

I made a face. "Ugh. Thanks, but no thanks."

He looked hurt. "You sure? They're the best. Koenigshavens. Fit for a king, but priced for the common man, or, in your case, babe. Five bucks a stick, and I can get 'em at the drug store."

Shane put one of the cigars back into the top desk drawer and slid it shut after taking out a long, wood-stick match. With a flourish, he struck it on a huge rock paperweight sitting on the edge of his desk. The dark granite stone had a thick base and tapered top. It must have weighed at least five pounds.

He powered up the cigar with the match and, in no time, a mushroom cloud of thick, gray smoke chimneyed toward the ceiling.

The smell of burning rubber was making me gag.

"So, tell me again. What are you going to do with Grampa's farm?" I asked, pushing my chair back to get away from the cigar stench.

"Location, location, location," he said, waving out the match and tossing it onto a glass coaster on his desk. He leaned back in his black leather throne and crossed his tasseled loafers atop his colossus of a desk.

"The property is perched nicely along the banks of the Rock River." He took a drag and blew a nimbus over my head. "Gonna develop it."

"Don't forget what you promised me about the trees," I said, wagging my finger at him, then coughed and tried to wave away the cigar smoke as it descended onto me.

"Right. Don't worry. I'll keep as many of those elms, oaks, and pines as possible. At least on that, you and I agree wholeheartedly," he winked. "So, whatcha gonna do with the money?"

"You have to write the check first." I nodded at the pen on the desk in front of him.

"Oh. That," he snorted. "Details." He made a dismissive wave of his hand, took his feet off the desk, and rolled his chair forward.

"Do it fast," I said, holding my nose. "I'm dying here."

He pulled a checkbook from the top drawer of his desk and began writing. "Geez, I haven't written a check this big in a long time," he said, guiding the pen across the pale green paper.

I watched, feeling giddy and a bit light-headed—and not only because the cigar smoke was suffocating me.

Shane blotted the ink and blew on it before tearing the page from his checkbook. As he handed the check to me across his desk, the shiny finish of the polished top reflected his French cuffs.

I accepted his check with a grin. "Thanks."

He sat back, crossed his legs, and took another drag. "So…travel? A new car? A house? Clothes? All of the above? What?"

"Not sure," I said. "Next stop is the bank. Then…well…we'll see. I'm so used to being without funds, I think I'd just like to let it sit and earn interest. Maybe invest it in something that will grow, and set aside a little bit in savings that I can get at easily for emergencies."

Shane nodded thoughtfully as he puffed a few times on the cigar. "You're a very wise young lady." His face was wreathed in gray smoke. "Not to mention being a fox."

Normally, that would have been my cue to scold him again and leave, but I wasn't listening. I was eyeing the check. Something wasn't right about it.

I sat up straight in my chair. "Hey, wait a minute!" I said, alarmed.

"What?" He scowled.

"There's something wrong here."

"What are you talking about?" He uncrossed his legs and leaned forward.

"You wrote the wrong amount on the check."

"No, I didn't."

"You did. It's supposed to be for $475,000 and change."

"No, it's not."

"Instead, you wrote me a check for $47,550. That's a big difference."

"I wrote it for that because we agreed on that." He waved the cigar at me dismissively and sat back in his chair.

"No. We didn't." I drilled him with my eyes.

"Look at the contract you signed." With his fingertips, he gave it a gentle push. It slid across the desk and came to a stop beneath my nose.

I put down the check and riffled through the document until I found the correct page. He was right. My signature committed me to accept $47,550 for Grampa's farm, but that's not what we'd agreed upon verbally. I was sure of it.

I slapped the contract onto the desk in disgust. "Shane. How can you do this to me?"

"Do what?" He looked hurt.

"Do you think I'm just some dumb broad who wouldn't notice?"

"Well—"

"Nice try, Shane." I picked up the check for more money than I'd ever had in my entire life, tore it into tiny pieces, and poured the scraps into my messenger bag.

"I still have your signed contract," he said, reaching across his desk for the papers in front of me.

"No. You don't," I hollered. I pounced from my chair and snatched the document before he could pick it up. "This contract is null and void." The pages flopped as I shook them at his face. Angrily, I shredded the closing statement with both hands, jammed the pieces into my bag and headed for the door.

"Lark! Wait!" he called after me. "You're making a big mistake."

I got to the door, spun around, and glared at him.

"My big mistake," I hissed, "was trusting you, Shane Duran. But I'm over that."

I could barely see him through all the cigar smoke as he sat slumped in his chair, mouth hanging open in disbelief.

I made sure to slam the door when I left.

Chapter Two

I was still seething as I stalked out of Shane's office and onto the sidewalk of Main Street, Pine Bluff, Wisconsin, population 21,303 and growing.

It was a dazzlingly bright spring morning a few weeks after my twenty-sixth birthday. Shane Duran's real estate office is on the south side of Main, on the shady side, I noted ruefully.

Dodging traffic, I trotted across Main for the two-block walk to the *Pine Bluff Standard*, the weekly newspaper where I'd been working as a reporter for the past six months.

The sun felt good. I tried to calm myself by breathing in deep gulps of the fresh, sweet-smelling air. At the center of the bridge over the Rock River, which cuts through the center of town, I paused to gaze at the water as it passed lazily beneath me.

"How could you be so stupid?" I asked my reflection.

Slowly, sadly, she shook her head at me.

Looking up, I saw my boss and mentor Lionel Stone sitting with a man and woman on a bench on the east bank of Riverside Park. After a moment, they all stood. It looked like their conversation was coming to an end, so I pushed myself back from the steel railing, hurried over the bridge and turned left into the park. I wanted to intercept Lionel on his way back to the office so that I could tell him about my run-in with Shane.

Lionel smiled as he saw me approach. "There she is," he called, jauntily.

The two people talking with Lionel turned around to look at me.

Before you go," he said to them, "I want to introduce you to Lark Chadwick, my star reporter. Lark, this is Laura and William Benedict. They're on their honeymoon."

"Congratulations," I said, with as much enthusiasm as I could muster under the circumstances. I shook their hands.

"Thanks," Laura said. She seemed to be the more outgoing of the two. She wore a yellow windbreaker and a red scarf around her head like a bandana. She was plumpish and probably outweighed William by twenty-five pounds at least.

He wore a dark gray down jacket. I guessed them to be in their late twenties.

"Pine Bluff's a great place," I said, "but why are you honeymooning here?"

"Oh, we're just passing through," Laura said. "We wanted to say hi to Holly's dad." She nodded toward Lionel.

"They were on the trip with Holly when she died," Lionel explained.

Holly had been dead for two years.

"We should be going, Mr. Stone," Laura said, turning back to Lionel. "Thanks for taking the time to talk with us."

"Long overdue," he replied.

"Do you mind if I take a picture of you?" Laura asked.

"Not at all," Lionel laughed, "but please don't sue me if I break the camera."

"I'd be glad to do the honors," I offered. "That way all three of you can be in the shot."

"That would be wonderful," Laura said, digging a compact silver camera from her jacket pocket. After fiddling with it, she handed it to me. "Just push this," she instructed, pointing to a button on top.

"Is it digital?" I asked.

"Uh huh. I'll email you a copy, Mr. Stone," she said turning again to Lionel.

"Let's move closer to the river bank," I suggested.

As we edged that way, Laura said to William, "Thor, you stand on one side of Mr. Stone and I'll stand on the other."

"Thor?" I asked, confused, "I thought your name is William."

"Thor's a nickname," he smiled sheepishly. "Long story."

I had to bite my lip to keep from laughing out loud. William's fragile build and meek temperament made him extremely UN-Thor-like.

I pride myself on taking good pictures. Most people stand so far back from their subject that much of the shot is framed by extraneous stuff. In the tableaux I saw through the viewfinder, William stood to Lionel's right and Laura on his left.

I stood close enough so that they filled the frame. Slightly out-of-focus portions of the Rock River flowed behind them from the top right to the lower left.

"On the count of three, everyone," I called. "Say cheese! One… two…Lionel, you're not smiling."

"Cheese," he grumped, clenching his teeth.

I snapped the shutter and inspected my handiwork. "Nice," I said, handing the camera back to Laura.

"Thanks again, Mr. Stone," Laura said, hugging Lionel, who then shook hands with William, a.k.a. Thor.

"Keep in touch," Lionel said to them.

After saying goodbye to me, Laura took William's hand and they walked along the sidewalk that curved up toward Main Street.

"They're nice," I said.

"Uh huh." Lionel sighed. He stooped to pick up a stone and tossed it into the water. Then he sat down on the park bench. Listlessly, he scooped up more pebbles and, one by one, pitched them into the river.

I walked over to where he sat. "Is this seat taken, sir?" I asked.

Lionel shifted his bulk to make a little room for me.

I sat next to him. "You okay? You seem a little bummed."

He flung a stone into the water, harder this time. Wisps of his white hair blew in the slight breeze. He wore a dark suit, white shirt, and a conservative tie with diagonal blue and red stripes.

"I tried to close on Grampa's farm today," I offered, trying to get something started.

"*Tried* to close?"

Quickly, I told him what happened. Only the trace of a smile played on Lionel's lips when I told him about my dramatic exit from Shane's office. But instead of commenting on my story, Lionel fished another stone from the palm of his hand, *plooped* it into the water, and said, "Ronald Reagan used to be a lifeguard on this river."

"Uh huh," I replied, not knowing what else to say.

Lionel knew all about Reagan from his days as National Editor of *The New York Times* during Reagan's presidency.

"Reagan wasn't a lifeguard here, of course, but downstream in northern Illinois. Dixon," Lionel continued, lazily. "He even saved some people from drowning."

"Ohhh kayyy…" I wasn't sure where this monologue was going.

More silence.

"What's on your mind, Lionel?"

He sighed. A heavy one. The bench shuddered. "I was just thinking," he said softly.

"'Bout what?" My voice matched the gentleness of his.

"About my little girl." His voice caught.

I glanced at him and saw his eyes glisten.

Tears came to mine, too.

I'd never met Holly. She'd died in an accident two years earlier—more than a year before I met Lionel just after he'd moved back to his boyhood home of Pine Bluff from Washington after retiring from the *Times*. Holly had just turned twenty-two. He'd never really talked much about her. Neither had his wife, Muriel, yet I knew how deeply they missed her.

He leaned forward, elbows on his thighs, but said nothing. Normally, Lionel is crusty, cantankerous, and opinionated—a big guy with a powerful personality, sort of like Gene Hackman. Lionel had won a Pulitzer for his reporting during the Vietnam War and he'd been on Nixon's enemies list. Lionel is the strongest, bravest man I know, but now he just seemed morose.

I'd never seen this side of him and wasn't sure what to do.

Haltingly, I reached up and lightly stroked his broad back with the palm of my hand. After more silence, I whispered, "Laura and William's visit brought back some bad memories, huh?"

He nodded, stood, stuffed his hands into the pockets of his suit, and paced in front of the bench. In a moment, he reclaimed his place next to me.

"The day before she died, we got into an argument over the phone," he said. "I was trying to talk some sense into her, but it only got her upset. She hung up on me." He sighed deeply and shook his head.

"Oh, Lionel. And that was the last time you ever talked to her?"

He nodded and buried his face in his hands.

After a moment, he stood. "There's something I've got to do."

"What's that?" I stood, too.

"There was a lot of friction between us. My hunch is she poured it into her diary. I've been putting off reading it for a long time."

"Maybe now's the time," I offered.

"Maybe," he nodded. "But here's the question: do I have the guts to face what I'll find there?" He looked at me and smiled, sadly. "We shall see."

Chapter Three

"So, Lark, do you love him?" Heather, my libertine girlfriend, is always pumping me about my love life—or lack thereof. We had just settled in with our drinks at a table for two at Marsh Shapiro's Nitty Gritty. It's a hip Madison hamburger joint on the University of Wisconsin campus near the Kohl Center.

"Have you ever been here before?" I asked, changing the subject.

Heather shook her head and looked around. "Nice place, though."

Upbeat music flowing from a jukebox mingled with the buzz of a crowd gathering for open mic comedy night. The clientele was a mix of U.W. students and professors, young singles who work at the shops, offices, and restaurants along State Street, and people whose jobs are in the government agencies and legislative offices at or around the capitol.

"This place was a watering hole for anti-war activists during the sixties," I told Heather. "Lionel told me that the guys who truck-bombed the Army Math Research Center at Sterling Hall did their planning at the bar over there."

"You're kidding, right?" She turned to look in the direction of my nod.

Two guys sat facing each other on barstools. They were in an arm-wavingly intense conversation—probably about sports, not politics.

Heather's tightly coiled blonde ringlets quivered as she turned back to face me. "A truck bombing? In Madison, Wisconsin?" Her blue eyes were wide.

"Uh huh. It was 1970. Apparently top secret weapons research was going on in Sterling Hall. The bomb went off in the middle of the night, supposedly when no one would be around, but a grad student, Robert Fasnacht, was in the building."

"Did he get killed?"

I nodded. "It was a huge story. Stunned the nation. Lionel wrote about it in one of his books. He told me it marked the beginning of the end of the anti-war movement."

"How come?" Heather was about to get her BA in psychology. Politics and history were the furthest things from her mind, but my stories never seemed to bore her.

"Bombing buildings in order to stop the bombing in Vietnam made no sense to most people, so the anti-war movement lost its energy and the war droned on for a couple more years."

Heather looked sadly at her drink. She wore a low-cut, tight-fitting sweater that left little to the imagination. Suddenly, she sat up. "Hey! You haven't answered my question, Lark."

"I haven't?" I laughed, feigning ignorance. "What question?"

"You know…" She smiled slyly and touched the sleeve of my red silk blouse.

"I do?"

"I'll ask it again," she said with exaggerated impatience. "Do you love Jason?"

I toyed with the straw sticking out of my rum and coke. "I don't know. I know I like him."

"But you've been dating him for more than six months. Aren't you getting horny?" Heather, it seemed to me, was always horny.

"Maybeeee…" I smiled, still fiddling with the straw.

"You're getting together with him later tonight, aren't you?"

I nodded and sipped my drink. "He's taking me up on the bluff."

Heather's gold bracelet clunked against the wood-planked table as she leaned toward me conspiratorially. Without even trying, I could see her ample cleavage. "So why not jump his bones?" she asked.

"That seems so predatory, Heather."

"If you won't, I will. Jason's hot. You obviously don't know what you're missing." She leaned back and slung an arm over the back of her chair.

"Ignorance is bliss," I said.

"No. Bliss is bliss." She lifted her glass in a toast.

I laughed and took another sip. It warmed my insides.

"Seriously, Lark. Ross was a long time ago."

"Not long enough." I set down my glass and scowled at the traumatic memory of my former English professor.

"But not all guys are like him," she said, impatiently. Her eyes swept the room, which was getting more crowded, and came to rest on the tight butt of a guy passing our table.

"In my experience," I said, "most guys just want to get laid and--"

"And I'm an easy target," Heather said, finishing my sentence. "Right. I know. That's what you always say, but you need to get over it, girl, and move on. Have some fun. Get laid. That's what you need."

I blushed. "Move on to where? I like where I am."

"Do you? Do you really?" She leaned forward again, aggressively.

"Yeah, I think so," I said, looking down.

"You think so?" Heather was almost in my face.

I looked up at her. "Are you that satisfied?"

"Sexually?"

"C'mon," I said. "Sex isn't everything."

"Unfortunately." She made a face and took another sip.

A voice on the PA system interrupted our conversation. "Ladies and Gentlemen, welcome to open mic comedy night at the Nitty Gritty."

Heather and I turned to look at the stage near where we were sitting. Marsh Shapiro, the bar's owner, stood center stage clutching a microphone in his hand. A compact man in his sixties with short, gray hair, goatee and glasses, Marsh is a local celebrity. For many years, he'd been a popular sports anchor on Channel 27.

"Our first contestant," Marsh announced, "is Jonathan."

Polite applause.

An extremely tall, good-looking guy with light blond hair took the stage.

Marsh looked at a sheet of paper in his hand. "Dude," he said to Jonathan, "there's no last name listed here for you."

The guy leaned into the mic. "I'm just Jonathan."

"Okay," Marsh shrugged. "Everybody, give it up for Just Jonathan."

More applause, a bit rowdier this time.

Heather's chair scraped on the wooden floor as she scooted it around next to me so that we could both sit facing the stage.

"He's hot in a bad boy sort of way," she whispered in my ear.

I rolled my eyes at her and laughed. "And you do like 'em bad, riiiiight?" I drew the last word out long and suggestively.

Jonathan coughed nervously and placed the microphone atop a silver mic stand. "Thanks, everybody. It's great to be here at the Nitty Gritty tonight. I want to do some impressions of a few celebrities—local or otherwise."

He had short, unkempt blond hair and did a good job of filling out his short-sleeved brown and white checked shirt. To me, he seemed more shy and vulnerable than bad.

"We'll make this a game," Jonathan continued. "I'll do someone and you tell me who it is."

He turned his back to us for a moment.

Heather nudged me. "Nice butt," she whispered.

I poked her.

15

When Jonathan turned back, he stood with his stomach distended, his mouth agape, and his index finger raised. From deep in his throat came a guttural sound that resembled an idling motorcycle engine.

"A man gargling with ashes," someone shouted.

A few people tittered.

Jonathan shook his head, smiled, and spoke in a raspy voice: "The geopolitical situation is extremely grave," he began in a voice that made me want to clear my throat.

"Henry Kissinger," someone called out.

"Who the hell is Henry Kissinger?" Heather said to me.

Jonathan smiled and nodded. "Very good."

"Wish I could say the same," muttered someone sitting behind me, but a few people clapped.

"Here's another one, Jonathan said. He turned his back to us, pretended to do an elaborate comb-over, then turned to face us again, his mouth a twisted sneer. "You're fired," he said, jabbing his hand at Heather.

"Donald Trump," Heather shouted excitedly.

I had to admit, his impression was pretty good. Others must have thought so, too, because he got a laugh and a smattering of applause.

Jonathan leered at Heather. "And you, baby, you're extremely hired."

More laughter.

"That's Shane Duran," I hollered. If my eyes had been closed, I would've sworn Shane was at the mic.

Everyone laughed because Shane's smarmy real estate commercials are a constant on Madison television stations.

Jonathan smiled appreciatively at me. "You've just given me another idea," he said. "Hold on a sec." He turned around, took a deep breath, and then turned back looking coquettish. "Oh dear me," he said in a breathy voice. "Here I am on the railroad track and here comes a big ole train. What will I do? Jason, save me."

More laughter and applause.

"Lark Chadwick," several people called out, including Heather.

"Very funny," I scowled. Apparently, I was still a local celebrity.

Chapter Four

Later that night, after Heather and I left the Nitty Gritty, I sat next to my friend Jason Jordan on a blanket atop Table Rock, an outgrowth of limestone towering 500 feet above the city of Pine Bluff.

We had driven in Jason's Jeep Cherokee to the top of Granddad's Bluff. The locals simply call it "The Bluff." At the top are parking areas; picnic benches; plenty of hiking trails; and a magnificent view of the town, the Rock River, and miles and miles of gently undulating Wisconsin countryside.

The evening was breezy and cool. Jason wore a dark blue windbreaker, jeans, and hiking boots. His thick, dark hair spilled over the turned up collar of his jacket. I had on jeans and hiking boots, too, and wore my buckskin jacket over a loose-fitting sweater. In the distance, nearly thirty miles away, we could see the lights of Madison and the gleaming alabaster dome of the capitol. The moon was a mere crescent fingernail; stars were scattered across the huge expanse of clear sky.

"You've been quiet all evening, Lark," Jason said. "Is anything wrong?"

"I've been thinking about Lionel," I said, hugging my knees against my chest. I told Jason about the talk I had earlier that day with Lionel in Riverside Park. "I'm worried about him," I concluded.

"What are you worried about?" He shifted to get a better look at me.

"He seems like a broken man. No hope, and hating himself."

"Hating? That's pretty strong." Jason said, tossing a pebble over the side of the cliff.

"He didn't use that word, but I can tell."

Jason's hand scrabbled around, trying to find another stone.

What is it about guys throwing rocks? I wondered.

"You don't think he's suicidal, do you?" Jason asked, gently.

His question was like a sucker punch. It immediately took me back to how I felt six months earlier when I'd discovered Annie's body lying in the doorway of our attached garage, carbon monoxide from her Nissan spewing toxic fumes into the house—and her lungs. The coroner had ruled the death of my aunt—the only mother I'd ever known—a suicide.

"Oh, God," I said, putting my hands to my face, "I hope not. That would be awful. I hadn't even thought of that."

"Maybe you didn't think of it because Lionel's not suicidal," Jason offered.

He found another pebble and flung it as far as he could. It reached the top of its arc, and then fell out of sight below the lip of the cliff ledge.

"Or that I'm in denial…as usual," I pouted.

Suicide runs in your family, Mizz Chadwick. The coroner's taunt echoed in my head, reminding me of the day I'd tried unsuccessfully to get him to change his ruling of suicide in Annie's death. His words—a reference to the gruesome deaths of my parents when I was an infant— were an effective bludgeon against my puny arguments. I shuddered as I remembered how I, too, had flirted briefly with suicide after Annie died, something I'd only confided to Lionel's wife Muriel.

Jason put his arm around my shoulders and rocked me gently.

"Lark, it's probably not as bad as it seems. Lionel is a very strong man." Jason emphasized the last three words.

I leaned against him. "I know, but seeing Lionel like this makes me worry," I sighed.

His hand rubbed my arm.

Tears trickled down my cheeks. "I really care about him, Jason," I whispered.

"I know," he said gently. He laid his cheek against the side of my head and I brushed away the tears with the back of my forefinger.

That's what I liked about Jason: he understood me, accepted me, and let me have my space. It was easy to be with him. He was about five years older than I—and mature. I'd met Jason—a reporter for WMTV, Madison's NBC affiliate—six months earlier when he was about to interview me for a bombshell story I'd broken in *The Pine Bluff Standard* about the circumstances surrounding my parents' deaths. But before Jason could even begin our interview, events quickly spiraled out of control and my life was suddenly in danger, threatened by a madman and a speeding locomotive.

The dramatic video of my escape and Jason's story about it were seen around the world. We didn't have our first real conversation until hours later after our appearance on a popular CNN interview program.

We sat quietly for a while on the bluff, taking in the peacefulness of the sky, the stars, and the city lights below.

"I'm kind of surprised you let me bring you up here," Jason said finally, chuckling.

"I am too," I laughed, grateful that he changed the subject away from my worries about Lionel.

Being together in a romantic setting had become a running joke with us: Jason nudging me toward more intimacy, me keeping him at arm's length. Lesser men would have lost patience with me a long time ago—and they routinely did.

A typical conversation:

ME: "Why should I trust you?"

THE GUY: "Because I'm not going to hurt you."

ME: "Get your hands off me."

THE GUY: "Lighten up."

ME: "Get lost."

Fortunately, Jason understood and accepted my "trust issues with men" and knew that I was still coming to grips with them.

"So, why did you come up here with me?" Jason pressed.

"I like you, Jason," I said, looking into his eyes. They were a deep and yummy bedroom brown.

"You're precious to me. You know that, don't you?" he replied.

I took his hand—the one still draped over my shoulder—and snuggled against him more closely. "You're pretty special, too, mister."

Time seemed to stand still, which is exactly what I wanted. A cool breeze gently tousled my wavy hair. The sound of a mournful train whistle drifted up from the valley.

"Lark?" Jason asked softly.

"Mmmm hmmm?"

"I have to ask you something."

"I'm too young to get married," I said in a little girl voice.

He laughed. "It's not what you think."

"And what do I think?"

"The usual." He chuckled.

I sat up and looked at him. "Oh? And what might that be?"

"You think I'm going to proposition you or something, right?"

"Maybe…" I smiled.

"Don't worry. I know you're not there yet."

"Yet?" I poked him in the side with my elbow.

"At all. And neither am I, if that helps."

"It does." I leaned against him again. "So, what did you want to ask me about?"

"Coming to work with me in television."

"Jason!" I stood and paced. "We've been through this a thousand times. I don't want to do that."

"I know. I know." He stood. "You've made that very clear and I respect that."

I stopped pacing and faced him. "Then why do you keep bringing it up?"

"Because this is different."

"What is?"

"My proposition."

"You just said you weren't going to proposition me," I said in mock outrage.

He laughed, but then turned serious. "There's about to be an opening for a weekend anchor to do the six and ten p.m. newscasts. I've already talked to the news director. He wants you to audition."

Slowly, I began shaking my head.

"It's just weekends," Jason said, hurriedly. "You wouldn't have to quit your newspaper job with Lionel."

Actually, this was different. I'd been learning so much from Lionel, and didn't want to lose that. I stopped shaking my head and began rubbing my chin.

"Well?" Jason asked.

"I'm not a show-biz kind of person, Jason. You know that."

"You don't have to be. Just be you."

I frowned.

"Just think of the wider audience you can reach than through a weekly newspaper." He paused, eyebrows raised expectantly.

Silence from me.

"And the money's a lot better," he nudged.

I nibbled around the edges of a thumbnail as I remembered the $47,000 check I'd torn up that morning in Shane Duran's office. I'd been counting on the sale of Grampa's farm to finally get me onto a more solid financial footing.

Slowly, I walked to him. "But you've forgotten your best argument."

"What's that?"

22

I stroked his sleeve. "We'd be working together."

He brightened. "Do you mean you will? You'll do the audition?"

"Yeah. I guess so."

"Yesss!" He pumped his arm.

"But I still need to talk to Lionel about it," I said.

Jason pulled me to him. When I put my head against his chest, I could hear his heart thudding. After a moment, he drew back, lifted my chin with his forefinger, bent down and gently kissed me.

I found myself eagerly returning Jason's kiss. It felt as if the heavy burden of loneliness I'd been carrying for years had been lifted.

Do I trust this guy? I asked myself. *Yes, I think I do.*

Chapter Five

Jason may have been relieved that I had agreed to do the audition, but he didn't know Lionel Stone as well as I did. Lionel would be a tough sell.

I sat in the front row of a lecture hall in the Vilas Communications Hall on the University of Wisconsin-Madison campus. Graduation for me was only a week away. I'd dropped out for a few years to deal with the personal trauma of nearly being raped by Ross Christopher, my English professor. I credit Lionel with urging me to return to school to finish my senior year and get my English degree. He also insisted that I take his Journalism 101 class. I did—and loved it.

Today was his final lecture of the semester. The place was standing room only. There must have been at least 600 people in the room. Many stood in the back and along the sides. Still others sat on the steps of the steep center aisle. Lionel's class was tremendously popular, and for good reason: throughout his forty-plus years in journalism, he'd covered the Kennedy assassination, the Vietnam War, and Watergate for *The New York Times*, and had written three bestsellers. The one on Vietnam, *Quagmire,* won him the Pulitzer. After Holly's death two years ago, he retired as the *Times'* national editor and moved with his wife Muriel back to their hometown of Pine Bluff where he purchased *The Pine Bluff Standard*, lectured at U.W. and had plans to write his memoirs.

Today's final "lecture" was actually a question and answer session. As he spoke, Lionel paced in front of the lectern like a caged lion. He wore a dark suit, white shirt and a conservative blue and white striped tie, and gripped a microphone in one hand. I could have sat listening to him for hours, but was sad to see that only five more minutes remained before the end of class.

"One last question," Lionel said. He pointed to a man in the center of the hall.

As the man stood, several young women near me seemed to swoon. The guy was an Adonis—tousled blond hair, great physique. The tight T-shirt and jeans helped.

"What's your name?" Lionel asked.

"Yeah!" a woman behind me said to the appreciative titters of other women—and even a couple of the guys.

"Um, Kirk Kensington, sir."

Kirk seemed a little older than many of the students in the class, but maybe a year or two younger than I am.

"You've told us how important it is for a journalist to be objective," Kirk began, "but isn't that a myth? Is it really possible to be objective?"

He sat.

"The short answer to your question, Mr. Kensington, is…no."

Laughter rippled through the room like a wave.

"But let me ask you: Is it possible to be a perfect person?" Lionel asked.

"Are you talking to me?" Kirk asked, looking around.

"Yes. Is it possible to be perfect?"

"No, of course not."

"Does that mean, then, that you don't try to improve yourself, to try to become a better person?"

"No. I still try." He smiled, sheepishly. "Most of the time."

More laughter.

"That's my point. You're right to say that objectivity is a myth. No journalist can be absolutely, one-hundred percent objective. He—or she—will always bring their past experiences and, yes, biases to any story. But this is what's important: you have to realize what your biases are, then step back, and try—really try—to see the story from the other person's perspective—the perspective you might not agree with, or understand. That's the mark of the true professional. And it's also, I might add, why God created editors."

We all laughed, almost drowning out the bell.

Lionel held up his hands. "Thank you, everyone. It's been a great semester. Now go out there and get a job."

As one, we all got to our feet. The applause was long and loud.

I lingered after class, waiting for Lionel to break free from the groupies surrounding him. Some had brought copies of his books to sign. I'd read them all—and he'd signed each for me months ago.

Finally, the size of the crowd waiting to talk with Lionel dwindled to two people: Kirk Kensington and me.

"You go ahead," Kirk smiled at me. His teeth were perfect.

"No, you," I answered. "He's my ride." I nodded toward Lionel.

For a second, Kirk looked confused, then his face brightened as a light turned on inside. "Oh, I recognize you now. You're Lark Chadwick. I saw you and Mr. Stone interviewed on CNN a while back."

I blushed.

"If I'd known you were in this class, I would have introduced myself eons ago." He held out his hand. "Kirk Kensington," he smiled.

"Nice to meet you." His grip was firm and his hand was smooth and warm.

Just then Lionel turned his attention toward us. "Good question, Mr. Kensington." Lionel shook Kirk's hand and smiled.

"Sir, I've been in your class all semester and have learned a lot." Kirk handed Lionel a sheet of paper. "Here's my résumé. I'd love to work for you."

Lionel accepted the page and scanned it, scowling.

Kirk waited impatiently, his eyes glued to Lionel's face.

"You're a senior now?" Lionel looked over the top of his glasses at Kirk.

"That's right, sir. I graduate next weekend."

"Ever do this kind of work before?"

"No, sir. Until this year, I didn't really know what I wanted to do. Majored in English. But your class has inspired me to go into journalism."

Kirk's expression was earnest, sincere.

Lionel looked at him for a moment and scratched his chin. "What is it about journalism that grabs you, son?"

"All of it," Kirk laughed. I could tell, though, Lionel's question had taken Kirk by surprise. He was groping to find an answer, but recovered quickly. "I'd say the main thing is being able to follow your curiosity wherever it leads."

"Uh huh," Lionel said. I couldn't read Lionel's expression, but I could tell the wheels in his head were turning—he had some plan in mind.

"Have you met Lark Chadwick?" Lionel asked, suddenly, gesturing to me.

"Yes, sir. We just met."

"I hired Lark about six months ago," Lionel said. "Her situation was similar to yours: not sure what to do, but had lots of curiosity. It's worked out pretty well. She's come a long way. But we certainly do need help, especially now."

"Why's that, sir?"

"There's something that needs some, shall we say, investigative attention."

"You mean I've got the job?"

"Not exactly. Not yet, at least. But there's something I'd like you and Lark to look into for me. I'll give you and Lark one week to investigate a story for the next issue of the *Standard*. She can be Woodward to your Bernstein. We'll see what you guys can come up with. If your reporting and writing are solid, then you've got yourself a job, Mr. Kensington."

Kirk's grin was dazzling. "That sounds great, sir. Thank you."

Lionel turned to me. "Lark, what do you think?"

I'd been impatient to do something substantive. During the last several months, I'd been cranking out obituaries and going to boring City Council meetings. Working with Adonis, er, Kirk Kensington didn't seem like such bad duty, either.

Don't sound too eager, girl, I warned myself.

"Sure," I shrugged, "sounds great."

"Do you have a car?" Lionel asked Kirk.

"Yes, sir."

"Where do you live?"

"On Badger Road, just off Park Street on the south side. It's on the way to Pine Bluff, as a matter of fact."

"Good," Lionel said. "When can you get started?"

Kirk looked at his watch. "Um, now?"

"Perfect," Lionel smiled.

Another class was assembling in the lecture room, so we went out into the hall. Kirk and I followed Lionel into an unoccupied classroom next door.

Lionel put his briefcase onto a desk and snapped it open. "I've received some phone calls over the past few weeks from a few older folks who live mostly to the south and west of Pine Bluff. They'd bought land along the Rock River years ago that they one day hoped to build on for their retirement. But then they ran into money trouble along the way— usually because of health problems—and they got behind in their payments. But, in trying to sell the land to pay off their debts, they've discovered they no longer own it, they're only paying rent."

"How can that be?" Kirk asked.

"That's what I want to know." He handed a sheet of paper to Kirk.

While Kirk read it, I looked over his shoulder. He smelled soapy-clean.

Lionel continued, "This is a list of the people who've called me. As you can see, it's got addresses and phone numbers, too. I think there are about four or five people. I scribbled a few notes as I was talking to them, but my writing's indecipherable—even to me," he laughed. "I didn't really have time to get the full story, but when it seemed like a trend was developing, I put the list together. Now I need you two to do some digging for me. Questions? Ideas?" he asked, looking at each of us.

Kirk and I both began to speak at once, stopped, and laughed.

"You first, Lark," Kirk said, bowing.

Score one for Adonis. "No, you go," I said. I wanted to see if he had a brain.

Lionel laughed. "Well, I see competition between you two isn't a problem—yet. That's a start. Kirk, go ahead. Let's hear what you think."

"Well, sir, here are the questions I'd want to have answered: what is each person's individual story? I'd like to capture the pain and suffering they went through. I'd also like to look at the contracts they signed. Another question I have: are the contracts legal? What do others in the real estate industry think about this? Is this a widespread problem? Are other people at risk?" Kirk stopped, still thinking of other questions.

"You certainly do have some curiosity to pursue, that's for sure. Those are all good questions, son." Lionel looked at me. "Lark, what's the best way to go about answering them?"

"Obviously, the first thing we need to do is interview the people on that list," I said. "Once we've done that, we need to identify the best person or persons who typify the story and focus on them, getting pictures of them to illustrate and personalize the story. We need to identify the people behind this possible land scam and get an explanation from them. Next, as Kirk said, we need to read those contracts and see if they're legal. If so, is the practice ethical? Finally, and I think this may be as far as we can get in a week, do laws need to be changed?"

"Excellent, both of you," Lionel said. "In fact, let's make 'Landscam' the slug."

"Not Landgate?" I joked, knowing Lionel hated how the gate suffix had become overused.

"Quit while you're ahead, kid," he snickered.

I did. I still needed to ask him about that TV audition.

Chapter Six

Kirk agreed to follow Lionel and me to the newspaper office in Pine Bluff where we'd meet to plan our Landscam investigation. I declined Kirk's invitation to ride with him because I wanted to talk privately with Lionel on the way.

"He seems like a pretty sharp guy," Lionel offered as he pulled his burgundy Volvo to the edge of the Vilas lot on University Avenue. "Good looking, too." Lionel glanced at me.

"So I noticed," I said, trying to be nonchalant.

"Keep your head on." Lionel put the car in park and switched on his flashers while we waited for Kirk to get his car out of the Lake Street parking ramp.

"I will, don't worry. Besides, I'm beginning to like Jason. A lot."

Lionel grunted. "Kids these days."

Pretty soon Kirk showed up driving a hunter green Corolla. He flashed his lights, waved, and slowed down so that Lionel could pull in front of him; then we convoyed to Pine Bluff.

"Have you started to read Holly's diary?" I asked.

Lionel shook his head. "Not yet. I rummaged around in the basement last night looking for the box that it's in. Every single one I opened seemed to unlock a fresh wound. God, it's tough."

"What about Muriel?" I asked.

"She thinks I'm nuts. She just wants us to give all Holly's stuff to Goodwill, without even going through it. Can't say that I blame her. Maybe we should."

"You don't really believe that, do you?"

"No. But following your curiosity wherever it may lead is awfully painful. I think part of me—a huge part—just doesn't want to know what Holly really thought of me."

He sighed.

We drove in silence a while. When we were out of town, driving south on US 14, I took a deep breath and decided to try my luck on the TV thing.

"Lionel?"

"Yeah?"

"Hear me out, okay?"

"You're not planning to quit, are you?" he shot a worried glance at me.

"Heavens no." I bit my lip. "Well, not exactly."

"Lark?" He drew my name out ominously.

"No, Lionel, I'm definitely not planning to quit."

"Uh huh." He waited for the other shoe from Imelda's closet to drop, his fingers tapping nervously on the steering wheel.

I took a deep breath. "Jason says there's an opening for a weekend anchor at his station. He wants me to audition."

Lionel began shaking his head.

"It would only be part time on weekends," I said, defensively.

His lips pursed as he continued shaking his head. "I thought you had more sense than that, Lark."

"What do you mean?"

"C'mon, Lark. TV news is not journalism. It's show biz!"

"That's what I told Jason."

"So why do you want to do it?"

"It might be fun."

"Geez!"

"I know. I know. Wrong reason."

"I'll say." He tossed me a scowl. "You get one more chance to come up with a reason. Make it a good one."

"TV news reaches more people—it has a greater impact."

"Than what?"

"Newspapers."

"Wanna bet?"

"Yeah."

"Go for it." His knuckles whitened as his grip tightened at the ten and two o'clock positions of the steering wheel.

"First example—"

"Yeah?" He was itching for a fight.

So was I. "The story I wrote on the death of my parents."

"Yeah."

"Big local story," I said.

"Right."

"Local story."

"I heard you the first time. What's your point?" He glared at me, sensing a trap.

"It didn't become a huge national, actually international story until Jason broadcast the pictures on television."

"You through?"

"Your witness."

"It became such a big story because of the dramatic pictures. I'll bet you there's not a person who saw those pictures who can remember the important nuances that brought it to that big, dramatic finish."

"Not so. I was spilling my guts on CNN for an hour, remember?"

He shrugged. "Yeah, but the next night they had on the entire cast of 'Desperate Housewives'—for the full hour."

"Okay, here's another example, from your experience: Watergate."

He laughed.

"Seriously."

"I'm listening," he smiled indulgently.

"You yourself wrote in your book *Obstruction of Justice* that Watergate never became a big national story until CBS News and Walter Cronkite devoted something like an unprecedented twenty-five minutes to explaining it to the American people over two nights."

Lionel became quiet, brooding. He even looked Nixonesque.

"Game, set, match, Ms. Chadwick. Thenk yew. Thenk yew verah verah much," I Elvised.

"Not so fast. I'm thinking."

"You know I'm right, Lionel."

"You make a very good point, Ms. Chadwick, but—"

"Here goes…"

"There's one important point you're missing: Watergate began as a newspaper story."

"But it ended," I cut in, "on national television in live hearings and Nixon's very public resignation which the entire country watched on television."

He turned to me. "You really want to do this, don't you?"

"I don't know. I've actually got mixed feelings. I'd at least like to try it. Who knows? Maybe I'll hate it. Maybe I'll suck."

"Or both. One can only hope. It's just an audition, right?"

"Right."

"When?"

"Sometime next week. I've got to get in touch with the news director and work things out."

"I'll make you a bet," he said.

"Yeah?"

"You won't suck. The camera's gonna love you. And that, my dear, is what it's all about. Broadcast journalism is more show than tell. They don't call it *broad*-cast journalism for nothing."

"Lionel!" I said, poking him in the shoulder.

"Oops," he smirked. "Remind me to install speed-dial to Human Resources for you when we get back to the office."

"First you've got to install Human Resources," I said. "Wait. Don't bother. I can talk to Muriel. She understands me."

Lionel smiled. "Ah, yes, Muriel. My Eleanor Roosevelt—only better looking."

Chapter Seven

We got to Pine Bluff about noon. The newspaper office is a nondescript storefront on the north side of Main Street with dark green wood trim. A bell above the door tinkled our arrival as Lionel pushed it open and led Kirk and me into the building.

Muriel looked up from the paper she had spread out in front of her on the expansive counter that took up the entire front of the office. She wore a lavender cardigan sweater over a white blouse. To me, she looked way younger than her fifty-five years.

"Muriel," Lionel announced, "I want you to meet Kirk Kensington. Kirk was in my class this semester, and he and Lark are going to be working together on an investigative piece this next week. Kirk, this is my wife Muriel."

Muriel gave Kirk a particularly luminescent smile and held out her hand to him. "Hi, Kirk." She had high cheekbones, reminding me of Meryl Streep.

"Hi, Mrs. Stone," Kirk said, shaking her hand.

"Now, Muriel," Lionel said, "I haven't hired the boy yet, but I just might, depending on what he and Lark come up with in the next six days."

"Well, good luck, you two," she said, brightly. Her dazzling smile had impressed me with its friendliness from the day I'd met her. "Where are you from, Kirk?"

"Elroy, ma'am. My dad owns a farm. Mom teaches fifth grade."

"You're not a freshman, are you? You look a little older than that."

"No. I'm a senior. I graduate next weekend. I'm an English major, but when I heard Mr. Stone was coming to U.W. to lecture, I took his journalism course as an elective. Had to wait until second semester to get it, but now I think journalism is what I want to do with my life."

"Yeah, me too," I chimed in.

"What do you do here, Mrs. Stone?" Kirk asked.

She laughed. "I keep Lionel in line. That's a full-time job right there."

Kirk chuckled.

"Basically, I try to make things run smoothly," she continued. "I guess you could say I'm the office manager. I used to teach English at the high school before Lionel and I got married."

"It's been the best twenty-eight years of my life," Lionel said. He'd moved around behind the counter, sidled next to Muriel, and kissed her on the cheek. To my surprise, she winced.

"How did you two meet?" Kirk asked, his eyes going back and forth between them.

"Met her at a book signing down the street at the library when I was in town flogging my latest book," Lionel said. He turned to Muriel. "I forget. Which one was it, hon?"

"*Quagmire,* dear," she said, an edge to her voice.

"Right. The Vietnam one."

"Did he sign a book for you?" Kirk asked Muriel.

"Oh, yes."

"Do you remember what you inscribed, sir?"

"Nah—"

"I do," Muriel cut in. "He wrote, 'Thanks for staying awake during my talk.' He was so romantic." She gave him a playful poke in the ribs.

"How was I supposed to know I'd fall for you?" he pouted. "That came later."

"How much later?" Kirk wanted to know.

"Years," Muriel said. "I was still in college. Lionel was the *Times'* White House correspondent. He's close to twenty years older than I am and was still sowing his wild oats."

"But she managed to wheedle my address out of me and then began bombarding me with letters," Lionel said, putting his arm around Muriel's shoulders and giving her a squeeze.

"Bombard?" She wriggled away from his embrace and batted his forearm. "I wrote you one letter and you responded."

"And then you wrote another one," Lionel grinned.

"That's not a bombardment," she scowled at Lionel, then turned to Kirk. "That's the beginning of what was a wonderful pen-pal friendship, don't you think, Kirk?"

Kirk nodded and smiled.

"As I remember, it was pretty intense," Lionel muttered.

"That's because you were in your cynical, life-is-meaningless phase, dear."

"Yeah, well, JFK, MLK, and RFK had all been assassinated," Lionel explained, "and the country was bogged down in a war that was killing two hundred kids a week with no end in sight."

I said to Kirk, "Lionel told me that Muriel actually proposed to him by letter."

"Really?" he asked her, chuckling.

She nodded and rolled her eyes.

"Any kids?" Kirk asked.

Lionel suddenly stiffened.

"We had two," Muriel said, her smile fading almost imperceptibly. "Paul's a Capitol Hill correspondent for the Associated Press in Washington."

"I see," Kirk said. "You must be very proud of him. And the other?"

Lionel walked away from Muriel and moved toward his desk at the rear of the office.

"Our daughter, Holly, died suddenly almost two years ago," Muriel said simply.

I noticed Muriel didn't use euphemisms like "passed away" or "we lost her." I'd always admired Muriel for the unflinching way she faced life—and death.

"Oh, I'm sorry to hear that," Kirk said. "If you don't mind my asking, how did she die?"

Lionel's voice came from the back of the room where he now sat at his desk. "Better get used to Kirk, honey. He tells me he has a lot of curiosity."

"The short answer, Mr. Kensington, is that she fell off a cliff while hiking in Peru."

"Hey," I said to Kirk, trying to rescue Muriel from more questions, "why don't we put our heads together and come up with a plan of attack on this Landscam thing. Time's a-wasting."

"Okay. Great." Kirk held out his hand to Muriel and she grasped it. "It was nice meeting you, Mrs. Stone."

"Delighted," Muriel smiled.

"Lionel? Do you have that list of contacts for us?" I moved to his desk.

"Yeah. Here." Lionel snapped open his briefcase, retrieved the sheet of paper, and handed it to me.

"You hungry?" I called to Kirk, who still stood by the door near Muriel.

"As a matter of fact..." he called.

"Good. We can catch a bite across the street at the Korner Café. My treat." I winked at Lionel. It was the same line Lionel used on me the day we met—the day I learned through a newspaper clipping the details about the car accident I survived that killed my parents when I was an infant.

* * *

The Korner Café is, ironically, in the middle of the block next to the Majestic movie theater. The restaurant is long and narrow. The counter and grill are to the left; tables, chairs, and booths are to the right. Millicent Korner is the owner and chief waitress. I introduced her to Kirk when she showed up at our table by the window with two glasses of water.

"Millie, this is Kirk."

"Hi, Millie."

"Hey, Kirk." She placed the waters in front of us and took pencil and pad from the front pocket of her apron. "What'll you kids have?"

"I think I need a minute to look things over," Kirk said.

"Anybody tell you that you look like a young Robert Redford?" Millie asked.

"All the time," Kirk smiled. "Either him or Brad Pitt. I just wish I had their money."

Millie laughed and then turned to me. "Just signal me when you're ready, Lark."

"Okay, Millie."

She hurried away. The place was getting crowded—and noisy.

Kirk put his elbows on the table and leaned across it toward me. "I shouldn't have asked about their daughter, should I?"

"You surprised me a little by wanting to know how she died," I said.

"I need to be more sensitive. I can see that Mr. Stone's still busted up about it."

"Yeah. That he is."

"Mrs. Stone said the girl, what was her name…Hillary?"

"Holly."

"Right. Holly. She died two years ago?"

"Uh huh. Muriel told me once that dealing with Holly's death is like trying to keep an inner tube under water."

Kirk furrowed his brow. "I don't get it."

"The emotions keep bobbing to the surface."

"Oh. Right," he nodded.

"I don't think you ever get over something like that," I said, remembering Annie. Her death is what had brought me back to Pine Bluff, setting in motion the events that would change my life and put me on my current path.

"I guess you're right," Kirk said, leaning back against his chair. "I'm a dope. I hope I didn't burn a bridge with Mr. Stone."

"You can call him Lionel, you know."

"I don't want to be presumptuous. I'll wait 'til he gives me the green light. Even if it only lasts for a week, I'm just thrilled to have this chance to work with him—and with you." He smiled.

I felt myself blush.

Chapter Eight

Over lunch, Kirk and I agreed to divide up the four names on Lionel's list. Each of us would interview two, and then we'd get back together to compare notes. The first person on my list was Naomi Johnson. She lived in Sussex, a small town midway between Madison and Milwaukee, just off I-94.

It was a nice day, so I decided to hop into Pearlie and go for a drive. Pearlie is my yellow VW bug. We're buds. She listens to me when I vent and doesn't tell me what to do. I wasn't really in a venting mood, so we just talked.

"Pearl, I gotta tell ya. That Kirk Kensington is one handsome dude. I know. I know. You're gonna tell me that it's Jason who loves me. And I'll admit I've begun to have feelings for him, too. I definitely trust him, which is huge. So tell me this, Pearl: how come I'm thinking so much about Kirk?"

Pearlie didn't say anything—she just hummed.

I hate taking the interstate, so I zigzagged along back roads. The winding, two-lane state and county highways passed farm after flat farm. I drove with the windows down, my hair blowing about wildly as I breathed in the pungent smell of freshly manured fields. Having spent lots of time on Grampa's farm as a kid, I didn't mind the smell at all. It brought back pleasant memories.

I used to love to play on the swing Grampa had attached to the bough of a big oak tree in the front yard. Sometimes he would push me.

"Higher! Higher!!" I'd scream delightedly as he'd rocket me so close to the cottony clouds that I was sure I could reach out and touch them, then I'd giggle as the flat-board swing reached the top of its arc then swooped down and back, causing a woozy-sweet thrill in the center of my stomach that was so intense I could barely stand it.

So many memories: cuddling with Grampa when he wore his snuggly, blue flannel shirt; helping Gramma with the dishes—she'd wash, I'd dry, and we'd talk about cats and flowers…and boys; picking blueberries with Annie down by the river; digging for worms at night with Grampa, then going fishing with him at daybreak in his leaky green row boat.

I sighed.

Gramma had been dead for several years, but the pain was still fresh from Grampa's death of a heart attack, followed only a few weeks later by Annie's sudden death. Apparently, time hadn't gotten the memo that by now it was supposed to have healed the ache in my heart.

When Annie died, someone had sent me a sympathy card with the comforting inscription, "God gave us memories so we could have roses in winter."

On this day, those roses were in full bloom—and fragrant. For that, I was thankful.

* * *

Naomi Johnson lived just down the street from St. Alban's Episcopal Church in Sussex on Maple Avenue. Her modest, one-story, wood frame house had a screened front porch and pansies blooming around the base of a stone bird feeder.

I went up two concrete steps, opened the screen door, walked across the porch to the metal storm door, and rang the bell. It made a buzzing noise like a science class experiment on rudimentary electrical circuits.

Immediately, I heard someone moving around inside.

In time, the door cracked open and a short, pleasant-looking woman peered out at me.

"Ms. Johnson?" I smiled.

"Yes."

"My name is Lark Chadwick. I'm a reporter with *The Pine Bluff Standard*. Not long ago you called and talked with my editor about some kind of land deal you became involved with, is that correct?"

The door opened all the way, revealing the reason it took her so long to get to the door: she was leaning against a metal walker.

"Why, yes, that's right. I just figured he thought I was some old biddy and tossed my name into the waste basket." Her voice had a built-in smile. She wore a dark blue cardigan sweater over a faded lavender housedress.

"No," I smiled, "he gave your name to me. Is now a good time to talk about it or should I come back some other time?"

"Now's as good a time as any, Miss Chadwick. Won't you come in?"

"Thank you." I stepped past her into a hallway and she closed the door behind me.

"Make yourself comfortable in there," she said, gesturing to the living room off to the right. It was neat with old furniture—a couple of easy chairs and a sofa, all adorned with white lace doilies.

I maneuvered past a low coffee table and sat on the edge of the sofa.

"Can I get you anything to drink? Some tea, perhaps?"

"No, thank you. I'm sorry I didn't call first."

"That's quite all right." She shuffled to an armchair just inside the room.

Steadying herself with a tight grip on the walker's sides, she slowly lowered her slight frame into the chair. The walker blocked our view of each other, but she nudged it aside with her foot.

We chitchatted briefly about the weather, but then I got down to business.

"Could you tell me what prompted you to call our office, Ms. Johnson?" I took my reporter's notebook out of my bag and uncapped the ballpoint I always keep tunneled through the spirals at the top.

"Oh, call me Mrs.," she said. "I'm too old for all that Ms. stuff," she smiled. "I'll be seventy-seven next month. I don't mind that people know I was married."

"Was?"

"Bill died a few months ago. Massive heart attack. Thank God he didn't linger. We wouldn't have been able to afford it."

"I'm sorry to hear about your loss, Mrs. Johnson." I opted not to use my handheld tape recorder, deciding to get an idea of the outlines of her story first, then, if necessary, I'd try to get some exact quotes during a more formal taping.

"Thank you, dear," she said. "Bill and I had been planning to build a little retirement cottage on the Rock River outside Pine Bluff. We paid $20,000—a big chunk of our savings—as a down payment on the property. The mortgage was $244.56, which we paid religiously every month for the next five years."

I wrote down the figures. "Then what happened?"

"Then, just as we were getting ready to build, Bill had that heart attack. He'd been a truck driver and was about to retire."

"Did you work outside the home?"

"Part time years ago, off and on. Mostly secretarial work. Then my hip began giving me trouble."

"Did you consider selling the property?"

"After Bill died, that's what I was going to do because it was really his dream to build there. He wanted to spend the rest of his days fishing. I was content to be there with him, but I didn't really want the property. Once he died, I knew I was going to need some income to supplement Social Security."

"Uh huh." I was scribbling notes.

"Turns out, though, I got behind in the payments."

"Uh oh."

"Not seriously behind. I just missed one, the one after Bill died. He'd been the one who made all the payments."

"Missing just one payment under those circumstances shouldn't have been a big deal." I said.

"Let me tell you, young lady, when I tried to put the property on the market, I was stunned to learn that we didn't own it anymore."

"But you said you put…" I shuffled back through my notes, "…twenty-thousand dollars down."

"Exactly."

"What happened? What went wrong?"

"The bank pointed to the small print in the contract. It said that if the buyer defaults on a mortgage payment by more than thirty days, ownership reverts to the bank, and any subsequent payments would be considered as rent."

"That's outrageous."

"That's what I thought."

"Did you get a lawyer?"

"I could barely afford my medications. I'm ashamed to tell you how many times I've eaten cat food for dinner."

"Oh, Mrs. Johnson. That's awful."

She fished a crumpled tissue from the pocket of her cardigan and dabbed at her moistening eyes, then glanced at a picture on an end table of her and her husband. He was a brawny guy with short, dark hair and a fun-loving smile. She sighed, turned from the picture, looked at me and smiled weakly. When she did, she reminded me of Gramma. I really wanted to help this woman.

"Do you have any of the paperwork that I could take a look at?" I asked.

"I certainly do." She pulled the walker around in front of her, placed her gnarled hands on the arms of the chair, and rocked herself to her feet. "I've kept everything in the bottom drawer of the chest there in the dining room."

I followed her as she shuffled and clumped her way into the next room. A large table surrounded by six chairs dominated it. A pine chest of drawers, stained brown, stood against the far wall with a large mirror hanging above it and a forest of family pictures cluttering the surface.

"Would you mind opening that bottom drawer for me?" Mrs. Johnson asked.

It took a little coaxing before the drawer slid open.

"It's that manila folder there on the top. Take that out and set it here on the dining room table," she directed.

I took the bulging folder from the drawer and placed it on the table.

Mrs. Johnson pulled out an end chair and eased herself into it, leaving her walker off to the side.

I sat to her left in a chair at the corner of the table.

She flopped the file open and began flipping through the contents. Every now and then she'd slide something toward me.

"This is the ledger Bill used to keep track of his payments."

His handwriting was surprisingly neat, probably from diligently keeping logbooks as part of his trucking job. Bill Johnson had faithfully paid $244.56 a month for five years. I didn't have a calculator handy, but it didn't take a math whiz to realize it added up to a big chunk of change in addition to the $20,000 equity of their down payment.

"Did you own the property jointly?"

"Uh huh." She continued to shuffle through papers.

"Do you have a copy of the contract you signed?" I asked.

"That's what I'm looking for. Ah! Here it is. Take a look."

She slid it over, her thumbnail on the paragraph that gave the lender the right to take over the property if the payments were in default. The print was so small I had to squint to see it.

"Did they ever send you a notice in the mail warning that you had defaulted and were about to lose the property?"

"No, they did not." Her face flushed.

"Amazing. Okay, let me write down some of the basic information."

We sifted through more papers together. I skimmed a generic welcome letter from the bank, noting the irony of how often the word "integrity" was used. I felt my blood pressure ratchet up. Mrs. Johnson also showed me the slick Rock River Estates brochure that had first caught her husband's attention. Tantalizingly pastoral pictures showed the Rock River with a few rustic cabins along the shore. Finally, she showed me the closing document she and her husband had signed. I almost fell off my chair when I saw the name of the seller: Shane L. Duran.

Chapter Nine

During the next several days, Kirk and I worked diligently on the Landscam story. Based on our interviews, we saw a definite pattern in which Rock River Estates had targeted low income, blue-collar workers in their fifties and sixties to buy property along the Rock River.

In each of the four cases we investigated, the property owners had missed a mortgage payment—either because of a health problem, or the death of a spouse—forcing the immediate forfeiture of the property without formal notification. Shane L. Duran was the real estate agent of record, the Secretary of State's office listed him as the Chief Executive Officer of Rock River Estates, and he was a member of the board of Integrity Bank.

By Wednesday, the day we had to write and file our story, it was time for us to confront Duran with what we knew. Kirk and I met at the newspaper office at eight that morning to go over our notes and try to make contact with Duran.

There was no answer at his Pine Bluff office when I called. I tried Duran's Madison office. His secretary told me he wasn't there, but said he would be in Pine Bluff at noon to meet someone for lunch at the Korner Café.

"Does he plan to be in his Pine Bluff office before that?" I asked.

"I don't believe so. Mr. Duran told me that he'll be in the field all day."

Duran's secretary gave me the number of his cell phone, but every time I tried calling there was no answer, just a recording telling me the "cell phone user is not available at this time."

At eleven o'clock, when there was still no answer on Duran's cell phone, or at his Pine Bluff office, Kirk and I decided to wait for our quarry outside the Korner Café. We got there early, at 11:30. I ducked inside, but Shane wasn't there, so I came back out to confer with Kirk. We agreed we didn't want to embarrass Duran by interviewing him in front of his lunch partner, so we waited for him out on the sidewalk.

"What does he look like?" Kirk asked, as we scanned the sidewalk in both directions.

"He's about forty, fairly short, probably five-five, but stocky," I said. "His hair's curly like he's had a midlife-crisis perm. Dapper dresser. Every time I've seen him he's been wearing an expensive suit, usually double-breasted, dark. He seems to like blue shirts with white collars and French cuffs."

"Does he wear ties with bold-colored designs?" Kirk asked.

"Right. How'd you guess?"

"I'll bet there's our man now," Kirk said, nodding over my shoulder.

I turned around. Shane was about half-a-block down the sidewalk, swaggering toward us from the direction of his office, looking just the way I'd described.

"Tell you what," Kirk said. "You talk to him because you know him. I'll hang back inconspicuously and study his demeanor. Otherwise, he might feel like we're ganging up on him."

As Kirk headed down the sidewalk away from me, I quickly pulled my hand-held tape recorder from my purse, switched it on, and turned to confront Duran.

"Hey there, Wonder Woman," he called jovially as he sauntered closer. It was as if the check-tearing incident six days earlier had never happened between us.

"Hi, Shane." My smile was tight—I don't like confrontations and just wanted to get it over with.

I walked toward him, my tape recorder clearly visible in my hand.

"Shane, I need to ask you some questions, on the record, about a story I'm working on."

His smile faded, but he kept coming toward me. When he got to me he stopped and looked at his watch. "What's the story?" he asked warily. He shoved his hands into his pockets and jingled his change.

"It's about Rock River Estates."

"What about it?"

"Could you tell me in your own words what Rock River Estates is?"

"It's three words. What's this about, Lark?" He was all business now, very serious, and scowling.

"The Secretary of State's office lists you as the CEO of Rock River Estates."

He just stood there, an impassive expression on his face.

"Are you?" I asked when he didn't respond.

His brow furrowed. "What's this about?" He spoke the words with an icy steeliness. "Why do I feel like I'm being ambushed?"

I tried a new tack. "Does the name Naomi Johnson ring a bell?"

Duran's tone turned formal and menacing. "I'm not going to say a thing until you tell me what this is about." He made a move toward the Korner Café entrance.

I stood my ground.

He stopped and waited.

"Bill and Naomi Johnson, Polly and James Michaels, Clyde Forsythe, and Mildred Cunningham all bought property from you," I said. "When they missed just one payment—even though they had built up thousands and thousands of dollars of equity—their mortgage payments suddenly became rent. They lost not only the land they were hoping to use for retirement, but their life savings. That's what this is about, Mr. Duran. Your thoughts?" My tone now matched his, but was tinged with indignation.

51

"I have no comment," he said softly through clenched teeth. Then he leaned close to the recorder in my hand. "NO COMMENT!" he shouted into it.

I continued to stand in his way, but he firmly brushed me aside and went around me. It wasn't exactly a shove, but it had the same effect.

After he completed his end run, he turned and stabbed a finger at me. "If you're still here waiting for me after my meeting, I'll call the cops and have you charged with harassment. Is that clear?" Not waiting for my answer, he stormed into the restaurant.

For a moment, I just stood there, with my mouth hanging open, my heart pounding. Finally, I jabbed the button that stopped the tape recorder and turned around to link back up with Kirk.

Kirk was across the street entering the newspaper office.

Chapter Ten

Kirk, were you watching? Did you see what happened?" I called breathlessly as I dashed into the newspaper office.

"Did I ever!" He rounded the counter and headed to the desk he'd been using on the right side of the office near the back. "Can we use the word 'pissed' in copy?"

"No!" Lionel bellowed from his desk in the middle of the room next to Kirk's. "But thanks for asking."

Wednesday was always the busiest day of the week. Lionel and Muriel were bustling about putting last-minute details on that week's edition. The telephone was a constant interruption, with many people calling to see if one last tidbit could be shoehorned into the paper. Muriel deftly fielded those calls. Lionel was also busy writing his weekly column, and when he was doing that, he was not to be disturbed.

Kirk and I were on our own. But that was okay. Lionel had been our coach during the week, debriefing us at the end of each day, going over what we'd found and how we should proceed the next day.

Lionel was particularly helpful to me right after I'd gotten back from interviewing Naomi Johnson and learned that Shane Duran was at the center of the Landscam scandal.

"Lionel," I asked.

"Yeah?"

"I'm wondering. Do you think it's a conflict of interest for me to be working this story?"

"Why do you think it might be?"

"Shane tried to cheat me when I was selling Grampa's farm."

"Tell me more."

Quickly, I told him how Duran tried to gaslight me into believing I'd agreed to sell the farm for a price more than $400-thousand less than what we'd agreed upon.

Lionel rubbed his chin for a moment.

"Is that something I should mention in our story?"

He shook his head. "The story's not about you, or about what he tried to do to you. It's about the people he actually wronged."

"But personally, I think he's a crook. Doesn't that disqualify me from reporting on him?"

"In a small town like this you can't avoid having personal dealings – and negative opinions – about the people you cover. It's good that you're aware of your bias. If anything, it means you'll do your best to balance your true feelings with an attempt to try to see him in a different light and be fair to him – even if he wasn't fair to you."

"That'll definitely be a challenge," I said.

"Thanks for letting me know," Lionel said.

Since the previous summer when Lionel had taken over the paper, he'd installed a nifty computer network with a centralized filing system, a top-line instant messaging capability, and a cool program that laid out the paper.

Both Kirk and I had shared with each other all the notes from our reporting and had written separate rough drafts incorporating all the information we had. Today we would try to meld our two versions into a final account. While Kirk typed furiously at his keyboard across the room, I searched our files for a picture of Shane Duran. I found one—a smiling head-and-shoulders shot that was used in a story written five years earlier when he'd opened his Pine Bluff office.

Kirk and I had taken pictures of the people we interviewed. I had also taken a close-up shot of Duran's signature on the document Naomi

Johnson had shown me. Then I updated my version of the Landscam story, inserting Duran's "no comment" near the end.

"Okay," I hollered across the room at Kirk, "ready to compare stories when you are."

"Lark," Lionel said, irritated. "Top-line him, will ya? I'm trying to concentrate."

"Sorry, Lionel. I keep forgetting that your new computer system has now reached the twenty-first century."

Lionel grunted and resumed hammering his keyboard.

Before I could send Kirk a top-line, the message light on my computer began to flash.

K; I'm done, Kirk messaged me. *Where's your version?*

I replied with a message directing him to my file and, a few seconds later, we began reading each other's story.

Kirk's version was good. Really good. Embarrassingly good. His ability to capture and empathize with the pain of the Landscam victims was brilliant and sensitive.

My writing felt clunky compared to his smooth style, but after a few moments I got another top-line computer message from Kirk: *You're a GREAT writer, Lark.*

Liar, I responded.

He sent a smiley-face, adding: *Let's print these out and decide how to cut and paste. Your "office" or mine?*

We met at the printer and huddled quietly so as not to disturb Lionel.

My lead was straight-ahead journalism 101:

Four area families complain they have lost their life savings in land deals administered by Rock River Estates. RRE is owned and operated by Shane L. Duran of Madison, who maintains a Pine Bluff real estate office.

Kirk took a more leisurely approach:

Naomi Johnson of Sussex had hoped that by now she and her husband Bill would be living in their retirement cabin along the scenic Rock River outside Pine Bluff. But that was before Bill died. It was also before she learned she'd been — as she calls it — "swindled" out of their investment property by area land developer Shane L. Duran.

"I like your lead better," I said to Kirk.

He was very diplomatic. "Thanks. Why don't we start with my lead, and then segue into your summary, then add more details of how Johnson and Forsythe were hurt so terribly. I think you're best at explaining how the whole Landscam thing worked."

So, for the rest of the afternoon, we worked on one computer, sitting side by side—me on the keyboard—Kirk making suggestions about what to put where and how to marry the two stories. It was a collaborative effort in its best, most fulfilling way: no arguments, each listening to the other's suggestions, always moving ahead as a team.

By five o'clock that afternoon, an hour before our deadline, we were ready for Lionel to take a look. Kirk was especially pensive as he scoured Lionel's face for any sign of displeasure.

"Good!" Lionel said, finally. "Young Kirk, you've got yourself a fulltime job, if you still want it."

Kirk beamed. "I do. I really do. Thank you, Mr. Stone."

"Call me Lionel."

"Yes, sir."

"Immediately."

"Yes, sir, um…Lionel."

Our story was on the front page the next morning:

LANDSCAM?
Area Residents Allege Rock River Estates "Swindle"
By Lark Chadwick and Kirk Kensington

Chapter Eleven

The newspaper office was quiet. Lionel had taken the Landscam story Kirk and I wrote—along with everything else—to the printer, and Muriel had gone home for the night. Kirk and I were alone.

We sat next to each other in front of my computer. His feet were crossed casually at the ankles atop my desk. He wore loafers, black socks, twill slacks, and a dark blue turtleneck.

Throughout the week Kirk and I had worked steadily on the story to the exclusion of everything else. For much of the time, we had gone our separate ways, conducting interviews, transcribing them, writing rough drafts, meeting with Lionel. In between, I had to study for two final exams. Fortunately, when I'd dropped out three years earlier, I'd almost fulfilled my academic requirements, so I didn't need to take a full load to graduate—and the classes were easy, especially journalism.

Kirk had a light load too, but between the Landscam story and the end of school, we really didn't have any get-to-know-you time.

"Want to get a bite to eat, Lark?" Kirk asked.

"Y'know, I would, but I promised my boyfriend we'd do something," I replied.

"Oh." Kirk's face fell and he was quiet for a moment. "I didn't realize you had a boyfriend," he said finally.

"Sorry. But it would be good to get together sometime, you know, to talk."

"Yeah. Maybe. Sometime." He stood and lifted his windbreaker from the back of his chair. "I'll catch ya later." He swung on his jacket as he walked toward the door.

"G'night," I called.

The bell tinkled as he closed the door behind him. Now it was just me and my thoughts in a tomb-quiet newspaper office.

My thoughts were about Jason—and Kirk.

I realized that I'd never before referred to Jason as my "boyfriend." *Why is that?* I wondered. As I considered the question, I acknowledged to myself that I actually hate the word boyfriend because it's too proprietary, yet I use it all the time to fend off guys who come on to me: "No, thanks. I have a boyfriend," or, "I don't think my boyfriend would approve." Those are great phrases to weed out the insecure guys with ulterior motives.

Of course, there are exceptions. When I first met Shane Duran, he'd asked me out to dinner.

"I'll ask my boyfriend," I'd replied.

Without missing a beat, Shane had a comeback: "Don't you think it's time for you to trade up?"

I couldn't help myself—I'd laughed. I've been fending him off ever since.

Jason was different. When I used my "boyfriend" evasion on him, he'd shrugged and said, "That's okay. I just want to get to know you. Bring him along."

I was instantly attracted to Jason because of his quiet self-assurance.

Soon, we were spending lots of time together, talking, mostly, but also doing things like playing tennis.

The first time we played, I challenged him to the best of three out of five sets. I was actually ahead by two sets before I got overconfident and he roared back to tie the match at two sets apiece. We remained even throughout the third set, but then he won the match in a tiebreaker.

I knew Jason was crazy about me, but I preferred to think of him as a special friend. I could tell him anything—including fessing up about my boyfriend fib—yet he accepted me totally and unconditionally.

Since our kiss on Granddad's Bluff, I found myself feeling more committed to him. But, as I sat ruminating alone in the newspaper office, I could tell I was actually more than a little bit attracted to Kirk—all the more reason, I sternly told myself, to go slowly and just observe him from a distance. I'd made the mistake before—a couple of times, actually—of impulsively plunging ahead, only to regret it.

Later that night, Jason and I met for dinner in Mount Horeb, a small town halfway between Madison and Pine Bluff. I hadn't seen him all week.

"How've you been?" he asked as we sat down. He wore a navy blue sport coat, a button-down blue shirt, yellow tie with blue polka dots, and khaki slacks.

"Busy!" I told him about the Landscam investigation, but avoided mentioning Kirk. The omission surprised me.

"Wow," Jason said, finally. "Sounds like a huge amount of work. When did you find time to study?"

"Fortunately, I had some extra assistance on the story."

"Oh? From Lionel?"

I shook my head. "He teamed me up with a guy in my journalism class who'd approached Lionel about a job. We worked on the story together. Lionel liked it so much, he hired the guy."

"What's his name?" I could tell Jason was doing his best to seem nonchalant.

"Kirk. Kirk Kensington." *Okay. The cat's out of the bag. Steady, girl.* "He's a really good writer."

"What's he like?" Jason was inching into reporter mode and the story he was investigating was Kirk—and Lark.

I shrugged. "Just a guy."

"Uh huh."

Suddenly, the peppercorn I found on my chicken Caesar salad was the most intriguing thing in the world.

Jason remained silent.

I peeked. His doe-eyed gaze nailed me. Quickly, I looked down and stabbed a piece of lettuce with my fork.

"You like this guy, don't you?" It wasn't an accusation. His voice was calm and steady. He was just stating a fact.

I shrugged. "He's just a really nice guy." Finally, I was able to look Jason in the eye again. "He wanted to go out tonight, but I told him I was going to be with you."

That seemed to satisfy Jason. He relaxed and bit into his burger and chewed thoughtfully.

"Oh!" he said, swallowing and wiping his mouth. "I talked with my news director today. He's arranged for you to tape an audition Sunday evening at five at the station. Did you talk it over with Lionel?"

"Yeah. He's not thrilled."

Jason grimaced.

"I told him it's just a taping and that I'd either hate it, suck at it, or both. He heaped all his scorn of television news onto me. But deep down, I just think he's afraid he'll lose me," I laughed.

"I know the feeling," Jason said. He didn't laugh.

Chapter Twelve

WMTV is located in an unimposing light brown brick building on Forward Drive in the boonies on Madison's far southwest side across the road from the Ray-o-Vac battery plant. As I drove into the station parking lot late Sunday afternoon, I called Jason on my cell to have him let me in.

He'd been tied up all weekend on a story and was in an edit bay when he took my call.

"Yeah?" He sounded impatient, distracted.

"I'm driving into the parking lot now," I said. In the background, I could hear the screeching of what sounded like chipmunks on speed.

"K. I'll be right there."

When he opened the door for me, he looked harried. The sleeves of his blue oxford shirt were folded up; his tie was askew.

"Sorry I don't have more time. I'm crashing a piece," he explained breathlessly. "Lemme quick introduce you to the director. She'll take it from there."

He hustled me through a couple narrow hallways before entering a tiny darkened room. A huge bank of television monitors dominated an entire wall. In front and below was a giant slanted table with all kinds of colored lights and buttons. Several people bustled about. Most of them were young, in their twenties. All of them looked frazzled.

The director was a young woman with frizzy black hair. She wore glasses and had a grim look on her face. Her jaw muscles flexed constantly making me wonder if she was grinding her teeth. She gave me a quick smile, not unfriendly, but all business.

"Jane, this is Lark Chadwick. She's here for the audition," Jason said. Jane and I shook hands.

"Right," Jane smiled. "We're all ready for you, Lark."

"I gotta get back to editing," Jason said. "Take care of her, Jane." He rushed away. "Knock 'em dead, Lark," he called over his shoulder.

A few butterflies began circling slowly in my stomach.

"Let me show you the newsroom," Jane said. She led me through a door into a cinder-block room with yellow walls and garish florescent lighting. An aisle bisected the room with desks and computers on either side. There were no windows. It felt like a bomb shelter.

Each desk was occupied. No one looked up. Keyboards clattered, phones rang, and the squawk of a police radio was constant. It was bedlam.

Jane introduced me to a guy in his thirties, bald, wearing a white shirt and suspenders. "This is Don. He's the assignment editor and six o'clock producer."

Don stood and we shook hands, but he was obviously distracted.

"So, you're our new weekend anchor," he said.

"Well, not exactly," I smiled. "I'm just here to tape an audition."

Don and Jane exchanged panicked looks, then he looked back at me. "Um, that's not the way I understand it. I was told you're doing the audition on the air. Live. Right now."

Suddenly I felt like I was going to barf on Don's shoes. My palms felt wet and clammy.

"Ron, the news director, told me it was going to be on tape," I squeaked.

"That's not what he told me and we don't have another anchor scheduled. You're it. It's already been promoed," Don said.

I could hear the desperation in his voice.

"P-promoed?" I asked.

"Promoted," he said impatiently. "We'll probably have lots of extra viewers interested in checking you out."

63

With Jason on deadline someplace else in this mysterious building, I was on my own.

"Have you ever done this before?" Don looked worried, probably a reflection of the panic he saw in my face.

"I was on CNN a couple months ago."

Don quickly relaxed. "Oh, well, that's different."

I didn't think it wise to tell him I'd never actually anchored before— just been interviewed.

Don looked at the huge clock on the wall. 5:45. "Lemme give you your scripts and get you set up in the studio," he said, guiding me by the arm into the control room. "I'll have someone come onto the set to do your makeup and your hair."

Jane said, "I'll go get Bridget," and dashed off.

Don pointed at my outfit. "You're not gonna wear that, are you?"

"Wh-what's wrong with this?" I looked down at the light brown her-ringbone jacket I was wearing over a pale blue blouse and a dark blue pantsuit.

"Are you kidding? It's awful!" Don's voice had just gone up an oc-tave. He threw another panicked look at the clock and began breathing faster.

"I know. I know," I said. "You probably think this isn't fancy enough. But for me, it's a stretch. I hate dressing up."

Don wasn't listening. "Jane!" he shouted.

Jane appeared, eyes wild. "What's wrong?"

"Houston, we have a problem. Look!" He pointed at my jacket.

"Oh, God." Her jaw dropped. "You aren't planning to wear that on the air, are you?"

"Well, ah, actually—"

"Quick! Take it off!" Already she was clawing at the jacket, peeling it from me.

"Why? What's the matter?" I felt sick to my stomach.

"Herringbone will make you look like a frigging test pattern out there. The cameras'll go nuts! There'll be epileptic fits all over the county."

Jane held my jacket daintily out in front of her as if it was covered with anthrax. She dashed into the newsroom. "Does anyone have a jacket we can use?"

In a moment, she was back carrying a navy blue sport coat.

"Where's my jacket?" I asked, alarmed.

She ignored me. "Here. Put this on. It's a guy's, but it's the right color."

I shrugged it on. It was two sizes too big—the sleeves were three inches past my wrists.

"It'll have to do," Jane sighed, shooting a worried look at the clock. "You've got to get onto the set."

She gripped me by the arm and dragged me to Don who was waiting for us in the studio.

It was quiet, cavernous, and cold. Three large cameras stood in front of a semi-circular desk on a dais in front of a huge picture of the Madison skyline at twilight. A man and a woman were already seated at the desk talking and joking. Don brought me over to them.

"You probably already know these two," Don said to me.

I didn't.

"This is Ginger Jones. She does weather."

Ginger was pretty, but her caked-on makeup made her look like a raccoon at a clown convention. She wore a tight cashmere sweater that accentuated her well-curved body.

"Hi, sweetie," Ginger said.

"Hi, Ginger. I'm Lark." We shook hands.

"And this is Grant Deloatch," Don said. "He's the sports guy."

Grant stood and kissed my hand. "Welcome aboard, Lark."

"Thanks, but this is just a tryout."

"Don't worry," Ginger said. "You'll do fine."

I took my seat at the only chair left behind the desk. It was between Ginger and Grant.

"Here, you might need your IFB." Grant handed me a wire with a squiggly plastic thing on the end.

"Oh. Thanks." Inside, I was panicking. *What the hell is an I-F whatever?*

Grant pointed to his ear, and winked at Ginger. He had a similar thing in his ear. A tightly coiled wire disappeared behind his neck and beneath the collar of his suit, making him look a little like a Secret Service agent.

Quickly, I unbuttoned my borrowed, two-sizes-too-big jacket and took it off, draping the I-F-whatever cord down my back. For a split second, I thought about ditching the ridiculous sport coat and just going with a blouse, but the studio was so cold I felt that my chattering teeth would inhibit my ability to speak.

As I slid back into the coat, I noticed Grant making meaningful eye contact with my chest, confirming my decision to stick with the more modest look.

"Don't button up, yet, hon," Ginger said, stopping me from pulling the curtain closed on Grant's entertainment. "You'll need to put this under the front of your jacket." She handed me another wire with a tiny microphone at the end and a clip around it for attaching to my lapel.

"Five minutes!" barked a huge guy standing next to the center camera.

My hands began to tremble. All of a sudden I craved a drink of water. I also had to pee in the worst way.

A tinny voice spoke in my ear. "Lark, this is Jane in the control room. Can you hear me?"

I nodded, dumbly.

A woman—actually a young girl—wearing a headset, Rugby shirt and jeans stepped onto the platform in front of the desk. She carried a tiny sponge and a tube of something. "Gotta make you up," the girl explained, squeezing brown gunk onto the sponge, then dabbing my face with it.

"Mike check," barked the voice of authority coming from the direction of the center camera.

Who the hell is Mike Check? I wondered, as the girl rubbed the makeup onto my face. It felt mercifully cool.

Ginger answered my unspoken question. "Check. Check. One, two, three, testing."

Grant did the same thing as Ginger.

Then it was my turn. The makeup girl continued to dab me in the face as I said, "Mic check, one, two, three. Can you hear me okay, Jane?"

"A little louder, Lark," came her voice in my ear, "stop whispering."

"Sorry." I cleared my throat and tried again. "Che-eck," my voice cracked, "one, two, three, testing. That better?"

"Sounds good. One minute, everyone."

The makeup girl powdered my face, seemingly oblivious to the time. If she didn't get out of the way of the camera, her butt would be the lead story.

I heard Jane in my ear, but she was talking to the makeup "artist."

"Bridget, can't you do anything about her hair?"

"THIRTY SECONDS," boomed The Voice.

Bridget leaned back, appraised me, frowned, leaned forward, plunged her fingers into my hair and fluffed it. "Looks hopeless to me, Jane."

"FIFTEEN SECONDS."

Bridget backed off the dais, trying to speak into her headset so I wouldn't hear, "Sorry. I tried, Jane. I can't help it if she looks like a hooker who just got outta bed."

I had a pile of scripts in my hands and had not had time to read a one. It wouldn't have mattered. They were all a blur. I couldn't keep my eyes still long enough to focus on anything. I was on sensory overload.

So this is what a deer in the headlights feels like.

All too soon, the commercial that had been on the air ended and the opening "music" began. It was actually some sort of cacophonous, nondescript, adrenaline-induced, synthesized noise, designed, I guess, to sound earnest and authoritative.

Then I heard the voice of God:

"THIS IS NEWSCENE 15, WITH LARK CHADWICK, PLUS GINGER JONES WITH WEATHER AND GRANT DELOATCH WITH SPORTS."

The music crescendoed.

Our floor barker barked again: "STAND BY!" He held up five big fingers, then, four, then—

I felt Grant stroking my sleeve. It made me feel like crawling into Ginger's lap.

Time seemed to stand still. The studio was dead quiet. I could hear the noise of the open in my ear, but it seemed far away. I willed myself to stay calm.

The counting fingers were now below the middle camera that had a huge, white number one on it. When he ran out of fingers, the floor director swept his entire arm beneath the camera and pointed at me accusingly.

I stared at the camera. A big red light on top of it came on. What looked like a mirror rested at a 45-degree angle in front of the camera lens and on that glass were big words, slowly scrolling upward.

"Go!" Jane screamed in my ear.

GOOD EVENING, the words said in all capital letters, so I spoke them. "Welcome to Newscene 15. I'm Lark Chadwick."

The act of simply speaking calmed me.

Sure. I can do this. It's just talking and reading. No big deal. I know how to do that.

The words on the teleprompter kept scrolling. If I didn't hurry, they'd be gone before I had a chance to speak them.

"Tonight's weather in a word: SOTMRY."

Grant smirked.

Raucous laughter from the control room behind me seeped through the wall into the studio. But I swear to God, "sotmry" was exactly what was typed on the prompter.

Ginger's face came up on the screen. She spoke. "Stormy! That's right, Lark. I'll be along in just a minute with all the weather."

My turn to speak.

"Grant?" I turned to my left and looked at the sports guy who was doing his best not to lose it. He rattled off something about the "Brew Crew."

Then I was the center of attention again.

"Tonight's lead story comes from Pine Bluff. Several elderly residents say they've been swindled out of their life savings."

A drop of saliva began rolling slowly down the back of my throat as I continued to speak. I couldn't stop midsentence to swallow, so I kept reading.

"They're pointing their fingers at Rock River Estates, based here in Madison." The saliva trickled farther down my throat.

"Newscene's Jason Jordan reports the… (*gotta swallow! gotta swallow! CAN'T swallow!*) "…whole thing is being referred to down there as Landsc—"

The saliva oozed over that spot in the back of my throat that told my brain to throw a switch to keep the liquid from going into my lungs.

The result: I gagged.

Right in the middle of the word "Landscam"—MY word, a word I coined—I gagged. In front of hundreds, maybe THOUSANDS of people, my mouth formed the word "scam" but nothing came out. Nothing, that is, except a croak.

Thankfully, Jason's piece replaced my stricken face on the television screen.

I swallowed. But the embarrassment I felt (more stifled snickering from my new buddy Grant) quickly gave way to indignation as I watched Jason interviewing Naomi Johnson at the same dining room table in Sussex where she and I had sat together just a few days earlier.

He's stolen my story! I fumed.

Jason's package ended with him standing in front of Shane Duran's Pine Bluff office on Main Street.

"We tried to contact Shane Duran for his reaction to all of this," Jason said, "but the real estate developer is unavailable for comment. Jason Jordan, Newscene 15, Pine Bluff."

I read more stories, deftly tossed to my two sidekicks, Ginger and Grant, and soon it was over.

Anger, I found, is a great motivator, and it had the ironic effect of relaxing me. I'm comfortable with my anger. Other than those opening jitters, things actually went fine.

Well, okay, once I looked at the wrong camera, and once -- maybe twice -- the camera was too far away for me to see the prompter very clearly, so instead of looking down at the script in my hand—like the pros do—I leaned toward the camera and squinted until I could make out the word.

And then there was the time when there was nothing—that's right, NOTHING—on the teleprompter. But before I could panic, Jane was in my ear: "GO TO BREAK! GO TO BREAK!" she screamed. (She always seemed to be screaming, come to think of it.) But her screaming was very…motivational.

I looked the camera in the eye, smiled, and said smoothly, "We'll be right back."

When the newscast was finally over, I slumped in a heap against the back of my chair. The few people who were with me in the studio— Grant, Ginger, The Floor Barker Guy, the camera operators (one of whom was Bridget the makeup artist)—all applauded.

Jane burst through the door from the control room. "You did great, Lark. There were a couple of anxious moments, of course, but it's in the ozone now."

Don, the assignment editor/producer, followed Jane. He carried a sheet of paper. "Here's the official audience reaction," he announced: "Two calls were, shall we say, pornographic in nature."

We all laughed.

"One call was a marriage proposal. That's balanced out by one caller who said you—quote—'suck royally.' I consider that to be a crank call," Don said. "Some were mildly critical, but the overwhelming majority— twenty-one calls, a new Newscene 15 record—think you're great, have a very natural delivery, and they want to know when you'll be on again."

More laughter—and applause.

"You'll have to talk to my agent," I laughed.

"Better find one quick," Don said, "because the ten o'clock show is just a few hours away."

Back in the newsroom, I checked my cell phone.

Heather had left a voice mail. She squealed for the first ten seconds of it, then gushed, "Lark. You were so awesome. I'm really proud of you. And," she added, "do you think you could hook me up with Grant, the sports guy? He's gorgeous."

"First, I have to find Jason," I growled to myself as I hung up. But, when I looked for him, he was gone.

Chapter Thirteen

I breezed into the newspaper office the next morning as if nothing special had happened over the weekend, hoping Lionel hadn't seen my debut as a television anchor.

I was wrong.

"Lark, step into my office, please," he said as soon as I walked through the door. I hadn't even had time to say hello to Muriel.

"May The Force be with you," Muriel smiled as I passed her at her usual perch by the front counter.

Kirk was already at his desk, squinting at his computer screen.

Lionel's "office" is his desk in the center of the room. He doesn't believe in privacy, apparently.

"Have a seat," he said, nodding at the chair alongside his desk.

I sat.

"I thought you said your TV audition was going to be on tape." He sneered the word "TV."

"Lionel, I can explain."

"I'm listening." His arms were folded in front of his chest. His mouth may have been closed, but his demeanor made me wonder—and worry—that his mind might not be open, either.

"It was supposed to be on tape, but there was some sort of scheduling mix-up." I told him what happened. "I'm really sorry, Lionel," I concluded. "How did you find out?"

"I was watching."

I laughed.

"What's so funny?"

"For all of your disdain for TV news, you still watch it, don't you?"

His face turned red. "Yeah. Sometimes. I called in afterward to give them some instant feedback."

"Yours wasn't one of the two pornographic calls, was it?"

"No," he replied indignantly.

"The marriage proposal?"

He shook his head vigorously.

"One of the twenty-one people who thought I was great?" I asked, my voice hopeful.

"Nope. I said you—"

"Sucked royally."

"Did they recognize my voice?" He looked worried.

"No," I chuckled, "but I should have recognized the syntax." I had the feeling my humor had thrown Lionel off stride from the scolding he'd been planning to administer. "Are you sore at me?"

He shifted uncomfortably in his seat. "I was at first, but I knew you wouldn't lie to me."

"You're right about that."

"I think TV is a step down for you, Lark and—I'll be honest—I'm afraid I'll lose you to it."

I started to say something, but he stopped me.

"I'm learning that I have to back off and let you be you." He touched my arm. "So, consider yourself bawled out." The grimace on his face was the closest he usually ever came to an actual smile.

I bit my lip, then grinned, relieved. "Where'd all this self-awareness come from?"

He nodded in Muriel's direction and leaned toward me. "I've been learning some things from Holly's diary," he whispered.

"You finally started reading it?" I kept my voice low.

"Yeah, but it ain't easy. In the bit I read last night, Holly really unloads on me."

"Oh, Lionel." I touched his sleeve.

He shook his head sadly. "I don't think I can read any more—it hurts too much." Before I could respond, he leaned back in his chair and, in his usual booming voice, changed the subject. "So, what happens next with this TV thing?"

"I don't know. I've got to talk with the news director. It's only supposed to be weekends. I don't intend to quit here."

"That's a relief, but I know that you're too good to be working at a weekly newspaper forever. Just keep me in the loop."

"I will." I stood.

"Oh, Lark?" Lionel said.

"Yeah?"

"And Kirk," Lionel called.

Kirk looked up from his computer screen.

"I've got something you both need to know." Lionel got up and strolled over to Kirk's desk. "Shane Duran's called a press conference for eleven o'clock in his Madison office. I want both of you there."

Chapter Fourteen

Kirk and I arrived at Shane Duran's Madison office about 10:45. It's on the top floor of the Integrity Bank building on Capitol Square. A small conference room overlooking the capitol dome was crowded with buzzing reporters, but hushed briefly as Kirk and I paused in the doorway looking for a place to sit.

Jason caught my attention with a smile and a wave. He sat off to my right at the far end of a massive oval table that dominated most of the narrow room. He gestured for me to sit in the luxuriously padded easy chair next to his.

TV lights standing in each corner glared down onto a small portable podium at the end of the table, nearest to me. A forest of microphones sprang from the podium, their cords spaghettied along the shiny table and into various tape recorders. About a dozen reporters sat around the table and several more people stood against the walls.

As I excuse-me'd my way toward Jason, I thought I heard someone whisper, "There she is."

I used to hear that quite a bit after I was catapulted to national attention, but much of that notoriety had, thankfully, toned down. I assumed the current stir was in response to my television debut the night before.

The room seemed to grow hotter and stuffier the deeper I got into it. I tried not to trip over outstretched legs and electrical cords snaking across the beige carpet. I squeezed past four television cameras sitting on tripods at the back of the room and slid into the soft, cool leather chair next to Jason.

"I looked all over for you last night," I hissed, leaning toward him. "Where were you?"

"Lark, I'm sorry. I didn't know it was gonna be live." He wiped sweat from his brow with the back of his hand.

"Why'd you take off?"

"I thought you'd be upset."

"You got that right."

He loosened his tie. "Are you still pissed?"

"At you? Of course. You abandoned me."

A few people turned to look at me.

I lowered my voice to an intense whisper. "I looked all over for you. I called your cell. No answer. I called your apartment. No answer. I stopped by. No one was home. It's like you didn't want to be found, just when I needed you."

"Lark, I'm sorry." He placed a cold hand lightly on top of mine. "Can we talk about this later?" Jason took his hand away, fidgeted in his seat, and looked around. He was clearly uncomfortable and contrite.

But I was still ticked.

"And one more thing," I said. "You stole my story."

Jason turned defensive and combative. "I did not."

This time it was his voice that drew head turns. Jason tried to talk softly, but now he was angry and his whisper wasn't all that soft. "Your story had already been published," he said. "All I did was try to match it. Naomi Johnson talked to me, just like she did to you. Once your story is out there, you don't own it anymore, Lark."

"Well, you could have at least talked with me about it first." I was seething.

Jason threw up his hands in exasperation, but said nothing.

After it was apparent Jason and I had stopped speaking, a guy to my left leaned over. "Ms. Chadwick?"

"Yeah," I snapped.

"I'm Jonathan Anderson with *MadCity News*." His paper was a funky, mostly entertainment tabloid—the Madison, Wisconsin equivalent of *Rolling Stone*.

"Hi, Jonathan," I said, my voice softening. "I've read your stuff."

Jonathan blushed.

"Haven't I seen you someplace before?" I asked, taking a closer look at him. He had a smooth, baby face and couldn't have been any older than I was.

He smiled, knowingly.

I snapped my fingers. "Comedy night. The Nitty Gritty!"

"Uh huh," he replied, his cheeks flushed and his smile got wider. He wore the same brown-checked shirt he'd worn the other night.

"You were funny," I said.

"Were?" He smiled.

I nudged him. "But you really need to work on your Lark Chadwick impression."

He laughed. "And I saw you on the tube last night."

"Oh, great," I smiled and rolled my eyes.

"You're gonna be our feature cover story next weekend," he said. A powerful smell of tobacco smoke radiated from his clothing.

"C'mon. This is a joke, right?" I said.

"I'm serious," Jonathan replied. "You're hot, Lark. Why else do you think I'm at this press conference?"

"You mean you don't cover land scams?"

"Nope. But I do cover reporters who uncover land scams and then suddenly show up on television as an anchor. You have that jump-through-the-lens quality, Lark, and I want to profile you. That's my photog over there." He nodded across the table at a scraggly guy in a T-shirt and wiry hair standing against the wall snapping photos—of me.

"Whatever," I grimaced.

Just then Shane L. Duran strode into the room from a door at the far end of the table immediately behind the podium. He wore a dark blue double-breasted suit with a bright red handkerchief sprouting from the top of his breast pocket. The pattern of his matching red tie looked like a tangle of white lightning bolts.

Several people sitting nearby stood and started their hand-held tape recorders on the podium.

I looked at Kirk leaning against the far wall, but his head was down as he fumbled with his notebook. Quickly, I dug a hand inside my purse and pulled out my tape recorder and notebook. At this point, it would have been too awkward and obtrusive to crawl down the table and set my machine on the podium next to the others, so I snapped it on, hoping it would pick up Duran's voice this far back in the room.

"I've got a brief statement to read and then maybe I'll take one or two questions," Shane began loudly, digging a hand inside his suit coat. He pulled out a sheet of paper and waved it. "My lawyer doesn't think I should even be reading this, not to mention lowering myself to answer questions, but I've got nuthin' to hide."

I studied Duran's face. It looked flushed. His hands shook so hard that the paper he held undulated wildly. In a moment, he put it down on the podium and began reading.

"I've called you all here following the slanderous piece of trash that passed for journalism last night on SnoozeScene 15." He looked up and smiled crookedly. "Excuse me. NEWScene 15." He chuckled, looked down, and resumed reading. "Jason Jordan's story is malicious and untrue. I categorically deny any intent to swindle people out of their life savings." Shane read in a rushed monotone. "The people interviewed for that story signed legal and legally binding contracts with Rock River Estates. Those contracts explicitly state that ownership reverts to Rock River Estates in the event of a default."

Duran started to say something else, but stopped. Sweat glistened on his brow and he seemed to wobble slightly. "That's all." He stopped suddenly, folded the piece of paper, and stuffed it back inside his suit.

I'd been trying to figure out what was different about him and finally realized it: Shane Duran was drunk.

"Questions? Anyone? Anyone? Bueller?" His bloodshot eyes darted around the conference room. He seemed to have trouble focusing.

"Mr. Duran," Jason asked, "Lark Chadwick broke the story in *The Pine Bluff Standard.* Why no criticism of her?"

"Gee, thanks," I whispered.

"She knows how to write?" Shane smirked. "Coulda fooled me."

"Ouch," said a guy sitting to my left. Several others chuckled.

I felt my blood pressure peak.

Jason continued. "You say last night's story was slanderous. What, exactly, sir, makes you say that?"

"It's slanderous, Mr. Jordan, because the charges—all of them—are not true. I already said that. If you'd been listening, instead of thinking up questions, you would have heard me say that." Spittle had accumulated at the corners of Duran's mouth. He plunged on, voice rising. "It's also slanderous because of the negative effect your report," he stabbed a finger at Jason and his voice rose a notch "—your *false* report—is having on my business."

"How can you say your business is being negatively affected?" Jason asked calmly. "Only twelve hours have elapsed since the story aired, and only three or so of those hours have been during what's commonly understood to be business hours."

Duran's face darkened and he glared menacingly at Jason. "I'm warning you. Back off, if you know what's good for you."

"Are you threatening Mr. Jordan?" I asked.

Shane shrugged.

"Just what do you intend to do?" I pressed.

"I intend to do whatever it takes to make him stop slandering me, Wonder Woman. Let him ponder what I'll do—and worry. No more questions," he snarled, turned abruptly, and staggered out the door behind the podium.

A chorus of questions followed him.

Chapter Fifteen

As soon as Shane Duran bolted from the press conference after threatening Jason Jordan, all the reporters in the conference room stood and began gathering their materials. There was murmuring, laughter, and some back-and-forth bantering.

"Geez, it smells like a brewery up here," said a man retrieving his tape recorder from the podium.

"Better watch your backside, Jason," laughed a well-dressed television reporter standing against the far wall.

"Yeah, Jason. You got insurance for attacks by drunken sleazebag real estate agents?" joked another.

Jason just laughed, but I could tell he was bothered by Duran's *ad hominem* attack.

"Just shake it off," I said, touching Jason's sleeve. "He was drunk."

"Yeah, I know," Jason smiled. "You want to get together later?" he asked. "I've gotta go now, but we should talk."

"Sure. When do you think you'll be free?"

"Probably not until after six. I'll call you."

"Okay."

"And what's up with this 'Wonder Woman' nickname?" he teased.

"Long story."

Jason took out his cell phone and called his assignment desk, then began helping his cameraman pack up gear.

Jonathan Anderson of *MadCity News* lounged next to me, his reporter's notebook splayed open in front of him on the massive conference table. His photographer continued snapping pictures of me.

"Is now a good time to talk?" Jonathan asked.

"Sure." Just then my cell phone rang. "Lark Chadwick," I answered.

"Lark, this is Ron Bourne."

I couldn't place the name. "Uh huh."

"I'm the news director at Channel 15."

"Oh, right. Hi. How are you?"

"I'm doing great. Listen, I'm sorry about the scheduling mix-up last night." He paused.

I kept my mouth shut. There was no way I was going to let him off the hook.

He went on. "I was watching and I loved what I saw."

"Y-you did?"

"I did. You were great."

"Thanks."

"Want to do it every weekend?"

"Not really. I don't think television is my thing, Mr. Bourne."

"Call me Ron."

"Okay, Ron. It's way too nerve wracking, plus I don't think I did a very good job."

"You did great, sweetheart. It always feels worse than it is."

"It felt terrible."

"That's not what the viewers said. And it's certainly not what this viewer thinks. Oh sure, there were some bumps in the road, but that's part of the appeal. You're natural. Smart and natural."

He was trying to be nice, but I knew in my heart I sucked. And, frankly, it didn't really bother me.

"Look," he went on, "I know you're still new at this and things probably feel uncomfortable right now."

"You can say that again."

"I'll make you a deal. Let's try it for one month. That'll give you a chance to get more familiar with it. If, after a month, you still don't want to do it, I'll understand. I'll go away quietly and never bother you again."

It seemed like a reasonable offer. "I need to think about it."

"I understand. That's fine. And, while you're at it, think about this: I'm willing to pay you thirty-five hundred for the month."

I was speechless.

Ron Bourne filled the silence. "I'll help ya do the math. That comes to about forty-thou a year. Not bad for just four hours on the air a week."

Not bad indeed. What I didn't tell him is that for two days a week, he was paying me double what Lionel pays for five days' work. And, because the deal to sell Grampa's farm had fallen through, I really needed the money.

I said to Ron, "I still want to think it over and run it past Lionel Stone, my boss at the newspaper."

"You do that. How much time do you need to make up your mind?"

"It depends on when I can talk to Lionel, but I'll probably be able to let you know later today."

We hung up.

Jonathan Anderson and Kirk Kensington, my sidekick at the paper, stood next to each other, waiting for me to get off the phone. They looked so much alike—good-looking, blond—that for just a second I wondered if Kirk was Jonathan's older brother.

"Sorry to keep you guys waiting," I said. "I've gotta make another call. I'll meet you downstairs."

I dialed the newspaper office as I walked out of the reception area of Shane Duran's Madison real estate office, into the elevator, and down to the marble lobby.

Muriel put me through to Lionel.

"Yeah, Lark. What's up?" Lionel barked.

I told him about Shane Duran's news conference.

Lionel said, "Okay. You and Kirk catch a bite to eat and meet me back here by 1:30. We'll regroup and decide our next move."

"That's fine. One other thing," I said.

"Yeah?"

"I just got a call from the news director at the television station."

"Don't tell me. He thought you were awful."

"Wrong."

"That's what I was afraid of. How much is he gonna pay you?"

"Twice what you're paying."

Lionel swore, an exclamation about the spiritual qualities of excrement. "What'd you tell him?"

"That I needed to talk with you first."

"I can't force you to work for me."

"I don't want to quit."

"So why do you need to talk with me? You're not seriously considering doing television are you?"

"Not seriously."

"Playfully?"

"Let's just say I'm open to the possibilities, but so far I don't think it's for me. He offered me a deal."

"I'm listening."

"Anchoring weekends for a month. If I don't like it after that, I'm free to walk away."

"And you'd do this while still doing your newspaper job?"

"Uh huh."

There was silence, then I heard Lionel breathing heavily through his nose like he always does when he's concentrating. Finally, he spoke. "You'll be serving two masters."

"You're my top priority, Lionel. Hands down."

"Here's the deal. You can anchor for him on weekends, but no reporting. You read the news for him, but you dig it up for me."

I didn't even hesitate. "Sounds reasonable. I'll give him a call back and see what he thinks."

By this time, Kirk, Jonathan and his photographer had emerged from the elevator and were waiting out of earshot on the other side of the lobby. When Jonathan saw me hang up, he came toward me, but I raised my finger to stop him.

"One more quick call," I said. "Sorry."

I called Ron Bourne back. He didn't flinch when I conveyed Lionel's conditions. "You'll do the six and ten Saturday and Sunday nights beginning this weekend," Bourne said. "Be there by five. We'll see how you feel about things in a month."

As I put my phone in my backpack, Jonathan sidled over to me. "Now can we talk?"

"Sure, but it's gotta be quick. Kirk and I have to get back to Pine Bluff."

We walked out onto Capitol Square. It was breezy, sunny, and mild.

"Let's go over there," Jonathan suggested, pointing across the street to a concrete balustrade by the capitol.

"Mind if I eavesdrop?" Kirk asked.

Jonathan deferred to me. "Not if Ms. Chadwick doesn't mind."

"Be my guest, but it'll be pretty boring," I smiled.

"Oh, I doubt that," Kirk said, winking at me.

Chapter Sixteen

The interview with Jonathan Anderson of *MadCity News* lasted about twenty minutes and was more like a conversation. Kirk stood nearby listening as Jonathan's photographer snapped more pictures. After a while, I wasn't even aware of his presence.

"Thanks for talking with me, Ms. Chadwick," Jonathan said, turning on his tape recorder and holding it between us in his left hand. We sat next to each other on a slab of concrete, his reporter's notebook flopped open next to his right leg.

"Sure. Thanks for being patient. And call me Lark, okay?"

Were it not for his slightly flushed cheeks, Jonathan Anderson was almost an albino. His short, blond hair was nearly white. His light eyelashes seemed to wash out his pale blue eyes. He seemed nervous. On stage at the comedy club, he seemed mid-twenties young, but up close, I judged him to be pushing thirty because he seemed to have that steely-eyed look of a hardened professional. Maybe Heather had been right about the bad boy thing.

"So were you in the middle of some high-powered negotiations back there?" he nodded toward the building where I'd been talking to Ron Bourne and Lionel on my cell.

I laughed. "I wouldn't call them 'high-powered.' I'll be doing the weekend anchor thing at Channel 15 for a month. We'll see if they like me... and if I like doing it."

"Pay?"

"Yes. I'll be paid." I knew where he was going: not where I was.

"Care to elaborate?"

"No. Next question." I smiled.

"But you'll still do your newspaper job?"

"Uh huh." I didn't like his prying, so I shut up, hoping he'd get the message and change the subject.

Jonathan smiled. "I see you're not gonna make this easy for me, are you?"

I returned his smile. "I'm shy. I'm much more comfortable asking the questions."

"Um…" He looked down and pawed through the pages of his reporter's notebook. Finally, he regrouped. "What's it like working for Lionel Stone?"

"He's wonderful," I beamed. "Sort of like the father I never knew, only better. Not only is he a journalistic legend, he's a great teacher. I've learned so much in such a short time."

"What's the most important thing you've learned?" Jonathan crossed his legs and leaned back.

"That's a tough one. I don't know where to begin. I guess the biggest thing I've learned is to be skeptical, but open-minded."

"What's your impression of television news?"

"Chaotic," I laughed. "I really don't know if it's right for me. There's so much going on. It's very tense during a newscast. You really have to concentrate and try to be friendly, but authoritative, all at the same time. It's hard trying to relate meaningfully to an inanimate object like a camera."

"Well, I, for one," Jonathan said, "was very impressed with what I saw last night."

"Thank you," I blushed.

"Is there anyone in your life right now?"

"Ooooo. Too personal."

"Jason Jordan?"

"No comment. Next Question."

"C'mon, Lark, there must be someone," Jonathan looked over at Kirk and wiggled his pale eyebrows.

Kirk held his hands up and shrugged. "Don't look at me," he smiled, "we just share a byline."

"And you are?" Jonathan asked Kirk.

"I'm Kirk Kensington, Lark's colleague at the paper."

They shook hands. "Here's my card," Jonathan said, digging a business card out of his pocket and handing it to him. "Do you have one?"

Kirk shook his head. "Not yet."

"Get some shots of him, too," Jonathan said to his photographer, then turned his attention back to me. For a moment, he seemed to have run out of questions. He looked down at his notebook and thought a minute.

"You're twenty-five years old and already you're something of a national celebrity."

"I just turned twenty-six," I corrected, "but that celebrity thing was a long time ago. I've already had my fifteen minutes of fame."

"But doesn't doing television mean you're still interested in fame?"

"Not really. I think television reaches a lot of people. It's the story I'm interested in."

"Landscam?"

"Yeah, but that's not the only story."

"What do you think about Landscam?"

"I think it's an important story, but there's a lot we don't know yet."

"Like what?"

"If I told you that, then I'd be tipping my hand to the competition. Let them ask their own questions."

"So, journalism is competitive, then?"

"Sure. You know that. Nothing's wrong with competition. It's healthy."

Jonathan was quiet again, thinking. Finally, he asked, "What kind of music do you like?"

"I'm eclectic: jazz, classic rock, indie."

"You're pretty definite about that."

"I know. It'll probably disappoint your hip readers. I'm quiet, contemplative. I don't like loud stuff."

"Favorite group?"

"Arizona. They're an indie band out of New York City, but they do a lot of recording in Asheville, North Carolina."

Jonathan looked quizzical, like he'd never heard of them, but should have.

"Their stuff's very melodic," I went on. "They're sort of folk/rock, but they call what they do 'heavy mellow.'"

"I like that," Jonathan laughed. He uncapped his ballpoint pen and began scribbling in his notebook, parking the cap of the pen between his teeth.

"Ben Wigler, their lead singer, has a unique voice. And they've got a cute drummer," I said.

"What's his name?" Jonathan asked, taking the cap out of his mouth for a moment to speak before putting it back.

"James something. It's ethnic. Greek, I think, and unpronounceable. They're on Spotify, if you're really interested."

Jonathan wrote furiously. "Do they have a web site?" The pen cap between his lips made "site" sound more like "phite."

"It's Arizona the band dot com – all one word. I'm one of their Facebook friends."

"I need to check them out," Jonathan said, placing the cap back on the pen.

"I also like Sade," I continued when he looked up. "Her stuff is very emotive."

"Emotive as in sad?" He gestured with his right hand, the pen between his index and middle fingers.

"Complex. There's lots of pain and passion woven into her songs. I can relate."

"Hmmm. Pain and passion. Tell me more about that." He rested his chin on his hand, his pen now pointed right at me.

I shifted, uncomfortable. "I never do pain and passion on the first date," I laughed.

Thankfully, Jonathan chuckled and didn't push me any harder.

Chapter Seventeen

Will you let me buy you lunch?" Kirk asked when the interview was over and Jonathan Anderson was out of earshot.

"Sure. Thanks." My prompt and eager response surprised me. I've found that a lot of guys use food as bait, so usually I'm more reticent about putting myself in a position where a guy might think I'm obligated to put out if he buys me something.

I glanced at my watch. Noon.

"Lionel wants us back by one-thirty, so we've got about an hour. Where do you want to go?"

"How 'bout we get a couple sandwiches and go down by the lake? It's a gorgeous day."

"Sounds great. I know just the place. Follow me."

I led Kirk down the steps of the capitol to a small building at the end of State Street that faced the square where we'd just been sitting.

"Myles Teddywedgers," Kirk read from the sign over the door. "What's a teddywedger?"

"I'll let you hear the story from the man himself," I laughed as we went inside.

The store was small, barely room for the two of us. A short, stocky guy with mutton chop sideburns was behind the counter taking a tray out of an oven. His rock-solid biceps bulged as he placed the tray filled with steaming pies onto a stainless steel table.

"Hi, Myles," I called. "I brought you a new victim…er…customer."

Myles turned around and beamed when he saw me. "Hey, Lark. Is this your new boyfriend?"

I blushed and dodged his question. "Kirk wants to know what a teddywedger is."

Myles took off his oven mitts. "Teddywedgers are meat and potato pies that the Cornish miners took with them in their lunch pails when they went to work below ground a hundred or so years ago. It's a full meal, neatly contained in a pie crust."

"I'm sold. Sign us up for two," Kirk laughed.

Twenty minutes later we were sitting at a picnic table in James Madison Park just off Capitol Square on Lake Mendota. A slight breeze played with my hair. I was glad I'd worn my jacket. A mother and her ducklings patrolled the shoreline near our table, hoping for handouts. I obliged by tossing them a piece of crust from my teddywedger. They quacked in unison as they pounced on the tidbit.

"It's really been fun working with you, Lark."

"Thanks. This has been fun, hasn't it?"

"It has. I can tell you adore Lionel."

"I do."

"He's pretty gruff, though, isn't he?"

I nodded and took another bite. Something brushed against my leg. Looking down, I saw a fuzzy little duckling scavenging for crumbs. I took a potato chip and dropped it for the little guy. While I was still looking down I heard what I swore was Lionel's voice.

"Lark! Step into my office. You're in big trouble now, kid."

Startled, I looked up. Kirk had a Lionel-like scowl on his face. His impersonation of our boss was dead-on, complete with growly, no-nonsense voice.

"That's awesome," I laughed. "Where'd you learn to do that?"

Kirk laughed. "High school. I did all the teachers. Must be some sort of anti-authority thing in my genes."

"You're incorrigible," I laughed.

He smiled and shrugged.

We ate in silence for a few moments. The sun sparkled on the lake.

"I could stay here all day," I mused.

"Me, too. But it wouldn't be as fun alone."

Even though Kirk's compliment was indirect, my heart did a little dance.

"So, tell me about you," I said. "What are your folks like?"

"Dad's a wuss; Mom's a shrew." He took a slug of water from his bottle.

"You certainly have a way with words."

"I don't do well with overbearing people, and my mom qualifies."

"So, lemme guess. You ran away from home."

"Something like that."

"Troubled childhood?"

"You a shrink?"

"Social worker."

"Same thing."

"You seem bitter."

He sighed. "I try not to think about it." He wiped his mouth with a napkin, balled the debris from his lunch and stuffed it into the paper bag it came in. "You through?" He nodded at my nearly empty bag of chips.

"Yeah. Want the rest?" I said, holding out the bag to him.

"You sure?"

"Take 'em," I said. "They'll just go right to my butt."

He laughed and took the bag from me. "You're many, many potato chips away from having that happen."

I felt myself redden.

He poured the last few chips into his hand and popped them into his mouth, then looked at his watch. "We've got time for a short walk, okay?"

"Okay."

We stood, gathered our litter and placed it in a trashcan on the way toward the water's edge.

"What about brothers and sisters?" I asked.

"Younger brother. And his dog." He sounded disparaging.

"What do you mean?"

"Just before I went away to college, my folks got Josh a dog to be his bud because he'd be all alone once I moved out. He loved that little pooch."

"What kind?"

"Dachshund."

"Cute."

"Yeah. Right."

"You seem bitter again."

"It was Josh's dog, but I ended up doing all the work: walked it, fed it, even had to clean up after it when it crapped in the house."

"Why you?

Kirk adopted the whiney tone of what probably sounded like his mother.

"Because you're Josh's big brotherrrrr."

"Not fair, right?"

"You got it. But then the dog died."

"Aww. That's too bad. Hit by a car?"

Kirk nodded. "Really broke Josh up."

"That's terrible."

We walked slowly along the shore in silence. The mother duck and her ducklings followed us.

"How do you like working for Lionel?" I asked.

Immediately, Kirk's face brightened. "He's great. I am so lucky. I idolize the guy. It's amazing how strong he is, even though his daughter died."

"Oh, don't be too sure."

"What do you mean?"

"Her death's been tough on him."

"How do you know?"

"He's told me some stuff."

"Yeah?"

"He's carrying a load of guilt."

"How come?"

"The last time they talked, they argued and she hung up on him."

Kirk winced and stopped walking. He stood looking out over the water, hands on his hips. I stood next to him. To our left, farther up the shore, a few sailboats scudded in front of Memorial Union by the U.W. campus.

We watched for a minute, or two, then Kirk turned to face me and said, "I like you, Lark."

I looked at Kirk, surprised. Before I could react, he leaned in and kissed me. He wanted it to be longer, but I pulled back, startled.

"What's the matter?"

"Nothing. Y-you just took me by surprise." I nervously shoved at my hair and tried to catch my breath.

He leaned in to try again.

"Kirk—" I placed my hand against his chest to keep him from coming any closer. "I need to go more slowly."

"Why?"

"It's complicated."

"It's Jason, right?"

I nodded, bit my lip and looked at my watch. "You and I have a meeting with Lionel in half an hour."

"But—"

"We have to go." I turned away from the shore and walked quickly away. My heart was racing.

Chapter Eighteen

The drive back to Pine Bluff was thunderously silent. I couldn't read Kirk's mood. He sighed several times. Was he embarrassed? Brooding? Depressed?

To kill time—and to avoid an uncomfortable conversation—I took out my tape recorder and listened again to the news conference in which a drunken Shane Duran had threatened Jason. The audio quality was good enough to hear what was said. I copied a few direct quotes into my notebook.

By the time I finished, we were back at the newspaper office.

Kirk and I met with Lionel, bringing him up to speed on the news conference.

"I've got my ideas," Lionel said, "but I want to hear yours first. Where should we take the story this week? Young Kirk?"

"Well, sir, I think we need to look more deeply into Duran's background. A records check to see what else he's involved in."

Lionel nodded. "Lark?"

"I agree. But I think it should also be part of an in-depth profile of Duran. Who is this guy? What's he like? What do his friends say about him? Does the guy even have any friends?"

"If he does, you'll find them," Lionel said.

"And, more importantly, what do his enemies say?" Kirk offered.

"Good. Both of you. That's what I was thinking, too. Kirk, you get going on the records check. Think you can handle it?"

"No problem."

"Great. On your way, then."

As Kirk headed for the door he said, "I'll be at the courthouse."

"Here or in Madison?" Lionel asked.

"I'll start here in Pine Bluff, but I'll do Madison, too. Maybe tomorrow on that."

After Kirk left, I made a move for my desk, but Lionel touched me on the arm to stop me.

"So, what's your impression of the new guy?" Lionel asked.

I sat down. Lionel leaned against an adjacent desk.

"I think he likes me," I blushed, "but I can handle that."

"I'm not asking about your love life, Lark. I want to know how he is to work with. Good journalist, do you think?"

"Oh sure. Absolutely. He does seem kinda shy, though."

Lionel scowled. "Are we back to bedside manner already?"

I laughed. "Noooo. He's just not very confrontational. My guess is he really gets off on digging around musty filing cabinets."

"Nuthin' wrong with that, plus he's a great writer."

"Yes, he is." *Much better than I am,* I thought to myself.

Chapter Nineteen

The rest of the week was spent digging into Shane Duran's past.

Kirk's records search came up with the names of Shane's first two wives, whose names and addresses he turned over to me.

Wife number one, Terri Blanchard, was more than eager to talk. We met at her palatial home in Shorewood on Madison's far west side.

"I got the house in the divorce settlement," she smiled as she poured tea for the two of us. We sat on a gold sofa facing a picture window. A spray of lilacs adorned the coffee table, emitting a deliciously fresh scent.

"Do you mind if I tape-record our interview?" I took a notebook and handheld recorder from my book bag.

Terri wrinkled her nose as if a skunk had suddenly scampered through the room.

"It makes for more accurate note-taking," I explained.

Terri looked at the recorder, which easily fit in the palm of my hand. She relaxed when she saw how small it was. "Sure. Go ahead," she said. "I've got nothing to hide." She brushed a strand of platinum blonde hair behind her ear. "What do you want to know?"

"What was Shane like when you first met him?"

Terri smiled, revealing perfect teeth. "He was so funny. And I was so stupid. God, how could I have ever thought he was worth a second look?"

"Because he's handsome?" I suggested, not because I personally thought so.

"You got that right, honey. It's amazing how we women sometimes put aside a man's shortcomings because he makes us hot."

"So, the attraction was physical?"

"Uh huh. But, as I said, he was funny, too. I used to go weak when those two attributes are manifested in the same person, but I'm older and wiser now."

"What would you say is his best character trait?"

She threw her head back and laughed. Finally she caught her breath. "If you give me a year, I might come up with one."

"Surely he has some redeeming attributes," I tried.

"Well, he certainly had a knack for making money. It's his jovial personality. I guess that counts, even if it's all a façade."

"At what point did the bloom come off the rose?" I probed.

"Not for a long time. He really had me fooled into believing I was the only one. I didn't find out until after we'd been married for a year that he is a serial cheater."

"How did you find out?"

"Caught him humping his secretary in our bed."

I shook my head. What she said didn't surprise me. "Until then, you'd had no clue?"

"None. Love is blind, as they say."

"You must have been devastated."

She lit a cigarette and inhaled deeply. "Devastated fits." She blew an enormous nimbus at the ceiling. "But the divorce settlement not only netted me this house, it paid for my therapy."

"What can you tell me about Shane Duran the businessman?"

"Nothing, other than what I already did—he really knows how to make money. Now, his second wife, Bonnie, she might be able to help you with that one." Terri stood and walked to the kitchen. In a moment she was back with a piece of paper with Bonnie's name, address and phone number written on it. "We've become good friends. She hates the bastard, too."

Chapter Twenty

At first, Bonnie Duran was hesitant to meet with me when I called to make an appointment.

"I don't want to make trouble," she explained. Her voice was breathy, like a frightened Marilyn Monroe.

I did my best to explain how I knew Shane and summarized the Landscam story for her. "We're really trying to get a better idea of who Shane is," I concluded. "Won't you give me your insights?"

She sighed and capitulated. Twenty minutes later I was ringing the doorbell of her elegant federal style home in Madison's University Heights.

The woman who opened the door looked nothing like Marilyn Monroe. Bonnie Duran is a petite woman with jet-black wavy hair that frames delicate features. I had expected that each of Shane Duran's wives would be gorgeous, and wife number two was every bit as beautiful as wife number one. But Bonnie was as quiet and shy as Terri was loud and extravagant.

Bonnie led me to a cozy living room just to the right off the entry hallway. Even though a fire burned in the fireplace, the room still had an early spring chill.

I asked permission to record our interview, but she politely declined.

"I'm sorry," she said. "I'm really uncomfortable about even meeting with you. And I don't want my name in the paper," she said. Her fists were clenched tightly in her lap.

I hate it when sources won't go on the record. It makes my job much tougher. "Will you at least let me attribute what you say as coming from, say, 'a person who knows him well'?"

Bonnie thought about that. "I suppose that would be all right," she said finally after taking at least two minutes to weigh all the options.

"But," I continued, "I would like to tape our talk so that any quotations I use will be accurate."

She sighed and shrugged. "Okay. But no names."

"No names," I agreed, and snapped on the recorder.

"How did you meet?"

"He hired me to be his secretary."

A mental image of her in Terri Blanchard's bedroom flashed through my mind, but I resisted the temptation to immediately confirm my suspicion that she was the secretary Terri had been referring to. Instead, I asked, "What was he like as a boss?"

"Sweet, at first. He was funny and flirtatious. And I was young and dumb."

"What was he like as a businessman?"

She shrugged. "Okay, I guess."

"Terri Blanchard led me to believe you might have some insights."

Bonnie scowled and shook her head. "Not sure why she'd think that."

"Maybe because you worked for him."

"Maybe."

"Did he work alone, have a partner, or any other business associates?"

She shook her head. "He's very much a lone ranger."

"Did he ever have you do anything that may have been unethical?"

She shifted her position. "Okay," she squirmed. "Like what do you mean?"

"You know, something, um, dishonest."

Bonnie didn't answer, but looked at me with wide eyes that implored me not to go there.

"No names," I reminded her.

She was quiet a long time, her fists clenched so tightly her knuckles were white. Finally she said, "Dishonest is his middle name."

"Go on."

"I don't even know where to begin."

"Try the beginning."

She must have thought that was funny because her tightly pursed lips curled slightly into what must have been her version of a guffaw.

"The beginning," she echoed. "Well, for starters, he instructed me that when I answered the phone, I should repeat the name of the caller out loud so he knew who was on the line. If he didn't want to talk with the person, he'd give me a thumbs-down signal. That meant I should tell the caller that he wasn't in the office and that I should take a message. That's for starters."

"Did that bother you?"

"A little, but it was just a white lie, so I didn't mind too much."

"Then what?"

"The lies got darker."

"Uh huh…"

She didn't go on.

"What do you mean 'darker'?"

"Let's just say I thought he was single."

"No wedding ring?"

She nodded. Her lip trembled.

"How'd you find out?"

Bonnie put her head in her hands and wept bitterly.

I felt like an insensitive voyeur. All I was doing was following the logic of the conversation. I'd been hoping to learn about Shane's business practices and perhaps the names of business associates I could interview. Instead, it seemed I'd become locked into a never-ending version of "Divorce Court."

"Bonnie, I'm sorry." I leaned toward her and gently touched her shoulder. "I really don't need to know about all this. I'm sorry."

But whatever had been holding back the water behind the dam had now been punctured. Following the gush of tears came a torrent of words.

"She found us. His wife found us. I didn't even know he was married. I thought he really cared about me."

"Then why did you marry him?"

"I don't knowwww," she wailed.

Something didn't compute. I waited and soon the emotional squall passed. I dug in my bag for a hanky and handed it to her.

"Why'd you marry him?" I asked again, gently.

She blew her nose and shook her head. "I loved him. I really loved him. The way his wife shrieked at him when she found us made me feel sympathy for him. I was so naïve. She seemed so mean, I figured I was the one who understood him. I was the one who cared for him. I was the one he loved."

She dabbed her eyes with the hanky and wiped her nose. "I know," she sniffed, "it makes no sense. I can see it now, but back then, to me, it made perfect sense. I'm so ashamed." She buried her head in her hands again and shook her head slowly back and forth.

I waited patiently. Finally, when she looked up, I asked, "What was it like to be married to him?"

She sat up and it seemed as though her back stiffened. "Tender at first. We lived together and I helped comfort him through the divorce. He lost everything to her."

"To Terri Blanchard?"

"Uh huh."

"She said you're friends now."

Bonnie nodded, and smiled through her still damp eyes. "We are now, but back then, I blamed her for his problems, just as he blamed her, too."

"What made you see the light?"

"It took a while. I guess it was when he hit me." She glanced at me timidly.

"Why did he do that?"

"Because I threatened him."

"In what way did you threaten him?"

"I threatened to go to the police."

"Why?"

"To tell them about his mob activities."

"Oh?" I tried to keep my face impassive.

"No names, right."

"No names," I repeated, even as I kicked myself for allowing her to reveal juicier and juicier stuff it would now be harder and harder to confirm.

"He was bribing the state insurance commissioner."

"How do you know?"

"I was the go-between."

"What do you mean?"

"Every week, I took an envelope bulging with cash to the commissioner's office."

"Did you actually hand it to the commissioner?"

She shook her head. "Not exactly. I'd leave it with the secretary. But it was addressed to him and marked personal."

"How much money was in it?"

"I never counted it."

"Hundreds?"

She shook her head.

"Thousands?"

She nodded.

"Hundreds of thousands?"

"I don't know, but a lot of hundred dollar bills."

"What would Shane get in return?"

"No hassles."

"So that he could do what?"

She looked at me. "Ever hear of Rock River Estates?"

Chapter Twenty-One

Back in the office, I updated Lionel on what I'd learned from Terri Blanchard and Bonnie Duran.

"Bonnie's stuff about the insurance commissioner is great, but you know we can't use it," Lionel said, giving me the hairy eyeball look over the top of his glasses.

"I know." Lionel and I once had a big argument about going off the record with a source. I knew he was right. "How should we go about trying to confirm it?" I asked.

"Not sure yet, lemme think." He paced around the office.

"I don't even know who the state insurance commissioner is," I said as I logged onto the Internet and found the department's website.

After a few minutes, I learned more than I'd known when Bonnie Duran dropped her bombshell: John Callahan, forty-three, had been insurance commissioner for the past six years. He was halfway through his second four-year term. His picture showed a smiling man with glasses and short wavy hair. He looked very honest and approachable.

Soon I became aware of Lionel standing behind me, reading over my shoulder.

"Do you know him?" I asked.

He shook his head as he rubbed his chin absent-mindedly. He was engrossed in the site.

"What do you think we should do?" I asked.

"This may take some time to sort out. For now, our focus should be on Duran, but it now seems obvious this goes much higher. Let's begin looking for who else may be involved and what ties they have to Callahan's office. And, we should keep our eyes open that this could go as high as the governor."

Just then, Kirk came in.

"Greetings, Young Kirk," Lionel called. "Come on over here. Let's compare notes."

"What's up?" Kirk asked as came around the front counter and joined Lionel and me at the computer.

"One of Lark's sources alleges that our boy Duran regularly pays off the state insurance commissioner so that he won't run into any regulatory trouble as he perpetrates his Landscam."

Kirk let out an amazed whistle. "Can we go with it?"

"Not yet," Lionel said. "We need to confirm it somehow. Let's keep an eye on this angle and look for other people whose links to Callahan might be able to help. What have you been finding out?"

Kirk cracked open his reporter's notebook and flipped through the pages. "Let's see," he said, thumbing his notes. "The main thing I found is that some of the same Rock River properties have been bought, sold, repossessed, and resold by Duran as many as sixteen times."

I asked, "What kind of money are we talking?"

Kirk flipped through a few more pages. "Over time, he's built himself up a nice little nest egg. He buys low, marks up the property about twenty-five percent, and rakes in regular payments at slightly higher than market interest rates. Then, when a person defaults, he's still taking in what's now a rent payment, even though the mortgage interest is still factored in. After repossessing the property, he turns it around. This time, he tries to keep the price low and affordable for his next victim. One property alone can fetch a pure profit of at least a million dollars during one of those cycles, which on average is about five years. He controls a hundred lots. I haven't looked at all the property records yet, but it's lucrative."

"Okay," Lionel said, getting impatient, which always happened the closer we got to deadline day. "Even if you can't get your arms around

John DeDakis

the whole story yet, let's do a piece that sketches the general outlines, but let's focus on the cycle of one property that seems representative of what you've been finding so far."

"Sounds good," Kirk said. He left us and went to his desk and logged onto the computer.

"And Lark," Lionel said, turning to me. "You organize your stuff and begin writing that profile."

I couldn't wait to get started.

Chapter Twenty-Two

The paper came out Thursday morning. Lionel, Kirk and I met for breakfast at the Korner Café. Going there for breakfast was a ritual on the morning *The Standard* came out because it was a way to get a feel for the public's reaction to it.

I sat between Kirk and Lionel at the counter. Kirk and I had side-by-side front-page stories that jumped to the inside. Kirk's was the lead story showing the breadth of Shane Duran's activities in Rock River Estates. A sidebar tracked the life cycle of one of the properties.

My profile piece on Shane quoted Terri Blanchard. I wasn't able to independently confirm any of what Bonnie Duran had told me about Shane's violent side, or the bribery of a public official, so I had to leave those angles out.

"You're famous again, Lark," Millie, the owner, said to me as Lionel slid onto the stool next to Kirk.

"You mean today's front page story in *The Standard?*"

"No. Front page, *MadCity News*." Millie nodded at the dispenser by the cash register.

I looked. A picture of myself on the front page smiled back at me.

"Take one," Millie said. "It's on me."

I got up and took the paper from the metal rack, but before I could rejoin Kirk and Lionel, two farmers sitting at a nearby table slid their copies toward me.

"Can we have your autograph, Lark?" one of them smiled.

"Sure, Wayne," I laughed. "Gotta pen?"

"Here, honey," Millie said, taking one out of her apron pocket.

I scrawled my name for the two men. Before I finished, I was surrounded by what seemed like everyone else in the diner, each with their own personal copy.

I laughed. "Jeepers. I haven't even read the thing. I'm assuming it's a good article, right?"

"This guy Jonathan Anderson apparently thinks you walk on water, Lark," Millie said.

Finally, I made my way over to Kirk and Lionel at the counter.

"Pardon me if I don't ask for your autograph, Lark," Lionel mumbled.

"But I'd like one," Millie said. "Lionel can look at mine from time to time, if he wants to."

"Don't hold your breath," he grumped.

"Is it any good?" I asked him.

"Embarrassingly so," he said, staring moodily into his coffee mug.

I took a minute to skim it. He was right:

LARK!
A Fresh Face on Madison TV
By Jonathan Anderson
Entertainment Reporter

She's beautiful, smart, "plucky" (to quote CNN's Wolf Blitzer), and coming to a TV screen near you.

Lark Chadwick, 26, reporter for *The Pine Bluff Standard,* has just agreed to anchor the weekend news on WMTV.

"It's just for a month," says News Director Ron Bourne, "but we're hoping to be able to persuade her to make a long-term commitment."

Judging from an avalanche of positive viewer phone calls after her debut last weekend,

112

the pressure on Ms. Chadwick to stay may be enormous.

A sampling:

"She has a down-to-earth delivery, not fake—and she's not hard on the eyes, either."

"Knows what she's talking about."

"Spunky."

"Fresh and refreshing."

"Just what Madison TV needs."

You get the picture.

Just who is this fresh face gracing the vast wasteland that is local TV news?

Most of us first became aware of Lark Chadwick last fall when she very publicly and dramatically solved the mystery surrounding the violent deaths of her parents when she was an infant.

Pulitzer Prize-winning former *New York Times* National Editor Lionel Stone hired her on the spot to report for *The Standard*.

"Lark is as solid as they come," Stone says. "I don't want to lose her."

"Aw, that's sweet, Lionel," I said, nudging him. "I'm surprised you talked to him."

"I am, too," Lionel grumbled.

I caught up with Lark earlier this week at a Madison news conference. All eyes were on her as she sashayed into the room where moments later embattled real estate tycoon Shane Duran would soon make an embittered attack on Newscene 15's Jason Jordan, with whom Lark is rumored to be romantically linked.

"No comment," Lark smiled coyly when I asked her about it. "Next question."

For the record, Lark, not Jordan, helped break the Landscam story, but more people watch TV news than read a small, but scrappy, weekly newspaper in tiny Pine Bluff, Wisconsin.

She wouldn't talk with me about Landscam, either, other than to say it's an "important" story.

Lark is also rumored to be dating her Landscam colleague, Kirk Kensington, but neither of them would confirm nor deny.

In fact, it's safe to say Lark seems genuinely uncomfortable in the spotlight. Throughout our interview sitting on the steps on the grounds of the capitol, she skillfully parried my attempts to get to know her better.

"I'm shy," she explained. "I'm much more comfortable asking the questions."

Will Madison viewers be seeing a lot more of Lark Chadwick? That's really for you to decide.

"Actually," I said folding the paper and picking up a menu, "it's for *me* to decide."

"He seems really hung up on your love life, doesn't he?" Kirk asked.

"Uh huh. I really don't want to go there."

Kirk turned to Lionel. "I listened as the guy interviewed her. She talked about all kinds of stuff, Lionel, but Anderson didn't use much of it. His piece reads like a first date."

Lionel leaned forward and turned so he could look at me more directly. "See what I mean about TV being showbiz, Lark?"

"Yeah, I do," I said.

"Welcome to life in a fishbowl," Lionel scowled, sitting back. "I just hope you can swim."

Chapter Twenty-Three

Weekend number two on TV didn't go nearly as uncomfortably as my initial appearance. I felt more at ease and bantered effortlessly with Grant and Ginger. But when the ten o'clock newscast ended Saturday night, and the spotlights dimmed, I felt a sudden emptiness—a tinge of loneliness that caught me by surprise, and troubled me.

"Ginger and I are going out for a drink. Care to join us, Lark?" Grant asked from the doorway between the studio and the control room.

"No, thanks," I sighed. "I'm kinda tired. You two go on without me."

"You sure?" He wiggled his eyebrows suggestively.

"Maybe some other time," I smiled.

"Suit yourself." He bowed. "G'night."

"Night, Grant."

I was alone on the set. Slowly, I gathered up my scripts, all the while trying to figure out the reason for my sudden, and uncharacteristic melancholia. My thoughts turned to Jason. I hadn't seen him since the Duran news conference on Monday. He'd said he would call me later that night, but he didn't. I'd thought about calling him, but I have a personal policy against chasing boys. I've found they need very little encouragement, so I do my best not to give them any.

But Jason wasn't just some random guy. He cared about me. And I cared about him. Deeply. Yes, I'd been angry with him, and I hadn't hesitated to tell him so. But my emotions had steadied since then. It occurred to me that the spat we'd had just before Shane's news conference was our first real argument. I'd never been in this territory with Jason.

I began to worry that the reason I had yet to hear from him was that he'd given up on me. He'd realized what a shrew I could be and decided to bail out while he could. Lots of guys had, but the thought of losing Jason felt different. It felt the same way as the day I found Annie's body: A powerful inner void—an ache that still hadn't gone away after six months.

As I sat at the news desk, absentmindedly shuffling through my discarded scripts, I thought about Kirk. I couldn't deny that I felt something for him, but I knew in my heart it was probably nothing more than a thrilling infatuation that was already starting to wear off, accelerated by his sudden come-on when he stole a kiss from me by the lake. Yes, he'd shown some respect and backed off, but he'd also crossed a line with me—a line that Jason had honored.

The longer I sat in the cold, cavernous studio, the more I was able to convince myself that my petulance had caused me to blow it with Jason. And that made me feel like crying.

"Hey there."

I looked up, startled.

Jason stood by the door where Grant had been only a few minutes earlier. Jason wore jeans and an untucked, dark blue corduroy shirt, unbuttoned, revealing a gray T-shirt.

"Oh, hi," I said. He looked so good. Just seeing him made me feel comfortable—and comforted.

"I thought I might find you here." His voice echoed in the darkened corners of the now-dim studio. He took a few steps toward me and leaned nonchalantly against a TV monitor.

I didn't know what to say. He'd taken me by surprise, so I blurted out the first thing that came into my head: "Where have you been all week? You said you were going to call."

I was disappointed to hear a steeliness in my voice that I didn't feel.

"I've been busy," he said simply.

"Busy avoiding me?" I tried to smile, but it felt fake.

He shrugged. "And busy thinking."

"About?"

"About us."

I felt my heart beat faster and with it, that feeling of emptiness in my stomach that signaled I was about to lose the best thing that had ever happened to me.

"W-wanna go out and get a beer and, um, talk?" I asked, trying to mask the sense of desperation clawing at my insides.

He made a face and bobbed his head indecisively.

"Or you could walk me to my car, at least," I tried gamely. "You know how I hate dark parking lots." I tried again to smile, but it felt like a grimace.

"Sure," he shrugged.

As we made our way through the studio doorway and into the control room, I secretly wished that he would reach out to me, maybe put his arm lightly across my shoulder. I'd missed his touch more than I realized.

We walked in silence through the empty control room and down a side hall. When he opened the door to the parking lot for me, I was surprised—and a little disappointed—to see a rather forlorn-looking Jonathan Anderson skulking just outside beneath a security light. His flaxen hair and pallid forehead were so brightly illuminated that he looked washed out, but his eyes and chin were in shadows.

"Oh, hi, Lark," he said, dazed. "I was just going to see if you wanted to go get a beer or something." He looked at Jason.

"Do you two know each other?" I asked. "Jonathan, this is my friend Jason."

Jason reached out his hand.

Jonathan considered it, then finally grasped it perfunctorily.

"I remember seeing you at the Duran news conference," Jason said, smiling broadly. He had perfect teeth. "Lark and I were just going to get a beer ourselves. Want to join us?"

We were? My heart did a little hop. *There might still be a chance to salvage our relationship.*

Jonathan's face brightened. "Sure. Thanks."

The lightness I felt dimmed just a little because with Jonathan around, Jason and I wouldn't be able to work things out—at least not right away.

We drove separately, agreeing to meet at a nearby pub on Whitney Way. The place was louder than I would have liked. But it was close.

"You did a good job tonight, Lark," Jonathan said once we got settled in a booth and the beers arrived.

"Thanks."

"I agree," Jason added.

The jukebox began playing Aretha Franklin's "Respect."

"Oh, and thanks for the nice article," I said to Jonathan. "It was very sweet of you."

"I'm glad you liked it. It wrote itself." He paused, still uncomfortable. "So, are you two an item?" Jonathan asked, looking back and forth between Jason and me.

"We're friends," I said quickly, perhaps too quickly and presumptuously because Jason said nothing. He merely scowled into his frosted beer mug.

Silence.

We all took simultaneous sips.

I turned to Jason and broke the ice. "When he's not writing for *MadCity*, Jonathan does standup."

"Oh, really?" Jason said, brightening.

"He did some great impersonations the other night at the Nitty Gritty," I said.

Jonathan blushed.

"How'd you get started doing that?" Jason asked. He leaned forward, rested an elbow on the table and cupped his chin in his hand.

I longed to be the person on the receiving end of Jason's attention.

"It started one day when I was really desperate," Jonathan laughed, relaxing. "I worked one summer at a department store. The boss had a distinctive croaky voice. One evening I called up this girl I worked with. Had a huge crush on her, but we worked different shifts. So, I called her and pretended to be the boss."

Jonathan put his hand to his ear as if holding a telephone and his voice took on a coarse whisky-soaked timbre.

"Hey, Marcie, it's Jack. I'm dyin' here. Somebody called in sick and I need ya here right away. Can ya come right in, doll?" Jonathan took his hand away from his ear and smiled, wistfully. "She was there in twenty minutes. It made my day, and she never knew the difference."

We laughed.

"Where do you get your inspiration?" Jason asked.

"Usually when I'm outside," Jonathan said. "I love to hike."

"Cool," Jason said.

"Yeah. I'm in a hiking club, actually. Every year we go on treks."

"Where to?" Jason asked.

"One year we hiked the Inca Trail to Machu Picchu in Peru."

"Wow," Jason said. "I'd love to do that sometime."

"It's inspiring, that's for sure," Jonathan said.

I enjoyed sitting back, watching Jason and Jonathan talk. It made me appreciate Jason. I liked how he was willing to unselfishly and generously include Jonathan in our outing, and then made Jonathan feel at ease by effortlessly engaging him in conversation. I found myself realizing again how lucky I was to have Jason in my life—but then worrying that he might not feel the same way about me.

Jason asked Jonathan another question—this time about the Madison music scene. It launched Jonathan on a seemingly interminable analysis of the current crop of MadCity bands, their personnel, their strengths, and their weaknesses.

I found myself getting bored, tired, and a little annoyed that Jonathan was dominating the discussion. I wanted Jason to myself.

I finished my beer. "Gentlemen, it's been lovely, but I've gotta push on." I stood. "I'll leave you two to get better acquainted. Talk amongst yourselves." I said, waggling my hand at them.

"I'll walk you to your car," Jason said. He dug out his wallet and slapped some cash on the table. "My treat," he said to Jonathan, who hadn't made a move for his wallet.

"Thanks," Jonathan mumbled.

Jason got out of the booth and stood next to me. "Nice meeting you, Jonathan." He held out his hand.

"Same here," Jonathan said without enthusiasm. They shook hands.

As Jason followed me to the door I glanced back to see a forlorn Jonathan drag himself from the booth.

Jason and I strolled into the parking lot. Neither of us had spoken yet by the time we got to Pearlie.

I put my back against the door of the driver's side and leaned up against it. "Your chivalry is much appreciated, kind sir," I smiled. I was ready for him to offer to go somewhere to talk. Anywhere. Even right here, if he wanted.

Jason clicked his heels together and tipped his head deferentially. "My pleasure, your grace."

"So…" I said, not sure what to say next.

"So…" he responded.

We faced each other, the gulf between us seeming to grow wider with every second.

I caught a glimpse of Jonathan watching us from across the parking lot. When he saw me looking, he quickly got into his car and squealed out into the street.

I turned my attention back to Jason. "So … you've been thinking?"

"Uh huh."

"About us?"

He nodded.

"What about us?"

"Dunno. I'm still thinking." Suddenly, he leaned over, kissed me lightly on the forehead, turned and walked briskly away.

I was so stunned and disappointed that I didn't react, but if I knew then what I know now, I would have run after him. I will always, *always* regret not doing it.

Chapter Twenty-Four

Sunday afternoon I was taking a nap when the phone rang.

"Hello?" I mumbled.

"Hi, Lark."

"Jason?"

"No…"

"Kirk?"

"Wrong again…"

Now I was fully awake, and annoyed. "A telemarketer?"

"No. It's Jonathan."

"Who?"

"Jonathan. Jonathan Anderson. I see I've made a big impression on you."

I chuckled. "Hi, Jonathan."

"Did I catch you at a bad time?"

"No," I lied. "I was just taking a little nap before going in to anchor the evening news."

"Thanks for including me last night."

"Sure. No problem. What's up?"

Jonathan cleared his throat. "Um, I was wondering. I want to do a follow-up piece on you. Would it be okay if I hung out at the station and watched you at work?"

Something didn't feel right, but I couldn't put my finger on it.

"Well, that would be pretty boring," I laughed.

He started to talk rapidly. "I got a lot of emails after that profile I did on you. People can't seem to get enough of you, Lark."

"That's sweet, but I'm concerned they're going to get too much of me. I'm actually a shy, quiet girl, Jon."

"But it'll be good for the station," he continued. "You guys are in last place in the ratings on weekends, you know."

I didn't know and didn't really care, either. I couldn't think of a rejoinder, so I said nothing and tried to come up with a good reason to say no. I did know that better ratings meant more money for the station. And more money for the station often trickled down to the anchor whose face on the tube helped to build a bigger audience. And this particular anchor could use the dough.

"I promise I won't get in the way," he pressed.

"I suppose, if you want," I said, reluctantly.

He brightened. "That would be great. Maybe we could go out afterwards for a drink."

"Hmmmm. I don't think so. I've got to be in to work at *The Standard* pretty early."

"Oh..." He sounded disappointed. "Anyway, what would be a good time for me to show up at the station?"

"I have to be there at five."

"Great. I'll see you then."

At five, when I pulled into the WMTV parking lot, Jonathan was waiting for me outside the front door, a good-sized camera dangled against his chest, hanging from a strap around his neck. He looked worried, but a big smile came over his face when he saw me.

"Hey there," he called to me as I got out of my car.

"Hi, Jonathan. You sure you want to go through with this? People are going to think you have a thing for me."

His face flushed instantly.

Inside, I introduced Jonathan to the crew, and to my sports and weather sidekicks Grant Deloatch and Ginger Jones. They seemed cool to him, almost as if they were jealous of all the attention being showered on me by the Entertainment Reporter for the *MadCity News*. As disdainful as

124

some TV-types are of being lumped in with "entertainment," I realized they still seem to crave the attention.

Am I becoming the same way?

I found Jonathan a chair and pulled it up to the desk where I sat at the computer, getting caught up on the news of the day and reading over my scripts. At first, Jonathan whipped out a tape recorder and notebook, but soon he switched off the machine because all he was getting was room ambience.

I was in my reading zone, saying nothing. At times, I noticed him jotting notes and taking pictures, not only of me, but of the newsroom chaos, as well.

After a while, Jonathan left me and tagged along with Grant, and a little later I saw him talking with Ginger. No doubt they were telling him what a rank amateur I am. I began to regret agreeing to let Jonathan come along.

About 5:45, I went out onto the anchor set. Jonathan tagged along and watched from the shadows behind the cameras.

The six o'clock news went without a hitch. Each time I did it, I felt more comfortable.

"What do you do between newscasts?" Jonathan asked.

"I get a quick bite to eat, then get going on helping put together the ten."

"Where do you go to eat?"

"Depends. Sometimes we order a pizza, or go to any one of the restaurants nearby."

"Will you let me buy you dinner?" He mentioned a nice place.

"Sure. Thanks." I was still wary, but also hungry.

At the restaurant, we sat in an out-of-the-way booth. The lighting was dim. Soft piano music came from somewhere. After the waitress took our order, he whipped out his tape recorder again.

"You're always working, aren't you?" I observed.

"Obsessively."

"How'd you get into this line of work?" I asked.

"Hey, who's interviewing whom?" he laughed.

"I'm interviewing you, for a change."

He switched off the recorder and actually seemed grateful for the opportunity to talk about himself. "I love movies. Watched them all the time as a kid. I can spend all afternoon at the cinema, seeing the same flicks over and over again. In high school, I tried out for plays, but wasn't any good. I wrote a screenplay, but it sucked. But I could write about movies. When I was still in high school, I got a part-time job writing movie reviews. It turned into a full-time gig after high school and expanded to all aspects of entertainment."

As he talked, he seemed to come alive. It was as if I had tapped an underground spring. His blue eyes, which usually looked sad and haunted, sparkled.

"What about college?" I asked.

His face suddenly darkened. "I flunked out. Too obsessed with my job and not obsessed enough with studying. That's okay," he shrugged. "I've made my peace."

Our food arrived and we ate in silence for a while, then Jonathan asked, "So, where's Jason tonight?"

"He doesn't usually work weekends."

"And how has it been working with Kirk?"

"Really great. He's such a good researcher, not to mention writer. I'm in awe."

"Is Jason jealous?"

"Off-limits, but nice try. What about you? Any groupies?"

"Very funny."

"Well, I can ask. You don't seem to have a problem asking me."

"Yeah, but with you, it's more interesting. My life's pretty empty when it comes to chicks."

"So, you live vicariously?"

"Something like that."

Chapter Twenty-Five

I was sitting with Kirk at the Korner Café having a cup of coffee about nine Monday morning when my cell phone rang. It was Jason.

"I'm going to be out your way on a story today and wondered if you wanted to get together for lunch," he said.

"What's the story?"

He hesitated. "I can't tell you."

"Jason!"

"I'm sorry, Lark."

"There's only one story that would bring you out here and we both know what it is."

"I can't tell you, Lark. It's nothing personal. I just can't."

"Maybe that's why the root of competition is petty."

"C'mon, Lark."

"It's Landscam, isn't it?"

Silence.

"Am I right?" I prodded.

Jason sighed. "I can tell you this much. I got a call from Duran. He wants to meet privately at ten o'clock, no cameras, off the record."

"Where?"

"Granddad's Bluff. He says he wants to show me some property and to help put some things in perspective for me."

"Jason, I'm worried."

"I'll be okay, Lark. He didn't sound hostile. It seemed like he wanted to bury the hatchet."

"In your head."

"Oh, that's a lovely thought."

"What if he's drunk?"

"He's not drunk—or at least he didn't sound like it. I think he knows the story's not going away, so he's trying to mend some fences."

Now it was my turn to sigh. "That doesn't sound like Shane."

"Tell you what. If I'm not at the Korner Café by noon, call me on my cell, okay?"

"Okay. Be careful," I said, and hung up.

"Where's he going?" Kirk asked.

I just shook my head. "I've gotta get back across the street." I fished my wallet out of my bag.

"I'm off to the courthouse in Madison," Kirk said, pushing back his chair and standing up. "When should we link up to compare notes?"

"Jason's supposed to meet me here at noon. How 'bout here at one?"

"Sounds good."

We paid our bills and went outside. Kirk got in his car and headed off toward Madison. When I got to the office door, I looked toward the opposite end of the street. Looming above it, the craggy sandstone face of Granddad's Bluff. I shuddered, and said a prayer for Jason.

Chapter Twenty-Six

I spent a relatively productive morning at the office. Lionel was out and Muriel needed to run some errands, but before she left she gave me some odds and ends to do.

"Is something bothering you, Lark?" Muriel asked, as she was getting ready to leave.

"I'm worried about Jason. He's meeting with Shane Duran on Grand-dad's Bluff. Jason didn't sound worried when he told me about it, but it gives me the creeps. You should have seen the hate in Shane's eyes at that news conference, Muriel."

She gave me a little hug. "It'll be okay," she murmured. "When will you know how things went?"

"We're meeting at the Korner Café at noon," I said.

"He's going to be fine, but if you feel you need to cut out early, go ahead."

"Thanks," I said. "I probably will."

"See you later." The bell over the door announced Muriel's departure.

All morning, I kept glancing at my watch. Finally, at 11:45, I could stand it no longer. I dashed out the door and across the street directly to the restaurant. I managed to get a window table for two just before the noon rush began.

Millie filled a coffee cup for me while I waited.

And waited.

I called Jason's cell phone. No answer. I tried again. Nothing. I tried the television station, thinking maybe the meeting had been called off. The assignment desk said he was in Pine Bluff. I called the newspaper office. Muriel had returned, but she said Jason hadn't called. This time she sounded a little worried, even though she still said comforting things.

I couldn't sit still. I paid the bill and dashed out the door just as Kirk's car pulled up in front of the newspaper office across the street.

"Hey!" I hollered. "Kirk!"

He waved. "Hi, Lark."

Dodging traffic, I ran across the street.

"I was just running some errands," Kirk said when I got to the side of his car door. "I'm not late, am I?" He glanced worriedly at his watch.

"No, but Jason is. He went to the bluff to meet with Duran. I need to make sure he's all right."

Immediately, Kirk read the note of panic in my voice and on my face. "Hop in."

He squealed a U-turn in the center of the block and we raced out of town toward Granddad's Bluff, its rocky edifice towering 500 feet above us. The trees populating the bluff's lower two-thirds were just beginning to bud.

It took us at least fifteen minutes to get to the top because the road twists and turns through many hairpins. On weekends, the top of Granddad's Bluff is crowded with people having picnics, or bringing out-of-town friends to see the breathtaking panorama. But today, the place was nearly deserted.

We found Jason's Jeep parked alone in the lot at the end of the road.

Kirk parked the car and I jumped out, almost before he'd come to a stop. I peered inside the Jeep, but Jason wasn't there. I tried the doors. All locked.

I looked around, but saw no one. I ran down a sidewalk toward a picnic pavilion passing several empty picnic tables along the way. Jason and Duran could have met at any one of these tables, but Jason hadn't told me exactly where the two had arranged to meet. All I knew is that I was close.

But was I too late?

Fear tore at my stomach.

Am I just being an irrational ninny? God, I hope so.

I prayed as I ran.

Kirk trotted well behind me. I ran all the way to lookout point, a narrow fenced-in area with a pay-per-view telescope.

Still no sign of Jason.

"Where could he be?" I whined, as Kirk finally caught up to me.

"JASON!" I called. "JA-sonnn!" My words echoed in the hills, but there was no reply.

Kirk called Jason's name, too. His voice was louder and deeper than mine, but we got no reply.

"I've got another idea," I said. I dashed back the way we came. The pavilion was at the pinnacle of the bluff. I poked my head inside.

"Jason?" I called, my voice echoing off the stone walls.

No answer.

I stepped inside. It took me a minute for my eyes to adjust to the relative darkness. The room seemed to be empty, but I called Jason's name once more.

Still nothing.

I darted from the building and past Kirk. I was heading toward another look-out point nearby. In recent years, the parks department had it fenced off because the rocky observation area had become hazardous.

"Lark, be careful," Kirk called as I clambered over the fence. "It's not safe out there."

I ignored him.

The rocky outcropping was, indeed, precarious. Rocks I'd dislodged clicked onto the boulders below me. Carefully, I peered over the edge and looked down.

Nothing.

I surveyed the rest of the panorama in front of me. Main Street stretched out from the foot of Granddad's Bluff and went all the way into downtown Pine Bluff a mile away. Beyond the town, the Rock River snaked through the lush Wisconsin farmland. I could see Shane Duran's Rock River Estates. It was adjacent to Grampa's farm, which I could also make out in the distance. Way off, I could see the glistening-white capitol dome in Madison.

But I couldn't see Jason.

I looked to my right. About a hundred yards away was Table Rock where he'd first kissed me. No one was there. I shifted my gaze down about 300 feet to a rocky plateau. Something there didn't look right.

I screamed.

"What is it?" Kirk called. He'd stayed safely behind the fence.

I screamed again.

That was enough to propel Kirk over the fence and to my side.

"What's wrong?" he asked, urgently.

"L-look!" I pointed.

Kirk followed my finger to what appeared to be a figure crumpled on the stones below Table Rock.

"I see something," he said, "but from this distance, I can't tell what it is."

"It's Jason. I just know it." I began to sob.

"Steady, Lark." He cupped my shoulders in his hands and looked me in the eye. "We don't know that yet. We can't even be sure it's a person."

I would hear none of it. I dug my cell phone out of a pocket and jabbed the 911 keys.

"Let's go have a closer look," Kirk said, guiding me back to the fence.

"This is an emergency," I blubbered into the phone. "I'm on Grand-dad's Bluff. It looks as though someone has fallen off Table Rock. You need to send an ambulance right away."

We scrambled over the fence and ran down the trail. Before we got very far, another hiking trail veered off to the left. I swerved onto it and ran with all my strength down toward the foot of Table Rock. At one point, I tripped on a tree root and went sprawling, but Kirk lifted me to my feet and I dashed ahead again.

After a desperate ten minutes of downhill zigzagging, the trail entered a rocky clearing. I could now clearly see the prostrate figure of a person facing away from me lying among the boulders and stones.

At first glance, it looked as though the person had chosen to lie down for a nap. The body, clad in a brown leather jacket, dress slacks, and loafers, lay on its left side, almost in the fetal position. A two-foot-long bloody smear extended from beneath the head.

I ran to the body to get a better look.

Jason's eyes were open in a dead stare.

Chapter Twenty-Seven

Jason Jordan lying dead at my feet was just too horrible for words. I'd already been in this situation once before when I'd found Annie's body sprawled on the floor of the home where she'd raised me in Madison.

That had been just six months ago.

Now this. Now Jason.

By comparison, Annie's death by carbon monoxide poisoning, though harrowing and awful enough, was not nearly as monstrous as Jason's murder. And I say murder without hesitation. Already my mind refused to believe that Jason had simply slipped and fallen off Table Rock. He had come here to meet Shane Duran. And even though Shane had admonished Jason to tell no one of their meeting, Jason had shared the information with me.

I wept and wailed bitterly. He'd been patient with me—and kind. He'd been more willing than any other man I'd ever known to wait me out, always adjusting to my whims and moods. Although I'd been afraid that he was going to break up with me, his casual phone call to see if we could get together after his meeting with Duran had given me hope. And the worry I had about his safety convinced me that I was on the verge of being more conciliatory and less the glacier I'd been to him. But our time together had run out.

I knelt next to Jason and held his hand in mine, but just as with Annie's, Jason's hand was cool and unresponsive to my touch.

I vaguely heard Kirk on his cell phone place another 911 call, this time to say that the person at the bottom of the cliff was already dead.

I lay my forehead against Jason's shoulder and waited for the authorities to arrive. Once Kirk tried to comfort me with the lightest of touches on my shoulder, but I angrily shook him off.

"Leave me alone," I snarled. "Get away and leave us alone."

Kirk backed away, and until the police arrived, I was only aware of being with Jason, just below the place where he'd first kissed me.

Sheriff Carl Olson was the first to arrive. I knew him well and liked him. He wore wire rim glasses, a Smokey the Bear hat, and a dark brown jacket over his tan uniform.

"What happened, Lark? Do you know the victim?"

"It's Jason Jordan."

"The reporter?"

I nodded. "And Shane Duran did this, Carl." I didn't bother looking at him; my attention was still focused on Jason and his blank stare.

"How can you be so sure?"

Still kneeling by Jason's side, I told Carl of Jason's phone call earlier and how I'd pried out of him that Duran had invited him to the bluff for a mend-the-fences meeting.

"He's the real estate guy, right? The one you've been writing stories about?" Carl asked.

I nodded. "Kirk and I both." I gestured at Kirk, who stepped forward and held out his hand to the sheriff.

"Kirk Kensington, sir."

They shook hands.

"And," I went on, "Shane publicly threatened Jason last week at a news conference. Kirk and I both heard it."

"That true?" Carl asked Kirk.

"Yes, sir."

"What specifically did he threaten to do?" Carl asked.

"The threat wasn't specific," Kirk said. "Duran just made it clear that if Jason continued doing Landscam stories, he—Duran—would use any means necessary to make him stop."

"Were those his exact words?"

"I'd have to go back and check my notes." Kirk turned to me. "Lark, do you remember?"

"It was something like that. It was real clear to all of us that Jason was being singled out, and was being explicitly warned not to do any more stories."

"But why Jason? You guys are the ones who broke the story," Carl said.

"Well, he didn't like us, either," I said, "but apparently he felt Jason's stories were more damaging because they were on television and reached more people."

Carl crouched next to me. "But didn't you tell me that Jason thought Duran was now trying to make up? Maybe Jason fell after the two met, or perhaps Shane never showed up, or maybe they got into a scuffle and Jason fell by accident. There are a lot of other possibilities, Lark," the sheriff said.

"I think the meeting was a pretext," I said, angrily. "Reconciliation, and perhaps the promise of an exclusive interview, may have been what Shane used to lure Jason up here. But I think he intended to push Jason off the ledge." I grabbed Carl's sleeve. "You have to arrest Shane Duran and make him pay for what he did to Jason," I cried.

"Hold on there, Lark. First I need to find out what Shane has to say. If he won't talk, he'll do some cooling off in the slammer. But we'll see." Carl stood. "In the meantime, I'd advise you—both of you—to stay away from Duran and let me and my guys do our jobs. I can assure you we'll conduct a fair and thorough investigation, okay?"

"You're right, sheriff," Kirk said.

"Lark, what about you?" Carl asked.

"Okay," I nodded, sniffing as I swiped at the tears running down my cheeks.

"I can understand how you both feel," Carl said. "We'll get to the bottom of this. Trust me."

Chapter Twenty-Eight

The next few days were a blur. I stayed with Lionel and Muriel. They'd taken me in once before, after an attempt on my life several months ago when I'd been investigating my parents' deaths. Lionel and Muriel had also helped point me in the right direction when my Aunt Annie died.

Now Jason.

I could barely function. Lionel and Muriel carried me through those first few awful days and helped me during the worst of it.

Kirk hovered around, trying to be comforting, but I stiff-armed him. His motives were probably wholesome and sincere, but the distrusting part of me figured he was merely angling to become Jason's replacement in my heart. I couldn't even bring myself to contemplate that possibility.

Kirk did sit with me at Jason's funeral—in the very same pew with Lionel and Muriel. He even squeezed my hand once and offered me a handkerchief, but I did nothing to encourage him, and he seemed to respect my need for space.

Jonathan Anderson was also in attendance at the funeral. He shyly approached me at the cemetery as I headed back to the funeral parlor limo after Jason's graveside ceremony in Madison.

"Lark, I know this is a terrible day for you, but I'm writing a piece about Jason and I'm on deadline. Could you please spare a minute or two to answer a couple quick questions?"

I smiled through my still-fresh tears. "Sure, Jonathan. It's good to see you."

And it was. I felt as though I'd been in a cocoon. The story of Jason's death had been front-page news, but Carl Olson had refrained from releasing any information about my suspicions. He'd held a news conference shortly after Jason's death, but, other than mentioning that I was the one who found the body, he'd shared very few details, not even the reason Jason had been on the bluff in the first place.

I'd been angered to read in *The Wisconsin State Journal* this quote from Sheriff Olson: "Mr. Jordan's death appears to be an accident, but the investigation is not over yet." To the question, "Is foul play suspected?" Olson would only say, "We're looking at all possibilities, but for now this is an accident investigation, not a murder investigation."

So far, Shane Duran's name had not been mentioned, so I welcomed the opportunity to share my hunch with Jonathan.

He switched on a tiny hand-held recorder. "How are you feeling? Dumb question, I know."

"It hurts. It really hurts. Such a waste. He was a wonderful, talented, patient man." My voice caught on the word "patient."

"How is it that you came to be the one who found the body?"

It took me a moment to regain my composure. "Jason had told me he was going to Granddad's Bluff to meet with Shane Duran. I urged him not to go, but he said he thought Shane sounded conciliatory."

The surprise on Jonathan's face was sudden. His eyes got wide. He opened his mouth to ask another question, but when he saw I hadn't finished, he bit his tongue and let me talk.

"Jason and I were going to get together afterwards, but when he didn't show, I went looking for him. That's when…" I couldn't say more; the memory was still too fresh.

"Did Jason and Duran meet?" Jonathan asked.

I shook my head. "I don't know."

"What do you think happened, Lark?"

"This is only my opinion, Jonathan, but I think Shane lured Jason to Table Rock for a reason other than reconciliation. You were at that news conference, Jon. You heard the menacing tone in his voice. I'll let you put two and two together."

"One more quick question and I'll leave you alone, Lark. What are your plans now?"

"Too soon to tell, but I know I can't just sit around."

"So, you'll be on the air again this weekend."

"You can count on it. And I'll be looking for Jason's murderer, too," I added.

"Anything else you want to say?"

"I cared about Jason very much. And I'll always miss him." I couldn't say more.

Jonathan turned off his tape machine, thanked me profusely, touched my arm gently, told me to "hang in there," and scurried off to his beat-up Honda parked behind the funeral parlor limo.

Chapter Twenty-Nine

Exhausted and drained after Jason's funeral, I returned to Pine Bluff with Lionel and Muriel, and promptly went to their guest room, exchanged my black mourning garb for my nightgown, and collapsed into bed for a nap.

My sleep was troubled, a kaleidoscope of disjointed images and sounds, including the shouting voices of a woman and a man. But as I gradually awakened, the shouts persisted, punctuated by a loud *bang* that seemed to make the house shake.

I sat up in bed, now fully awake.

The angry voices of my dream were real and were coming from downstairs.

I slipped out of bed and tiptoed to the door, opening it a crack.

The voices became clearer.

Lionel was shouting. "I was NOT being overbearing. I was being protective. Don't you dare accuse me of not caring about her."

Then I heard Muriel's voice, almost a shriek, as she responded, "You only cared about your career—and keeping her under your thumb."

"I don't have to take this crap from you," Lionel yelled.

I heard his footsteps thud across the living room and then I heard the front door slam.

I went to the window and watched as Lionel stomped to his burgundy Volvo parked at the curb in front of the house. His white hair was disheveled, his face was flushed, and his mouth was a twisted snarl as he yanked open the door to the driver's side, got in, gunned the engine to a roar and then squealed away from the curb.

The house was suddenly quiet, but my heart was banging loudly. I was frightened and troubled by what I'd just witnessed. I'd always thought Lionel and Muriel were rocks of Gibraltar. The stability and strength of their relationship had steadied me through some of the worst storms of my life. But now I suddenly felt adrift and rudderless, buffeted by their anger at each other.

As I pondered how I should handle this troubling new development, I realized my arms were crossed at my stomach, a feeble attempt at hugging myself. Quickly, I threw on jeans and a rugby shirt and raced downstairs in my bare feet.

Muriel was standing at the picture window looking out at the street where Lionel's car had been parked a moment before. She turned in my direction when she heard me coming down the stairs.

"I suppose you heard all that," she said, her voice still edged with an anger I'd never heard from her before.

"Just the tail end," I said. "I'd been asleep." I got to the bottom of the stairs. "Are you okay?"

She shrugged. "I'm sorry you had to hear any of it."

I stood at the foot of the stairs, not knowing what to do, or say. She turned her back on me and gazed out the window again.

Finally, I spoke. "Maybe it would be better if I went back to my place. I think I'm in the way here."

Quickly, she turned to face me. "No. Please don't go." Her voice was now soft, almost pleading.

"Is ... is there anything I can do to help?"

"Stay." She sat down on the couch and patted the seat next to her. "Talk with me."

I padded across the room and sat where she'd indicated. Her eyes were damp. She fished a wrinkled hanky from the pocket of her cardigan sweater and blew her nose, then sighed heavily.

"What's going on?" I asked, my voice a gentle whisper.

Muriel sighed one more time. "The inner tube just bobbed to the surface again."

"Holly?"

She nodded. "About a year after she died, we moved back here from D.C."

"Why?"

Muriel shrugged. "A change of scenery. Lionel was more than ready to retire…and this is home…a fresh start. Lots of reasons. But then my depression set in."

She stopped talking and looked at me, probably to gauge my reaction.

Her revelation about depression stunned me because Muriel had always been so optimistic and steady. Depression is not a word I would have ever associated with her.

I kept my face impassive, neutral. "How did the depression manifest itself?"

"I slept a lot. Sometimes my emotions were a flat line. Other times I was volatile and angry."

I could relate. "Did you think about suicide or abuse alcohol?"

She smiled. "No, thank God. None of that."

"What did you do to deal with it?"

"I began seeing a therapist."

"Did it help?"

She nodded and smiled. "A lot. She prescribed an anti-depressant. I was spooked about that at first because I didn't want to live the rest of my life medicated." Muriel made a face. "But I went along with it. My therapist explained that the medication would steady my emotions and allow me to examine their underlying causes more objectively. She considered my depression to be mild, so she said her goal would be to wean me off the meds."

I touched her sleeve. "This is none of my business, but are you still in therapy? You don't have to tell me."

She put her hand on top of mine and smiled. "We're in the cone of silence, right?"

I nodded. "Of course."

"Yes. I'm still in therapy. I've even tried getting Lionel to go."

"Is he depressed, too?"

"He's certainly angry. And, of course, I seem to know which buttons to push."

"So, you're not getting along," I said, stating the obvious, but hoping it would be a graceful segue into learning more about the blowup I'd only partially heard.

Muriel nodded and sighed. "In many ways, we really do get along well. He's a good man and I've always loved him, but when it comes to Holly…"

"I've read that the death of a child can create stresses that can kill a marriage. Is that true?"

"Sad, but true." She dabbed at her eyes with the hanky.

"How can I help, Muriel?"

She sighed. "You're already helping, dear."

"So, what caused the Holly inner tube to bob to the surface this time?"

"It was the visit we got a couple weeks ago from Laura and William Benedict."

"I met them. They were on the hiking trip with Holly, right?"

Muriel nodded. "When they showed up, all the memories came rushing back—for both Lionel and me."

"And all the old tensions and friction?"

"In spades. Today's little…" she paused, searching for the right word, "episode was about the day we gave Holly permission to go on the trip to Peru."

"What was significant about that?"

"Lionel thinks it's my fault for letting her go."

I was getting into territory way beyond my ability to be of any help, other than to provide a sympathetic ear. At that moment, I decided not to take sides, but to be a sounding board. Maybe, I reasoned, as Muriel talked with me, she might be able to find a way to amicably resolve her differences with Lionel. And, failing that, perhaps our conversation would at least provide her with some comfort and encouragement.

"I'm sure his opinion prompted all kinds of feelings on your part," I said, trying to remain neutral. I didn't know the facts and felt uncomfortable digging for them.

Muriel nodded, and began to answer my unspoken question about why Lionel blamed Muriel for being complicit in the tragic death of their daughter.

"The trip was a graduation gift," Muriel began. "Holly was going to go with her friend Meredith, but Meredith had to back out at the last minute, so Holly would be going by herself. I was worried about it, but Lionel wanted to cancel the trip. That led to a big family argument.

"Holly was not a patient person and, well, you know what Lionel can be like." Muriel rolled her eyes. "He and I were sitting in the living room. He was in his favorite easy chair, feet up on the footstool, reading the paper—as always," she added, her voiced tinged with disgust. "I was on the couch reading a book when Holly came in to tell us that she'd just learned that Meredith had to back out.

"Lionel wanted to know why. Holly explained that Meredith needed to earn money for grad school and that she had just landed a very lucrative job. 'Looks like you won't be going then, either,' Lionel told her.

146

"'Like hell I won't,' Holly said. They were always clashing about something. I was always the peacemaker.

"Lionel said to her, 'You're just a kid.' He was glaring at her over the top of his glasses.

"'I'm twenty-two.' Holly yelled. She was standing over him, thumbs hooked through the belt loops of her jeans. She sneered, 'I don't need your permission.'

"'Actually, you do,' Lionel said, 'because I'm paying. It's the golden rule: he who has the gold, makes the rules and I rule that it's too dangerous.' And with that pronouncement, my husband angrily wrestled his newspaper back into position.

"That just got Holly more upset. 'I'm an adult!' she shouted.

"Lionel lowered the newspaper and took his feet off the footstool. I could tell he was getting ready to confront her standing up, if necessary. 'Don't yell at me, young lady.'"

Muriel smiled, a distant look on her face as she remembered something about the scene. "Lionel's 'young lady' line prompted Holly to have a quick come-back: 'Well, at least I'm not a kid anymore.' Then Holly turned to me. 'Mom, help me out here.'

"I must say, Lark, I was torn. I was sympathetic to Holly, but I told her that Lionel and I were very uneasy about letting her go to South America all by herself. I was trying to be a calming influence."

"Did it work?" I asked.

"Trying to find middle ground between two hotheaded, highly opinionated people isn't easy. You run the risk that they'll both turn on you. Fortunately, Holly stopped short of directing her anger at me. When I told her that both Lionel and I were uneasy, she spread out her arms imploringly and said, 'Don't you guys trust me?'

"I said, 'Honey, it has nothing to do with trust. A woman traveling alone—especially a young, attractive woman like you—is especially vulnerable.' I tried to keep my voice low and reasonable."

Muriel turned to look at me, seeming to need affirmation that she was being reasonable.

I merely nodded that I understood.

Muriel went on, "Apparently, it worked. Holly's voice softened. 'I know,' she said, 'I'll be careful.'

"But that prompted Lionel to jump back in. He leaned toward her. 'How?' he demanded. 'How will you be careful when some knife-wielding Spic comes at you?'

"Holly exploded. 'That is so totally racist.'

"Lionel didn't say anything, he just continued glaring at her.

"'It's not gonna happen,' Holly said.

"'Saying so, doesn't make it so,'" was Lionel's comeback. He rustled the newspaper to punctuate his point and put his feet back up on the footstool.

"I tried to bring something practical to the conversation," Muriel said, "so I asked Holly, 'What'll you do during your six-hour layover in Miami on a Saturday night? Your flight to Lima is at 1:30 in the morning!'

"Holly smiled. 'I could catch a cab and check out the nightlife.' She meant it as a joke, knowing it would set Lionel off. Which it did.

"'No frigging way!' Lionel roared from behind his raised newspaper.

"'Dad, I'm kidding. I'll stay at the airport,' Holly said.

"Lionel peered around the side of the page. 'And do what?' He was challenging her again.

"'Have dinner. Window shop. Read.'

"'You'll be a sitting duck.' Lionel told her and went back to reading the paper.

"'Dad, it's the Miami airport, not an Armenian brothel. I'll have passed through security, so I'll be in a safe place.'"

I laughed at Muriel's comment. Holly had said what I probably would have in the same situation.

Apparently, Muriel and I had a similar reaction, because she said, "I tried not to laugh out loud. Holly was making sense, so I stepped in on her behalf and said as much to Lionel. The newspaper shifted and he shot me an incredulous look. 'You're not letting her go, are you?'

"I told him, 'Not yet. I'm just trying to consider some ways that this can be done safely.'

"'I don't like it," he grumped and resumed pretending to read.

"'I know. I'm uneasy, too,' I told him, 'but let's try to brainstorm.'

"Holly came and sat next to me on the couch. The conversation was shifting her way, so by aligning herself with me physically, she was making it two against one. She said, 'I could call you regularly just to check in.'

"I asked if there would be cell phone service in the mountains while she was on her hike.

"'Not until the third day,' she told me.

"'How do you know that?' Lionel asked, lowering the paper just a little.

"Holly told him she read about it on the travel agency's website, adding that the tour guide would also have a satellite phone in case of an emergency.

"Lionel still wasn't satisfied. 'But for three days, you'll be out of touch, right?' he asked.

"'Probably,' Holly said, 'but by that time I won't really be alone any more. I'll be with an organized group of about fifteen other people.'

"Their sparring continued.

"Lionel: 'Fifteen strangers'

"Holly: 'Potential friends.'

"Lionel: 'Potential predators.'

"Holly: 'Dad, not all guys are like you used to be.'"

Muriel said, "I jumped in before it got ugly. 'Let's do this:' I said to Holly, 'call us when you can. There'll be times when you're on a plane, or sleeping, or hiking, but otherwise, just keep us in the loop.'

"Holly knew she was on the cusp of victory. 'I can do that. No problem,' she said.

"I suggested that she look for people along the way who would be safe companions, like a middle-aged couple traveling together. I told Holly, 'If they're like your father and me, they'll be protective of you, plus you won't stand out as being alone and vulnerable.'

"Holly agreed, but by this time, Lionel had gotten quiet and sullen, so I asked him what he thought.

"He scowled at me. 'I don't have to like this, do I?'

"I said, 'No, dear. You don't.'

"He muttered something under his breath, snapped the newspaper back into place, and resumed his reading—once again, father and daughter were separated by a wall of pulp and ink."

Muriel turned to look at me sitting next to her on the couch. Her eyes were sad and haunted.

Chapter Thirty

Slowly, Pearlie and I patrolled downtown Pine Bluff. It was about six o'clock. I was worried about Lionel, especially because of how angry he was when he zoomed away from the front of the house after his argument with Muriel two hours earlier.

Muriel assured me that he would be all right—"he always comes back in one piece" she'd told me—but I wanted to be sure.

"Pearl, I'm really freaked out about Lionel and Muriel," I told my car. "They've both been there for me in the past—the least I can do is help them."

I drove past *The Standard*, but Lionel's car wasn't there. Nor was it at Riverside Park. I was about to give up, but then I spotted his Volvo parked in front of Bank Shot Billiards, a dump at the far end of town. I parked behind him and went inside.

It took me a minute for my eyes to adjust to the dim lighting. The nearly deserted place smelled of stale beer. Classic rock thumped from the jukebox. A middle-aged guy with a scraggly beard sat at the bar just inside the door and to my right. He nearly fell off his stool when he turned to look at me, but quickly righted himself.

"Howzitgoin', sweetie?" he leered. He patted the seat next to him. "Sit right here and I'll buy ya a drink."

I smiled, mumbled "no thanks" and quickly walked past him to the far end of the bar where the room widened. Lionel was by himself in the back standing next to a pool table. He hadn't seen me, so I stopped to watch.

He wore a wrinkled white shirt, sleeves rolled up beyond his elbows. His suit coat lay in a heap on an empty pool table. He chalked the tip of a pool cue, then set the blue cube on the edge of the table next to a tumbler containing ice and an inch of something amber. He picked up the glass, took a slug, and set it back down. His cheeks bulged intermittently as he sloshed the liquid around in his mouth.

I turned to the bartender. "Has he been here long?" I asked in a low voice, nodding toward Lionel.

"He's starting his second solo match and finishing his third Scotch rocks."

I nodded. "Thanks."

"Can I get you anything?" he asked.

"Bud Lite." I wasn't yet sure of my plan, but I didn't want Lionel to think I was merely there to drag him back home. I'm not a hard booze kind of girl, but I wanted something comfortable and comforting in my hand when talking with Lionel.

He was now circling the table—cue ball in one hand, pool cue in the other. The balls were all racked up. He placed the white ball onto the green felt, quickly lined up the shot, and took it.

CRACK!

The white ball hit the others with such force that it looked like the splitting of the atom in a nuclear chain reaction—almost all the balls in the triangular cluster scattered in every direction, spinning in a wild kaleidoscope of colors, careening off the side bumpers and clicking into each other. Two balls—one striped, one solid—rolled into pockets at the two corners of the far end of the table where Lionel now stood, surveying the damage he'd done to what had been a nice, neat arrangement.

I stepped into the circle of light surrounding Lionel and the pool table.

"Winner buys the next round?" I smiled.

Lionel looked up, surprised. He held my eyes for only an instant before he pursed his lips and turned his attention back to the remaining balls on the table.

"You just know I'm gonna whip your ass, don'tcha?"

I chuckled. "You've already sunk a stripe and a solid. What'll it be?"

He surveyed the table to see if he had any easy shots. "Solids," he announced, bending down to line up another shot. He sank it easily.

As he prowled the table, looking for his next shot, I chose a cue and chalked it. Lionel quickly drained two more balls.

"Hey, mister. You gonna let me play?" I teased.

"Not if I can help it." He smacked another ball into a pocket, chuckled, paused briefly to take a swig from his glass, then lined up another shot. This time, he wasn't so lucky.

"All right, buddy. Give the lady some room." I hadn't played pool in at least a year, so I knew I was not only rusty, but was up against a seasoned pro. Nevertheless, I gave it my best shot, which isn't saying much. My feeble first attempt merely rearranged the balls on the table.

"So, now you know my dirty little secret," Lionel said.

"What's that?" I asked, pushing myself up from the table and facing him.

"That Muriel and I aren't getting along."

I shrugged. "Lots of people fight."

"I suppose she told you what a bastard I am."

"She told me that you're a good man and that she loves you."

He laughed. "Yeah. Right."

"Those were her exact words."

"Along with a few others?"

"Look, Lionel, I'm not here to take sides or divulge secrets. I care about you *and* Muriel—and I know you care about each other. Holly's death has been tough on both of you."

"Ya think?" He drained his glass and ambled to the bar. In a moment, he was back with another fresh drink.

I wanted to get him talking, but I felt it wise not to take a direct approach. We stood silently next to each other, looking at the pool table, but lost in our thoughts. The ice clinked in Lionel's glass as he stirred it with the short cocktail straw sticking out of it. I took a sip of my beer.

"Let's sit down over there," Lionel said, pointing at a table for two next to a wall. "I wanna tell you a story."

He slid the cue stick from my grasp, and laid it next to his on the pool table.

Chapter Thirty-One

The chairs scraped against the cement floor as we sat at opposite ends of a small, rickety table, our drinks between us. Lionel's flushed face was the only indicator that he'd been drinking. "Satisfaction" by The Rolling Stones poured from an overhead speaker and echoed throughout the still nearly-empty place, although a few more people—mostly older men — now sat at the bar.

"Two years ago," Lionel began, "Muriel and I were still living in Georgetown when I got a phone call one night from a guy named Mike Sutherland. We'd met at Khe Sanh back in '68 when I was covering the Vietnam War for the *Times* and he was a Marine lieutenant. We got drunk together one night in Saigon, so at first, I thought he was calling just to shoot the breeze about the good old days, but when I realized he was the U.S. Consul General in Lima, Peru, I got a hinky feeling."

Lionel took a sip from his drink, then continued with his story. "'This isn't about my daughter Holly, is it?' I asked Sutherland. 'She's on vacation down in your neck of the woods.'

"'I'm afraid it is,' Sutherland said. I heard him take a deep breath before he charged on. I only had a second to brace myself for what came next." Lionel hesitated and bit his lip, then continued. "He got right to the point and gave it to me straight, just like a good journalist. He said, 'I'm so sorry to be the one to tell you this, but your daughter Holly—'" Lionel's voice caught and he stopped suddenly, clenching his teeth and battling his emotions. He managed to croak one more word—"died"— before he had to stop again, but then lurched on to the end. "'Died this morning in a fall from a cliff along the Inca Trail.'"

Lionel put his hand up to his face. His shoulders shook violently, but I only heard two staccato sobs.

Tears coursed down my cheeks. I placed my hand comfortingly on his forearm and waited until he was ready to go on.

"I'm sorry, Lark. I've never talked about this before and I need to get it out."

"It's okay, Lionel. I'm right here."

In a moment, he regained his composure. "The news was a gut-punch. I staggered to the dining room table and sagged into a chair. Instinctively, I reached for a pen and found the back of an envelope to scribble on. I was struggling with my emotions. The best way to bludgeon them into submission is to force your mind—and your curiosity—to take over, and that's just what I did.

"'Okay,' I told Sutherland, 'give it to me straight: what happened?'

"He told me that Holly died instantly in a fall and that police in Urubamba were still investigating. I asked when it happened. He told me her body was found about eight that morning. I checked my watch. It was 8:15 at night—one hour ahead of Peru. I asked why it took twelve hours to let me know.

"Sutherland said it happened in a remote area, so it took a while for the cops to get to the scene, retrieve the body, identify it, and take it to Urubamba for an autopsy.

"I was scribbling furiously," Lionel went on. "I asked if anyone had seen it happen, but he said he didn't know because police were still investigating.

"When Sutherland told me that it would take another day—maybe two—before Holly's body would be returned to the states, I told him that I couldn't wait that long and that I was coming down there.

"He tried to wave me off. Said it wasn't necessary, that he could handle things, but I told him I wanted to go there and check things out on my own. He said he'd try to help in any way he could."

Bluff

"Lionel, I can only imagine how awful this must have been for you. How did you deal with your emotions?"

"I just sucked it up. You pay absolutely no attention to your feelings because feelings just get in the way of doing a responsible job. To be a good journalist, you have to be tough on yourself. Emotions can cloud your judgment."

"But you weren't being a journalist. You were being a father."

"All the more reason to keep a lid on things. After nearly fifty years in the trenches, I've grown a thick callus around my heart. I try not to let anything get to me."

He took a sip from his drink and swallowed. "Oh, sure, every now and then something sneaks up on you when you least expect it. My mom's death was tough because it was sudden—I never had a chance to say goodbye. Dad's death was more troubling than tough, maybe because Alzheimer's had simply turned the old man's mind to mush. It was hard to watch him waste away, so I simply backed off and let the nurses do what they were paid to do."

"But Holly's death was different?" I asked.

He nodded. "Things hadn't been good between us. I had eighteen hours to think about it during the trip to Peru."

"Muriel didn't go?"

He shook his head. "Nah. Our son Paul was with her. She knew I would have felt claustrophobic sitting at home waiting for Holly's body to arrive like some sick FedEx shipment. For me, being on the move was the best way to handle my grief. So I kept moving. I worked her death like I worked any story, by asking questions: What happened? When? Where? How? And the most maddening question of all: Why? It's the journalist's credo. All stories answer those questions."

"You left out 'who'," I said.

Lionel chuckled mirthlessly and took another swig of whiskey. "Ah, you're so right. Who indeed? The 'who,' of course, was Holly, but did I really know her? Believe me, I thought about that a lot on the trip down there, too.

"On the flight from Washington to Miami, I kicked myself for all the missed opportunities. When she was born, I was moderating a presidential debate at some university in the South. When she turned six, I missed her birthday because I was meeting with my publisher in New York. When she went to the prom, I missed the ceremonial moment when her date presented her with a corsage. It was Muriel who took the obligatory pictures in front of the fireplace. I had to work late because of a major story that threatened that night's deadline. It seemed important at the time, but I can't even remember what the story was now."

He shook his head, sadly.

"Had you ever been to Peru before?" I asked.

"Nope. Never. Spent the entire flight between Lima and Cusco with my face pressed against the window getting nose grease on the glass. The Andes Mountains are rugged. Reminded me of the Sierra Nevadas near Reno—varying shades of brown, craggy and wind-swept, with precipitous drop-offs.

"Mike Sutherland, the U.S. Consul General, met me at the Cusco airport. Once we were inside the white consulate Suburban, he brought me up to date. He handed me a manila folder containing the English translation of the police report. Bottom line: the cops ruled Holly's death an accident. No witnesses. She was alone at the time. Nobody saw her fall.

"That pissed me off. 'How could she be alone?' I asked. 'I thought she was with a group. Where was the tour guide?'

"Sutherland said he didn't know.

"I told him I wanted to talk with the guide, but first I wanted to see Holly.

"Sutherland had his driver take me to the morgue. It was a bone-jarring ride through narrow streets."

Lionel was now in full-blown storytelling mode. It was almost as if he was on deadline dictating his narrative over the phone to the rewrite guy back in New York.

"Along the way to the morgue," Lionel continued, "I got quick glimpses of street scenes: a mongrel dog drinking from a puddle on the side of the street; two young girls wearing backpacks and matching blue and white Catholic school uniforms eating ice cream cones and giggling as they walked down the sidewalk; two men working on a puny, turquoise taxi jacked up on the side of the street.

"The Cusco morgue is a relatively new lime green stone building at the top of a hill on a busy street corner. The surrounding structures could easily have been a couple of hundred years old. Many of them were two story ramshackle adobe buildings with roofs made of red tile or corrugated tin.

"The morgue is in a medical center for abused women and children, so you've got people waiting to identify the dead sharing the same space with beaten wives and molested children. It was a sad mix. The lobby was clotted with small knots of tense people, talking in hushed voices. A small, wooden coffin—the size of a small child—stood on the marble floor in front of two sad-looking young men. They were in their late twenties or early thirties. I figured they were brothers.

"A receptionist sat in a cubicle protected by two-inch-thick Plexiglas. Sutherland said something to her in Spanish and pretty soon the medical examiner came out from somewhere in the back to meet with us. I was surprised that the M.E. was a woman because it's a pretty macho culture. She was tall, good looking, about forty, and wore a white lab coat. I think she said her name was Dr. Rodriguez. Her English was nearly perfect.

"She led us down a hall, around a corner and out a back door into a walled compound. We crossed a small courtyard and entered another building. Two senses immediately overpowered me: a pleasant coolness and the strong stench of formaldehyde tinged with a whiff of decaying flesh.

"'Your daughter is back here,' Dr. Rodriguez said. 'Are you sure you wish to see the body?'"

"I gave her a curt nod. 'I must,' I said."

"She led us into a large, reasonably antiseptic room dominated by a stainless steel examining table in the center. Sunlight streamed through windows in the roof. She had us wait there while she opened a metal door that revealed a small, walk-in refrigerator. She went inside. A wall of cold air oozed into the room and seemed to pool at my feet. I squeezed my eyes closed for a moment, took a deep breath, and ordered myself to get ready."

I studied the expression on Lionel's face as he talked. His eyes were glazed over as if in a trance. The scene still seemed fresh and indelible in his mind.

Lionel continued, "I opened my eyes when I heard the squeak and squeal of a gurney as the medical examiner wheeled the covered body feet first into the examining room and closed the refrigerator door. Blotches of dried blood soaked through the white sheet that completely covered the corpse.

"The medical examiner reached for the edge of the sheet covering the head, paused briefly, and gave me a look that seemed to silently ask if I really was willing to go through with this. I nodded and Dr. Rodriguez slowly pulled back the sheet."

I reached over and gently put my hand on top of Lionel's. He didn't seem to notice.

He said, "I remember gritting my teeth and willing myself not to throw up. Holly's head was tilted back, chin extending upward at a forty-five-degree angle. My first impression was that the back of her head was recessed into a concave area of the table, but then I realized that it looked that way because the back of her head was missing. Her long blonde hair was ratty and matted with dried blood. Her skin was as white as porcelain, except around her cheeks and closed eyes, where angry bruises masked what had once been her typically insouciant expression. But it was Holly."

Lionel paused, fished a white hanky from his back pocket, dabbed at his damp eyes, and blew his nose. He clenched the hanky in his hand and plunged ahead with his narrative.

"I recognized her by her lips. Even in death, one side curled up as it used to when she was about to crack a joke."

Lionel smiled faintly. "I stared at her for a moment. I don't remember feeling anything. I reached under the sheet and found her right hand. Rigor mortis had turned it into a stiff claw. On her right ring finger, she still wore the ruby-stoned ring her mother and I had given her for her twenty-second birthday. I let go of her hand, and reached for her cheek, stroking it gently with the back of my hand."

Lionel's voice now was barely a whisper. I had to lean forward to hear it above the din from the jukebox, now playing something by the Beatles.

"Her skin felt like cement. That's when I lost it. I remember sobbing, but then I must have blacked out for a second because the next thing I remember is Sutherland and Rodriguez restraining me. I'd been banging my fist against the metal door of the walk-in fridge. I pounded it again and again and again and again—until it dented. It was only later that I realized my hand was broken."

He looked with sad eyes at his right hand and flexed his fingers as I patted his left hand with mine.

From the overhead speaker, Paul McCartney sang sweetly, "She's leaving home, bye, bye, bye, bye."

Chapter Thirty-Two

After telling me the story of identifying Holly's body, Lionel sat back in his chair, fully spent. The anger that had contorted his face as he left the house had given way to what seemed like resignation.

"Let me drive you home, Lionel. We can pick up your car later."

"Like when I'm sober?"

"Something like that. Friends don't let friends—"

"Drive drunk. I know. I'm not—"

"Drunk. Maybe not, but let's not take any chances."

He shrugged, then smiled. Super Tramp was playing on the jukebox. "Take the long way home," Lionel tried to sing. "Good advice." He chuckled. "C'mon, let's go."

Lionel signed his tab. "A lot cheaper than therapy," he said as he scribbled his signature on the credit card receipt.

"Where do you want to go?" I asked, once we were inside Pearlie.

"Surprise me," he said, and closed his eyes.

I drove to the cemetery in Madison where some six hours earlier we'd laid Jason to rest. Lionel dozed and snored heavily throughout the half-hour drive, his chin on his chest, head lolling when I'd make a turn.

Resurrection Cemetery is where Regent Street and Speedway come together near Madison West High School. Lionel woke up just as I came to a stop near Jason's grave. The days were longer now; the sun was low in the sky.

"Where are we?" Lionel asked, looking around. When he saw all the gravestones, he turned to me, mock alarm on his face, "Am I dead?"

"Not yet," I laughed.

"Why are we here?"

"You said, 'surprise me.'"

We got out of Pearlie and trudged the short distance to Jason's grave. Flowers from the funeral were heaped onto the fresh mound of earth that covered Jason.

"I like graveyards," I said.

Lionel gave me a look.

"No. Really. They're very peaceful."

We stood in silence, but Lionel shuffled uncomfortably. A crow cawed from the limb of a nearby tree, then flew gracefully to another tree deeper in the cemetery.

Lionel put a strong hand on my shoulder and squeezed. "It's tough, kid, but you're gonna get through this."

"Thanks, Lionel. I hope you're right, because it sure does hurt." I took a long look at the grave. I knew I'd be back. "We should go. It's getting dark and Muriel will be worried."

"Oh, I doubt that," Lionel scowled.

As we walked back to Pearlie, I said, "Look, it's none of my business, Lionel, but how bad are things between you and Muriel?"

"There are good days and bad days—mostly good, but today was particularly bad."

"Are the spats usually about the same thing?" I asked, getting into the driver's seat.

Lionel got in on his side and buckled up. "Variations on a theme," he said.

"What's the general theme?" I started the car and pulled away.

"That I was too hard on Holly."

"Any truth to it, do you think?"

He sighed. "That's a matter of interpretation. From Muriel's perspective, yes. From mine, I was merely trying to be a strong guide."

"Have you and Muriel tried marital counseling?"

He laughed. "I'm not into psychobabble."

"But aren't you concerned that things may be heading to a point where the marriage can't be salvaged?"

He thought a long time before answering. Finally, he said, "I don't know. I honestly don't know. Sometimes I think the marriage is doomed. Other times I have hope. Today? I dunno."

We were driving east on Regent Street. To our right, we passed the stone structure of St. Stephen's Episcopal Church where I'd been attending before moving to Pine Bluff. If I'd been alone, I might have dropped in on Dan Houseman, the rector. He lived next door to the church. Instead, I drove toward Park Street where I made a right turn and headed out of Madison toward Pine Bluff. I felt a little guilty that I hadn't transferred my membership yet to a church in Pine Bluff—and felt even guiltier that I hadn't been going to church at all.

We drove in silence for a while. I watched as the setting sun threw pink light onto fleecy clouds.

"Why don't you know if the marriage can be saved, Lionel?" I asked, finally.

He thought a moment. "I think it's because Muriel is different now."

"What do you mean?"

"She's quicker to find fault with me," he said. "But the faults she brings up are old ones. It's only lately that she started unloading on me."

"Maybe she'd been keeping a lid on her emotions all these years, but she couldn't do it anymore," I offered.

"Could be," Lionel replied. "Could be." He looked out the window at a passing farm. "Doomed," he said simply.

"Maybe marriage counseling will help."

"Yeah. Maybe." He sounded unconvinced. Soon, he was dozing again.

It was nearly dark by the time we got back to Pine Bluff. I was a little nervous because I didn't know what to expect when Lionel and Muriel would be in the same room together—the secret of their marital strife now no longer a secret—at least to me.

Would they argue again? Would things return to normal? Would we all be awkward and uncomfortable with each other as we tried to ignore the proverbial elephant in the room?

Muriel was sitting on the sofa reading a book, a glass of white wine sat in front of her on the coffee table.

"Welcome back, you two." She sounded like the pleasant Muriel I knew and loved.

"Hi," I said. "We played some pool at Bank Shot Billiards, then I took Lionel on a ride back to the cemetery in Madison."

"There's some soup simmering on the stove," she said. "I've already eaten."

"Mmmm. That sounds good," Lionel said. "Do you want some, Lark?"

"Sure. Thanks."

So far, I noticed, they hadn't exactly talked to each other, but the atmosphere, though a little tense, wasn't confrontational. Muriel kept reading.

I ambled into the kitchen to help Lionel who had taken two soup bowls from the cupboard and was now rummaging through a drawer, looking for a couple spoons. He handed one to me, along with a bowl, then ladled into it what looked like vegetable noodle soup. After serving himself, he put the cover back on the pot, turned off the heat and followed me into the dining room where we sat across from each other.

At first, the only sound was clinking and slurping, but then Lionel said, "Kirk's been looking into Jason's death."

"Oh?" I said. "And?"

"He's developed some sources inside the investigation and it actually looks as though they're closing in on Duran."

"Really? What kind of stuff does he have?" I asked excitedly.

"He's got two sources close to the investigation who tell him a half smoked cigar, the brand Duran smokes, was found on top of Table Rock."

"Was the cigar fresh?"

"Yep. Still warm, as a matter of fact."

"Fingerprints?"

"They're not saying."

"It's as if Shane was having a smoke while he waited for Jason to arrive,"

I said, "Or maybe he had one of his 'celebratory stogies' after he pushed him."

"Could be," is all Lionel said.

Lionel's revelation gave me a sense of hope. For the first time, I had a reason to be encouraged that Sheriff Olson was really taking my suspicions seriously. I ate with gusto, my mind spinning with the possibilities. I began to relish the idea of helping Kirk get to the bottom of Jason's death.

But then Lionel brought my enthusiasm to a sudden stop.

He cleared his throat. "Lark, for now I'm taking you off Landscam and the Jason stories."

"What?" I asked, dropping my spoon. "Why?"

"C'mon, Lark. Do I really need to spell it out for you?"

"No. I guess not. I know better than to argue with you, Lionel," I said wearily. "I'm now definitely too close to the stories, right?"

"I'm glad you understand."

"I do, but I still don't like it." I finished my soup and took the bowl and spoon back to the kitchen and placed them into the dishwasher. Then I walked through the dining room back to the living room where Muriel still sat reading.

"What am I supposed to do, Lionel? I can't just sit around moping and missing Jason. I've got to be doing something."

Muriel put her book aside and walked over to where I stood looking out the front window. She put a gentle hand on my shoulder. "Just come in to work whenever you feel like it. I can always find something for you."

I sighed deeply and began to weep. Muriel draped an arm around me and pulled me close as I hugged my waist and cried. Pain and regret poured out of me in torrents. For the millionth time I berated myself for the way I'd treated Jason.

Muriel guided me to a place on their Chesterfield sofa and kept her arm firmly around my shaking shoulders. She fished a hanky from the pocket of her cardigan, but I waved it away and dug out one of my own from the front pocket of my jeans.

Gently, Muriel rocked me and whispered, "There, there. It's going to be all right, Hol—" she caught herself. "Oh, dear me," she gasped. Then Muriel, too, began crying.

With both my hands I grasped her free one lying in her lap, and raised it to my face. "Oh, Muriel," I wept. I kissed her hand and pressed it against my cheek. "Don't cry."

I sensed Lionel quietly passing through the living room and heard the stairs creak as he walked up to the second floor, leaving Muriel and me keening and comforting one another on the couch.

We sat swaying and crying for the next few minutes, both of us giving in to our emotions. I'd never seen Muriel cry. I'm sure she had, privately, but she was always strong for everyone else. We each knew, deep down, how the other felt. I remember reading somewhere that you're never closer to someone than when you pray—or cry—together. I'd never felt closer to anyone in my life than I did then with Muriel. It was a precious and sacred moment.

After a while, our emotions spent, we sat quietly on the couch holding each other. Soon Lionel came back downstairs and tiptoed back into the room carrying a book.

I looked up at him and he smiled. "I thought I'd leave you two alone," he whispered.

Muriel stood. "I'll make some tea," she smiled.

"I'll help you," I said, making a move to stand.

"That's okay. I'll be fine. Thanks."

Lionel sat in a chair across from me.

"Have you had a chance to read any more of Holly's diary yet?" I asked, wiping my nose and putting the hanky back in my pocket.

He slumped against the back of the chair. "I had to stop."

"How come?"

"It hurt too much." He fiddled with the book he held in his lap. "I can dish out the criticism, but I can't eat it, especially when it's coming from my own daughter. And now it's too late to fix things." His face was pained.

"Has Muriel read any of it?"

He shook his head. "I don't think so. She calls it 'wallowing in the past.'"

I reached over and touched his sleeve. "I'd be glad to take a more objective look at it, Lionel. Maybe there's more hope in there than you think."

He touched my hand. "Looking for hope. Nice line. I like that. It's just what I hoped you'd say. Here." He handed me the pastel-colored book he'd been holding. "It's Holly's diary. Happy reading." Then, he got up and walked slowly into the kitchen where the teapot had just begun to whistle.

Chapter Thirty-Three

I began reading Holly's diary that night. I want to say that I would have liked her, but I'm not sure that's true. She seemed extremely hard on Lionel—and way more licentious than I am. Yet I tried to read with an open mind. I kept telling myself that the person Lionel is now might no longer be the one Holly railed against in her diary.

As for Holly's libido, a part of me envied how carefree she was about sex compared to my uptightness, partly the result of the psychological damage Ross had inflicted upon me. I'd testified against him, but it was the testimony of two women he'd actually succeeded in raping that resulted in his conviction. He was sentenced to ten years in prison.

I felt he got off easy.

I desperately wanted to be able to trust men in the same way Holly seemed able to do, yet in my experience, most men gave me ample reason to have grave doubts about their motives and trustworthiness— even as my sexual side ached for physical intimacy with someone to whom I could give myself completely.

Just as I hate to peek ahead while reading a novel, I resisted the temptation to jump to Holly's final entry. I opted, instead, to get to know her as best I could as she revealed herself.

Here are some excerpts:

May 4—

Graduation is almost here, and once again, Daddy is on my case about going into journalism. My God! He still doesn't get it. I talk about my love for digging up detritus from old civilizations, and he goes on and on about how it's just like a journalist digging up hidden information.

I talked to Mom and she said she'd talk with him—again.

May 15—

Today I graduated from college.

Daddy gave the commencement address.

I felt myself slink deeper into my chair as I watched my famous father stride confidently to the podium. His white, wavy hair contrasted with the black robe and crimson hood he wore.

Light glinted off his glasses as he acknowledged the applause. Fervently, I hoped he wouldn't embarrass me. He'd teased me that he might.

"Oh, Daddy," I told him. "Don't. Please don't. I'll die. All my friends will make fun of me."

"At least you'll be listening to what I have to say for a change," he said with a twinkle in his eye.

I knew he'd meant it as a joke, but there was an edge of truth to it. Things hadn't been good between us. We're too much alike: opinionated and stubborn.

I felt a bead of sweat trickle down my back as I sweltered inside my graduation gown. My head ached from all the alcohol I'd consumed the night before. Two cups of coffee and two aspirins before the ceremony weren't enough to deaden the pounding between my temples. Even the buzz from toking up with some of my friends before the ceremony didn't help.

I squirmed impatiently as the applause died down and he began to speak.

"My daughter Holly—who sits among you today—has, in her typically emphatic way, urged me to be brief."

His amplified voice echoed throughout the stifling auditorium. A smattering of applause washed over the crowd.

"Hold your applause," he adlibbed, holding up his hands. "I'll keep it short. It's my graduation gift to you, Holl." He nodded at me. "It's a lot cheaper than the Corvette I would have gotten you, instead."

The crowd roared.

I groaned and sank lower into my chair.

May 16—

Just found out today that Meredith won't be able to go with me on the trip to Peru. Bummer. I was really looking forward to going with her, but she's got to stay home and earn money for grad school. It's too late for me to bail out without losing my deposit, so I'll go by myself.

Daddy, of course, thinks this is unwise. He thinks I'll now be vulnerable to every pickup artist and con man south of the border.

I tried to explain that I'll be going in a group, but he still thinks it's a bad idea. I really am getting tired of his oppressiveness. Doesn't he see that he's just pushing me farther and farther away?

"But you're my little girrrrl," he keeps whining.

Geez! I'm 22-years old. I can drink. I can vote. I'm an ADULT!! I can do whatever I damn well please. Doesn't he get it? Won't he let GO?!

"Let me make my own mistakes," I tried to tell him, but he's always got a response:

"Some mistakes can kill you."

He's Mr. Worst Case Scenario. For everything I try to do, he's got a detailed explanation as to how it could kill or maim me. I can't wait to get out of the country.

May 17—

Went shopping today with Mom. Went to REI and got some stuff for the trip, then she took me out to lunch. She's so much different than Daddy. I really don't see why she sticks with him, but she says they have a good rapport. Maybe so, but I'll never let my husband boss me around like he bosses her. But she doesn't seem to mind.

Mom understands me. She says Daddy is just having a hard time accepting that his little girl is growing up.

"Grown up, Mom; I'm grown up, not growing."

Mom pointed out, diplomatically, I must say, that we're all "works in progress." She says we should never feel that we've "arrived."

Of course, she's right. Why is it easier for me to accept what Mom says, but resist what Daddy says? I know deep down that a lot of what he says makes sense. Is wise, even. So, why can't I tell him that?

I think the answer is that if I tell him that, it will only spur him on and give him more encouragement to sink yet one more talon into me. I don't want him—or anyone—to control me, and I guess that's what I'm fighting. I love my parents; they've given me so much, but I instinctively rail against anything that feels like it's smothering my own person. My SELF.

May 18—

So, who am I, anyway?

I'm Holly Stone. Daughter of the world-famous, New York Times journalist and Pulitzer Prize-winning author Lionel Stone.

Long before I was even born, HE would define my identity. At first it was cool. I got attention because of who my dad is. And, at first, I really idolized him because of that.

Maybe that's when he first began to entertain the thought of taking that raw adulation of mine, and molding me into the female version of himself.

But why was that necessary? He already had a clone in my big brother Paul.

May 19—

I'm still thinking about who I am. It's hard to get out from under the stifling burden of Dad's fame. I want to be known for who I am, not who my father is. That's why I chose anthropology.

Do I love it? Will that be my career? My profession? Sometimes, it's so tedious. Sometimes. Other times, I lose myself in reveries about ancient societies. But, will I ever tell Daddy that sometimes I have my doubts that I really want to go into anthro? No frigging way. He'll just use that as a way to get into the next "I told you so" lecture.

But do I like journalism? Not really. I like writing. But I think journalism puts you around too many creepy people who don't tell the truth and do all sorts of unsavory things.

Why would anyone want to spend time getting to know these crooked people, then write things that often put them on pedestals?

Bluff

True, Daddy helped bring down Nixon, but that was a one-shot deal. Most of what I read in the papers is so BORING or DEPRESSING!

May 20—

I'm still not sure I want to go to grad school. A part of me just wants to say goodbye and good riddance to books, exams, studying and all that other crap. I applied for a job at the Gap, but Daddy thought I'd lost my mind.

He complained about how I'm lowering my standards. I didn't wait around to hear the rest. I left while he was in mid rant. It felt good to slam the door. I just want him to leave me the hell alone.

May 21—

I'm getting excited about Peru. Meredith wishes she could go, and it would be fun to have her along, but I'm honestly not freaked that I have to go alone. I'm looking forward to it. Kinda hoping I meet and fall in love with some hot guy. Somebody older and more mature. College guys are such immature morons.

Daddy's never really liked any of the guys I've dated. And he's made me so deathly afraid of getting AIDS that I don't hook up with anyone unless he uses a condom. In fact, that reminds me: I need to get a big box of condoms for the trip—maybe two. Or three. Yeah!

May 22—

I really am at a crossroads in my life. Now that I'm a graduate, I need to start being responsible for making my own way. But not yet.

Whenever I think of life after college, I get scared and don't want to leave the protective cocoon. But while being surrounded by all that protectivity, I just want to throw off the shackles and have fun.

Peru will be my life's pivot point—one last fling before I settle down.

Nah. Settle down is too strong. I think I'll always want to have fun, even as I begin moving toward being a responsible member of society with something positive to contribute. But what?

May 23—

I applied for a job as a copywriter at a PR firm the other day, but Daddy blew his top. (Why do I keep subjecting myself to his fits of rage??) Daddy really hates public relations. "They spin and lie," he said. "They spend tons of money putting things in an unrealistically good light. It's evil, Holly. Don't do it."

I start at the PR firm two days after I get back from Peru.

May 24—

Peru is getting close and I am so psyched. There's a guy I've been talking to online who's going to be on the trip and he sounds like he'll be a lot of fun. (Daddy: if you're reading this, don't think that this time I'll be foolish enough to provide you with any names. I did that the last time, and you know what happened).

That last entry got my attention. Had Lionel been snooping in Holly's diary? I debated whether to ask him about it, but fell asleep before I could decide what to do.

I had a troubling dream. In it, I was on Table Rock. Jason was there, too, but he stood apart from me with his back slightly turned and his arms folded indifferently.

I tried to move closer to him, but in my haste, I tripped over something, lost my balance, and toppled over the cliff. I was still falling when I woke up.

Chapter Thirty-Four

Lionel and Muriel's house was quiet when I woke up the next day about mid-morning. Patience is definitely not one of my virtues. I couldn't sit still, so I ambled over to the newspaper office.

Lionel and Kirk were gone; Muriel and I had the office to ourselves. "Muriel?"

She looked up from the newspaper spread out on the counter in front of her. "Yes, Lark."

"Has Lionel told you that he gave me Holly's diary to read?"

She winced. "Yes."

"Have you read it?"

She shook her head. "I just can't."

I touched the sleeve of her burgundy cardigan. She turned to look at me. Her eyes glistened. "But I don't mind that you're reading it."

"Are you sure?"

"I'm sure."

"Do you ever wonder what's in it?"

"Sometimes. But not enough to find out. What I really wish is that we had pictures of her from her hiking trip."

"You don't have any?"

She shook her head, sadly. "They never found her camera."

I paused, unsure how to say what was on my mind. Finally, I took the plunge. "I began reading Holly's diary last night."

Slowly, Muriel closed the newspaper and folded it neatly in half. She seemed willing to hear more, so I continued.

"At one point, Holly makes a comment directly to Lionel, and implies that he'd read her diary in the past."

Muriel shut her eyes tightly and bit her lip.

"Had he?" I whispered.

Muriel's nod was almost imperceptible.

I waited, but Muriel remained silent. She ran her fingers along the fold of the newspaper, pressing down so hard that her fingertips where white.

"What happened?" I asked finally.

Muriel sighed, walked to a nearby desk and slumped into it.

I pulled up a chair and sat down, too.

"Holly had a boyfriend her senior year of college," Muriel began. "Lionel didn't approve."

"Had he met the guy?"

Muriel smiled with a distant look on her face. "No. But that didn't matter. He didn't like anyone who threatened to come between him and his little girl. Holly was very reticent to talk about the young man, but Lionel was persistent. He told me later that Holly was his hardest interview. All he could really extract from her was that she was interested in someone. But he felt that was enough to justify him sneaking a peek at her diary."

"How did you know that he'd done it?"

"Because he told me"

"What was your reaction?"

"I was horrified that he'd been snooping, and told him so. He didn't see anything wrong with it. Said he had 'probable cause' to 'investigate' to see if Holly was in any way being 'lured and enticed' into any illegal or immoral activity." With her fingers, Muriel put air quotes around Lionel's comments.

"Was she?"

"Heavens no," Muriel laughed. Holly wasn't a bad girl. She was just trying to grow up and have some fun. But Lionel was trying to read between the lines for any clue that he possibly could use against the relationship."

"Did he find any?"

She shook her head. "Not as far as I was concerned, but he seized on some comment she had made about 'withholding sexual favors' from Mike. I think that was his name. Lionel assumed Holly was up to no good when she was only being funny and metaphorical."

"What did he do?"

"He confronted Holly with the entry."

"I'll bet that was a tender moment."

Muriel laughed, but then turned serious once more. "They had a nasty argument. I have to say, I was on her side. Later, it always amazed me that he kept wondering why she seemed to be stiff-arming him, telling him fewer and fewer things. I'm sure he now regrets having been so obsessed."

"I can see why he hasn't been able to read her diary anymore," I said.

"Why?"

"Holly was writing a lot about him in the entries leading up to her death. He told me that the comments he read about himself were so painful he couldn't continue, so he took me up on my offer to read ahead to see if there's any hope."

Muriel shuddered. "I don't think you'll find much, but good luck. You're very brave, Lark." She pulled her open cardigan tightly together.

Just then the bell over the front door tinkled. We both looked up to see who had entered. It was Shane Duran—and he didn't look happy.

"There you are," he thundered, pointing at me menacingly.

Muriel and I both stood. My blood turned to ice. I'm ashamed to say it, but my first reaction was to run out the back door, but I stood my ground and held his glare with one of my own.

"May I help you with something?" Muriel asked soothingly, trying to calm him. She stepped to her place at the counter, which separated him from us.

Shane looked past her at me. "No, but maybe she can." He jabbed his finger at me again. Strangely, for the first time, I missed him calling me "Wonder Woman."

Muriel edged closer to the phone, I assumed so she could quickly stab 911 if things turned suddenly violent.

I continued standing and staring back at the man I firmly believed had murdered Jason.

"If you don't calm down, Mr. Duran, I'm going to call the police," Muriel said.

That got his attention. He turned and looked at her for the first time, then looked back at me. He brought his other hand into view from below the counter.

For a panic-stricken moment I thought he was raising a gun, but, instead, his hand held a crumpled newspaper. He pushed it toward me and said in a softer, but still angry tone, "Did you have anything to do with this, Lark?"

"I don't know what you're talking about," I said. I hoped he didn't hear my voice waver.

"Here!" He thrust it at me. "Read it for yourself."

Muriel took it from him and handed it back to me. It was today's edition of the *MadCity News*. Shane's picture was on the front page next to Jason's.

Quickly, I scanned the article that accompanied it:

John DeDakis

JORDAN ON BLUFF TO MEET DURAN BEFORE FATAL FALL
By Jonathan Anderson

WMTV reporter Jason Jordan, who died in a fall from Table Rock Monday, was "lured" there for a meeting with embattled real estate developer Shane Duran, according to Lark Chadwick, a friend of the victim.

In an exclusive interview with *MadCity News*, Chadwick said Jordan called her the morning of his death to tell her confidentially that Duran "sounded conciliatory" and had invited him to Granddad's Bluff to talk.

Chadwick, a reporter with *The Pine Bluff Standard*, found Jordan's body a few hours later at the foot of Table Rock near Pine Bluff.

Chadwick, who also moonlights at WMTV as a weekend anchor, said she told police about the meeting.

The Bluff County Sheriff's Department will neither confirm nor deny Chadwick's allegation.

Duran is at the center of the so-called "Landscam" controversy involving several area residents who claim Duran's Rock River Estates organization "swindled" them out of their life savings.

The Pine Bluff Standard broke the story. It gained wider attention when Jordan reported on it for WMTV.

At a tense news conference a week before Jordan's death, Duran angrily denied the Landscam allegations and pointedly warned Jordan against continuing to report the story.

> Although Duran did not say what he would
> do, reporters who were present--including this
> one--came away with the sense that Duran had
> threatened Jordan.
>
> "I think Shane lured Jason to Table Rock
> for a reason other than reconciliation," Chad-
> wick said after Jordan's funeral.
>
> She implied, but did not say, that she be-
> lieves Duran murdered Jordan.
>
> According to Bluff County Sheriff Carl Ol-
> son, the investigation into Jordan's death "is
> still ongoing."
>
> When contacted by this reporter, Duran had
> no comment and referred me to his lawyer, who
> also had no comment.

"Well?" Shane demanded. "Did you have anything to do with this?"

My mind raced as I tried to think of what to say that was truthful, yet wouldn't further inflame Shane's passions. I kicked myself for not going off record with Jonathan. In my stupidly naïve passion to see justice done, I'd deliberately pointed a very public finger of suspicion at Shane Duran.

Not only did I now fear a libel suit, I also had the very real fear that at any second, Shane could—and might—vault over the counter and begin throttling me. I'd already seen him angrily threaten Jason.

"W-what do you mean?" I stammered, stalling for more time to think—and praying that Lionel, or Kirk, or both of them would come charging through the door to my rescue.

"C'mon, Lark. You may think I'm stupid, but I'm really not. Did you tell that reporter that you think I killed Jordan?"

"I never made that accusation, Shane. Read it again." I did it for him. "It says here, 'she implied, but did not say' etcetera, etcetera." I knew I was splitting hairs.

"Do you really think the average reader is going to pick up on that little maneuver?"

"I never made an accusation, Shane. I just stated the facts."

"Your facts suck," he shouted.

Muriel picked up the phone. "I've asked you once to calm down, Mr. Duran. Now I'm asking you politely to leave. If you don't leave right now, I'm calling 911," she said sternly.

He was fighting hard to keep his composure. His face was nearly purple with rage.

I kept my mouth shut, not wanting to get into an argument with someone who I felt was capable of unspeakable violence. I found myself glancing furtively to my desk and the ones nearby, looking for a weapon I could use, like a scissors or a letter opener, if Shane lunged at me.

Shane spoke again, but more softly this time. "I don't know where you got your information, Lark, but it's not true."

"Are you denying that you and Jason met on the bluff?"

"Yes. I'm denying it," he yelled.

"Dialing now," Muriel said, punching the nine on her phone.

"Don't bother. I'm leaving." He turned for the door and opened it, causing the bell to ring merrily again. "You'll be hearing from my lawyer, Wonder Woman," he sneered. Then he was gone.

Muriel came back to me and we hugged. She was shaking as badly as I was.

Chapter Thirty-Five

Shane's sudden visit unnerved me. I needed to be alone for a while. I thought about driving to Madison to sit and meditate at Jason's grave, but I didn't want to run the risk of having Shane see me driving alone and do something drastic. I'd already been attacked once on that lonely stretch of road between Pine Bluff and Madison. I didn't want to risk it again.

Before leaving the newspaper office, I waited for several minutes to give Shane time to take his anger elsewhere, preferably as far away from me as possible. As I stepped out the door, I checked up and down the street, but saw no evidence of Shane anywhere. I scampered to Pearlie where she was parked in front of the office and drove up Granddad's Bluff where I sat for a long time on Table Rock. That's where I felt closest to Jason—and to God.

God and I hadn't been on speaking terms lately, so I thought I'd break the silence.

"God," I began. And that's sort of where things stayed for several minutes as I gathered my thoughts and emotions. Finally, I took a deep breath and went forward.

"I'm scared, I'm lonely, and I'm really pissed at You right now. Deep down I think I know You're there and that You love me, but I really feel abandoned—by my parents, then Grampa and Annie, and now Jason. I feel so alone." I sighed and, for the umpteenth time, let the tears roll down my cheeks.

Disgusted with myself for being so weak and selfish, I stood and paced. "I know what You'll say, Lord. You'll say that I should shake it off and quit wallowing in self-pity. You're right, of course, but I can't help how I feel and I can't help but feel that You could have protected me from all of this."

I was pacing and gesticulating wildly. Anyone watching would have thought I'd lost my sanity. But I was on a roll and the words kept coming.

"You're supposed to be All Powerful and All Knowing, yet You sat on Your Divinely Royal Duff and let Jason die." I was shouting now. "Why, God, WHY?"

The sound of my voice dissolved into the air. I'd come to a stop at the edge of the cliff. Looking down, I saw the spot where I'd found Jason. Some of his blood, now dark and dried, still stained the rocky plateau where he landed.

For an instant—just an instant—I thought about jumping.

For an instant—just an instant—I considered it.

Yes, I missed Jason dreadfully.

Yes, I felt guilty for treating him so poorly.

Yes, I was afraid of what Shane Duran might do to me.

Yes, life sucked sometimes.

Yes, suicide was a tempting alternative.

And yes, I'd considered it—really considered it—once before.

But I'd decided then that, for me, suicide would be cowardly.

But that was then.

For a long several minutes, I stood at the edge of Table Rock where Jason had once kissed me, and looked down at where his broken body had come to rest.

Finally, I lifted my head, focused on the horizon, took a deep breath…and stepped back from the edge.

Chapter Thirty-Six

The day after my showdown with God on Table Rock, I felt strong enough again to be on my own, so I moved out of Lionel and Muriel's and back to my apartment nearby.

I slept and read most of the weekend. Muriel and WMTV had forwarded to me several nice cards and letters from people I didn't even know who were touched by my loss. They wrote to express their support and sympathy.

Part of my time off was spent answering some of those notes.

Soon, however, the urge to get back into the fray began to build. Contemplating life without Jason, though unthinkable, was something I struggled to consider. It was time, not necessarily to move on, but to allow myself to face the loss and, eventually, go forward from there.

I did my weekend anchor gig. It went smoothly, and people were very supportive; they were grieving for Jason, too.

On Monday, a week after Jason's death, I went back to the office, mostly to putter and to be around other people. Landscam and the story of the investigation into Jason's death were off limits to me, so I basically did whatever Muriel needed doing—mindless stuff: filing, screening press releases, an obit or two.

By Wednesday, I was bored and mopey. Near the end of the day, I meandered over to the desk next to Kirk's, plopped down on a chair and rolled it next to his desk where I sat facing him. The sleeves of his blue oxford shirt were rolled up and he was busily typing.

"Hiya," he said, eyes fixed on his computer screen. "Can't talk right now. I'm crashing."

"I'm just hanging out. Take your time."

I watched him work. His tie was askew. As he typed, one of his sleeves slowly came unfurled and dangled precariously close to the cream cheese atop his half-eaten bagel. His sandy hair was tousled. I noticed he had deep blue eyes. There was some stubble on his chin where he'd missed a spot shaving. Every now and then he'd stop typing, scowl at the computer then read back a sentence, quietly mouthing the words.

I'd never really noticed his lips before. They were pouty, in an Elvis sort of way. I scolded myself for having "thoughts" about Kirk. I still felt guilty about the way I'd treated Jason.

As Kirk typed, my eyes wandered to a back issue of *MadCity News* lying next to his keyboard. A picture of Jason smiled back at me.

I picked up the paper and began reading.

JASON JORDAN
An Appreciation
By Jonathan Anderson

Like many of you, I admired Jason Jordan from afar. The Newscene 15 reporter's death in a fall from Table Rock near Pine Bluff has stunned the Madison area.

Jason was the kind of guy the rest of us mere mortals envy: fresh-from-an-Eddie-Bauer-catalogue good looks, no-nonsense reporter, and a megawatt personality that made you feel like you mattered.

Yet, my admiration was from a distance.

I keep asking myself why I remained aloof. Even though we covered some of the same press conferences, I shied away from cultivating his friendship. That's an indictment of myself, not him.

From my distant perch, I watched as Jason routinely helped his cameraman lug around cumbersome gear. He made friends easily with strangers.

Jason even reached out to me.

It was just a few days before his tragic death. I was at the WMTV studios on another matter when he graciously invited me to join him and a friend for a beer at a nearby pub.

To my surprise, as soon as we got settled into a booth, Jason turned his attention to me. He asked me questions about myself and he listened intently as I gradually relaxed and opened up.

The image that I'll always have of Jason Jordan is of him resting his chin in the palm of his hand as he focused on me and what I had to say.

Jason Jordan: He really listened; he really cared; he'll really be missed.

"Aw, that's sweet," I said. "Did you see this, Kirk?" I asked holding up the story for him to see.

"Just a sec," he said raising his hand. "Lionel," Kirk hollered across the room.

"How's my ace reporter? Lionel called from the counter where he'd been standing next to Muriel.

I felt my stomach tighten. Lionel had never called me that.

"My Landscam piece is done and ready for you to look at," Kirk called.

Lionel walked quickly back to his desk, hit a couple of computer keys and brought Kirk's story up on his screen.

While waiting anxiously for Lionel's reaction, Kirk looked at me and winked. "This is the hard part," Kirk whispered.

"I know what you mean," I whispered back. "So, what's in it?" I nodded in Lionel's direction.

"I found two sources in Callahan's office who say—"

"Whose office?"

"John Callahan, the State Insurance Commissioner."

"Oh. Right. Sorry. Go on."

"The sources say that their boss not only received bribes from Shane Duran, but from a whole bunch of other people who wanted special treatment."

"Good for you. Nice going." I was jealous. It could have been me earning Lionel's effusive praise.

"I saw that appreciation piece on Jason," Kirk said, picking up a more recent issue of the *MadCity News*, "but did you see this?" He riffled the pages until he found what he was looking for. "Here," he said, handing me the paper, "take a look. Jonathan's daily paper can run rings around our weekly," he frowned.

It was the story Shane Duran had confronted me with a few days earlier.

"I already saw it," I said. "Shane stopped by the office Friday and rubbed my face in it."

"He did?" Kirk, asked, surprised.

Quickly, I told him the story, including Shane's denial and threat to sue me for libel.

"Have you been served with papers?" Kirk asked, all business.

"Not yet. I think he's bluffing."

"Lionel!" Kirk shouted across the room. I need to add a quick graf or two to the Duran story."

Lionel walked over to where Kirk and I were sitting. "What's up?"

Kirk filled him in on what I'd just told him.

"I heard he was here, Lionel said, annoyed, but Muriel didn't tell me the part about his denial or lawsuit threat."

"I mention Lark in my piece," Kirk said. "How should we deal with that?"

"Let's take a look." Lionel stood over Kirk's shoulder. "Pull up the story," he ordered.

With a few clicks of his mouse, Kirk had his story up on the computer screen.

We all read it in silence.

CIGAR LINKED TO DURAN FOUND AT
JORDAN DEATH SCENE
By Kirk Kensington

Two sources close to the investigation into the death of WMTV reporter Jason Jordan say a fresh cigar found near Jordan's body may be linked to area real estate developer Shane Duran.

The sources spoke on condition of anonymity.

Jordan died last week in a fall from Granddad's Bluff.

A friend says Jordan had gone there to meet with Duran a week after a tense news conference in which a belligerent Duran made menacing statements to Jordan.

Duran initiated the meeting in order to make peace, according to Jordan's friend Lark Chadwick, but it's not known if Duran and Jordan met.

Neither Duran nor Bluff County officials
are commenting publicly on the case.
According to the sources, a cigar -- the
brand preferred by Duran -- was found on Table
Rock a few hundred feet above the spot where
Jordan's body was found.
The cigar was "still smoldering," according
to the sources.
The sources refused to name the brand of
the cigar. Nor would they say if any fingerprints were found on it.
Publicly, Bluff County Sheriff Carl Olson
will only say that the investigation into Jordan's death is "ongoing."

Kirk's story went on to include my assertion that Shane had "lured" Jason to the bluff.

"What do you think?" Kirk looked up at Lionel.

"Take out Lark's assertion that Shane 'lured' Jordan to the bluff."

"What about my statement that Duran called Jason and set up the meeting on the bluff?" I asked. "I'm thinking that should go away, too. I don't want to upset Duran any more than I have to."

"You mean don't report the news?" Lionel asked, incredulous.

"Just keep me out of it," I said.

"No can do. *MadCity* already has you on the record. If we take you out of the story completely, it looks like we're covering something up. I'm fine with letting you off the hook by not accusing Duran of murder, but it is a fact that Jason told you Duran called him to set up a meeting, isn't it?"

"Yes."

"Then do this," Lionel said to Kirk, whose fingers hovered above the keyboard, ready to type.

"See the line that begins with the assertion that Duran set up the meeting? He pointed at the screen.

"Uh huh," Kirk replied.

"Change that to say that Lark said Jordan told her that Duran called him to set up the meeting. That way Lark is merely conveying what Jordan told her."

"Got it," Kirk said, his fingers tapping on the keys.

"Read it back to me," Lionel said.

Kirk finished typing, then squinted at what he'd written. "Jordan's friend Lark Chadwick says Jordan told her that Duran initiated the meeting on Granddad's Bluff in order to make peace, but it's not known if the two actually met."

"Also," Lionel said, "insert a new graf right after that which says something like, 'Duran denies the two met.'"

"Okay." Kirk continued typing.

"Lemme see it when you're done." Lionel walked back to his desk.

Kirk finished quickly, saved the revised story, and had Lionel take a look at it.

It was a bit surreal to watch them writing a story about me. It made me feel like a person in a coma: able to hear everything being said, but unable to reply or influence the conversation. Like it, or not, I felt Shane Duran was about to be handed more information he—and his lawyer— could use against me.

"It looks great," Lionel called. "That's two really strong stories, Young Kirk. Good job."

Lionel's praise of Kirk, though well-deserved, made me feel blue. It could have been me breaking wide open the stories about Landscam and Jason's death. Instead, I was off both stories while I mourned for Jason and read Holly's diary. But Kirk's piece on the investigation into Jason's death gave me reason to believe that Shane Duran might indeed be a suspect, even if Sheriff Carl Olson was downplaying that possibility. To have Kirk fan that ember flamed my optimism—and my gratitude. Kirk was doing what I would have liked to do.

"Got time to go for a walk?" Kirk asked.

"Sure."

Moments later we were on a stroll down the street to Riverside Park. The day was sunny and warm, but not yet hot.

"Who are your sources on the cigar story?" I asked.

"You know I can't tell you that, Lark," Kirk said, "but you can bet Lionel grilled me up and down before he let me write the stories."

"I can imagine what that must have been like," I said, remembering a heated argument Lionel and I had gotten into once about anonymous sources.

Kirk rolled his eyes knowingly.

We walked for a moment in silence before Kirk asked, "How are you doing?" He touched my arm gently.

I shrugged. "Not the greatest, but let's talk about you. Looks like your career has just gotten a shot in the arm."

"Yeah. Things are going pretty well," he beamed. "This Landscam story seems to be getting bigger and bigger. It's the gift that keeps on giving."

We got to the park and ambled in silence along the sidewalk next to the riverbank.

"How are you feeling?" he asked, coming to a stop and turning to look at me. "You seem a little wistful."

I stopped and gazed past him at the river. Coming up with words was hard. I looked at Kirk. We stood inches apart. His eyes eagerly searched my face.

I leaned my forehead against his chest and sighed. I felt his lips graze the top of my head, then he put his arms around me.

Involuntarily, my arms went around him and I began to sob.

Gently, Kirk stroked my hair, my cheeks, my shoulders, all the while cooing, "It's okay, just let it out. Don't try to hold back. Just let it all out."

I did.

Chapter Thirty-Seven

The phone was ringing when Kirk and I returned to the office. As usual, Muriel fielded it.

"Lark?" she called, her hand over the mouthpiece. "It's Jonathan Anderson with *MadCity News*. Line two."

I stabbed the button and picked up the receiver. "Hi, Jon. Nice piece you did on Jason," I said.

"Thanks. In fact that's why I called."

"Oh? Has there been a break in the investigation?" I sat up, alert. "Sort of."

"Really? What gives?"

"Can we get together for lunch?"

"Absolutely. Name the place."

We agreed on the Mount Horeb Diner, halfway between Madison and Pine Bluff. Jason and I had often met there. I took a deep breath to prepare myself for a rush of memories as I pulled into a parking space behind Jonathan's car. He was leaning against it, waiting for me.

"Have you been here long?" I asked as I got out and locked my car door.

"Nah. I just got here."

The place didn't have the charm of the Korner Café—just cinder block walls, 1950s vintage Formica tables, and chairs made of stainless steel metal tubes with plastic-covered seats of various pastel colors.

Thoughts of Jason overpowered me. A young couple holding hands and gazing into each other's eyes occupied the table where Jason and I had last sat. My chest felt so heavy I could hardly breathe.

Jonathan must have noticed. "You okay?" he asked, touching my arm.

I gave a curt nod. "I'll be okay. Jason and I used to eat here all the time."

"We can go someplace else, if you want."

"That's okay," I smiled weakly. "Really. I'll be fine, but thanks." I appreciated Jonathan's sensitivity.

The place wasn't crowded yet. Seating was do-it-yourself, so Jonathan led us to a small table in a corner near the back. After we ordered, he reached down next to his chair, pulled his backpack up onto the table, removed a small tape recorder and switched it on.

"I thought you were going to update me on the investigation," I said, confused.

"Well, sort of."

"Sort of? That's what you said on the phone."

"I gotta tell you, Lark. You wouldn't believe how good you are at selling papers. Your picture on the front page more than doubles our normal sales."

"Look, Jon. As flattering as all the attention is, I don't like being manipulated into doing another interview."

"I'm not manip—"

I reached over and hit the *stop* button. "So, has there been a break in the case, or not?"

"I wouldn't call it an actual break—yet," he said. "But there are some leads I'm checking." He fidgeted and seemed to be having trouble making eye contact with me.

"What kind of leads?" I probed.

Jonathan coughed, uncomfortably. "As you know," he began, "Jason was a very popular reporter, and his, um, mysterious death is big news. Both of our papers have run stories suggesting that Shane Duran may have killed him, but, given the dearth of information coming out of the sheriff's department, responsible journalists—like myself—would be remiss if we didn't pursue other possibilities."

"Meaning?"

"Meaning," he paused, groping for a word. "Meaning," he switched the tape machine back on, "I need to ask you a couple of questions."

"Wait a minute!" I grabbed the machine and jabbed the *stop* button. "Questions about what?"

Jonathan looked around nervously, but the few people who were eating at the diner were far enough away that they couldn't hear us. Gently, he lifted the recorder from my grasp. "I need to ask you a few personal questions about your relationship with Jason."

"You need to?" Sweat broke out on my brow and I felt a hot flash redden my face.

"Lark, this isn't easy for me. I like you. I really do. But, yes, I need to ask you a few questions." He pressed the *record* button.

I stabbed the *stop* button. "Why?"

"C'mon, Lark. Help me out here. I'm just tryin' to do my job."

"Who's making you do this story?" I asked. "Did some editor assign you to come grill me about my personal life? You're the editor of the Entertainment section, aren't you?"

"I am." He hung his head in what seemed like shame.

"So, you assigned yourself to this story, is that right?"

He nodded. Suddenly, his shoelace seemed much more engrossing than my face.

My blood was boiling. "Jon, my relationship with Jason is personal—and precious." I felt my lip quiver.

"Is?" He looked up at me.

"Yes. 'Is'" I glared at him.

He quickly rechecked his shoelace.

The silence between us was deafening and uncomfortable. Soon shuffling and laughing overtook the silence as more people began to come in.

The waitress delivered our food, but neither Jonathan nor I so much as touched a utensil.

Finally, I sighed. "Off the record?" I asked, trying to make peace.

Jonathan paused for a long minute, then frowned. "Oh, all right." He stuffed the tape recorder deep inside his backpack sitting on the table next to him. "So anyway," Jonathan said, "how would you describe the relationship you had with Jason Jordan?"

"That's personal," I whispered. Now hot tears were damming up behind my eyes. *You will NOT cry*, I ordered myself.

Jonathan tried again, his voice soft, gentle. "At Shane Duran's press conference—the one in which he threatened Jason—before it got started, a couple of us overheard you and Jason having a bit of a—how should I say it?—tiff, or argument about something. What was it about?"

I actually had to stop and think. "I barely remember," I shrugged. "It seems so totally inconsequential now."

"You seemed pretty angry at the time," Jonathan observed.

"Oh! I remember," I laughed, "I was irked at Jason because my TV audition was supposed to be on tape, but it was live. I was thrown off balance by that, but hadn't been able to talk with Jason about it after the newscast because he'd already left the station."

"Why were you angry at him?"

"Oh, I don't know. It seems so long ago. I guess I was irked because I felt abandoned. He'd been the one who'd been urging me to do the audition—he even got the news director to agree to let me try out. But then, when the scheduling got fouled up, it felt like he'd run for cover. That's all. It's really not that big of a deal, Jon."

"So, you felt he was ducking you?"

"Something like that. Why?"

Jonathan didn't reply. He was stoic and in full just-the-facts-ma'am mode. "But if he ducked you because he feared your wrath, then could it be you'd gone off on him other times in the past?"

"Am I a shrew? Is that what you're asking?" I spoke softly, but I could feel my anger rising and my self-control fleeing. The room seemed to get smaller and stuffier.

Jonathan ignored my question and offered one of his own, instead. "Wasn't there something else you two argued about that day?"

Again, I was struck dumb. "Whatever disagreement Jason and I may have had that day, I am so over it that I can't even remember. It was weeks ago. You were there. What did you hear?"

"You were upset about him stealing—your word—'stealing' your Landscam story—the one you and Kirk Kensington broke. Jason matched it and you even introduced his story live on the air."

Jonathan's eyes held mine.

"Is there a question in there somewhere?" I felt myself getting deeper into a snippy mood.

"Were you angry at him for stealing your story?"

I shrugged. "Sure, at the time, but I got over it."

"Did you?"

I leaned forward so that my face was only inches away from Jonathan's.

"Yes," I hissed. "I was angry, but I got over it." I enunciated every word clearly and distinctly.

He didn't blink. "When?"

"Almost immediately."

"Almost?"

"Yeah."

"Did you apologize to him?"

I hesitated, trying to pinpoint a time when we'd kissed and made up—but couldn't. In fact, I realized, I had only a few of Jason's kisses to remember. I bit my lip.

"When did you make up?" Jonathan Anderson nudged.

"I-I honestly can't remember, Jon," I said softly, "but there was nothing wrong between us the last time I talked with him."

"That raises another question."

"Oh brother."

"You claim Jason told you he was going to meet with Shane Duran."

"That's right."

"Can you prove that?"

"Yes, as a matter of fact, I can. Kirk Kensington was with me when I got the call from Jason. He'll back me up. Just ask him."

"I already did."

I felt as though I'd been punched in the stomach. "And?" I managed to gasp.

"He says you told him you got a call from Jason, but Kirk says he never actually heard Jason on the line."

"But Kirk was with me!" My voice went up an octave.

"Yes. But Kirk says you then went your separate ways. The next time he was with you was when you found Jason's body."

Through clenched teeth I said, "Are you accusing me of murder?"

"No. Not first degree, anyway, but involuntary manslaughter is a possibility. Maybe you didn't intend to kill Jason, but perhaps you were angry at him and he slipped during an argument."

"And maybe he was pushed by Shane Duran, the man who'd publicly threatened him," I shot back.

Jonathan shrugged. "Or not."

I stood up suddenly and glowered at him. "I hope you gag on all the papers you're gonna sell, you son of a bitch."

It wasn't until I'd sped halfway to Pine Bluff that I pulled onto the shoulder and wept bitterly.

Chapter Thirty-Eight

It took me a while to regain my composure. Once I did, I drove aimlessly, not sure what to do or where to go. I thought about going into the office and whining to Lionel about how I was being wronged by Jonathan Anderson.

I ran a few trial conversations with Lionel in my head:

ME: (whiney voice): Lionel… Jonathan is picking on me. Make him stop.

LIONEL: (gruff voice): Lark… Grow up.

Or:

ME: (angry): That Jonathan Anderson makes me so mad.

LIONEL: How come?

ME: He pulled a bait and switch on me.

LIONEL: Oh?

ME: He lured me to lunch by making me think there's been a break in the investigation into Jason's death, then he ambushed me.

LIONEL: What do you mean?

ME: Shooting questions at me as if I'm the one who pushed Jason over the cliff.

LIONEL: Well? Did you?

Or:

ME: (crying—just tears, no words)

LIONEL: Lark, you poor dear, what's the matter?

ME: (sniffling): Jonathan Anderson just interviewed me.

LIONEL: So what else is new?

ME: He's doing a piece that will suggest that I killed Jason.

LIONEL: Sounds like he's just doing his job.

ME: You're kidding, right?

LIONEL: Don't you think Carl Olson has thought of that possibility, too?

ME: (gulping): Y-you mean, I might be a suspect?

LIONEL: Believe it.

Instead of going into the newspaper office, I drove home and went to bed, but first I had to pull over to the side of the road and puke into a ditch.

Chapter Thirty-Nine

I awoke to the sound of persistent knocking on my front door. The room was dark. I felt entirely disoriented. Was it the middle of the night? The next morning? I couldn't tell.

Groggily, I checked the clock by the side of the bed. The emerald digits glowed 6:18.

I staggered to the door and looked through the peephole. Sheriff Carl Olson's face filled the fish eye lens.

"Lark?" he called, "I know you're in there. You car's parked out front."

I panicked. I thought wildly about sneaking out through a back window.

"C'mon, Lark. I can hear you breathing on the other side of the door. Open up."

"I...I was sleeping. Wh-what do you want?"

"I need to ask you a few questions."

I sighed. "Just a sec."

I unlocked the door and let him in.

"Thanks," Carl said as he brushed past me. He was alone.

"Can I get you anything?"

"A glass of water?"

"Sure. Have a seat."

Sheriff Olson followed me to the kitchen as I snapped on lights all the way. But the brightness didn't take away my sense of gloom.

Carl sat at the kitchen table while I got out two glasses.

I felt his eyes on the back of my head as he watched me open a cupboard, choose two glasses, move over to the fridge, open the freezer, scoop ice into the glasses, then sidle to the faucet to fill them. By the time

I brought our glasses to the table, my hands were trembling so much some water sloshed from Carl's glass and puddled on the Formica.

"Thanks," he said. In less than five seconds he had drained the whole thing.

"More?"

"Sure, thanks. I'm drier than I thought."

I refilled his glass, brought it to him, then eased into a chair across from him at the table.

I liked Carl and trusted him. We'd first met six months earlier when someone tried to run me off the road. In all my dealings with him, he always seemed to be a good and decent man. He didn't have a threatening appearance, but he was a strong man who could take care of himself. He filled out a uniform in a way any red-blooded woman would appreciate. He had close-cropped auburn hair, glasses, a kind face and a wedding band.

He took a sip of water, and smiled at me. "How are you doing?"

I shrugged. "Good days and bad days."

"Which kind is this?"

"A not-so-good one, I guess."

He coughed uncomfortably, but said nothing.

"Any news?" I asked hopefully.

"Not yet." He coughed again and shifted in his seat. "Um, Lark?"

Uh oh. Here it comes.

"Yeah?" I said, as my eyes searched for his handcuffs.

"This isn't easy for me. I like you and I respect you, but I have to ask you some questions about Jason. Personal things."

"Do I need a lawyer?"

"Do you think you need one?"

"No."

"You sure?"

"I don't have anything to hide, Carl."

He sighed and bit his lip.

"You gonna read me my rights?" I tried to smile.

"Can we just talk friend to friend?"

"Even though anything I say can and will be used against me in a court of law?"

"Something like that," he shrugged.

I leaned toward him. "I didn't kill Jason, Carl."

He raised a hand, palm forward. "Whoa. Let's back up."

"How far?" I sagged against my chair.

"First, describe your relationship."

"Very close."

"Intimate?"

"In some ways."

"Physical ways?"

"Kissing. Handholding. Jason would have liked it to be more, but I'm a bit of a prude, and he respected that." I could feel the tears welling up.

"Ever have a fight with him?"

"Ever have a fight with your wife?"

Carl smiled, disarmingly. "You know what I mean."

"We disagreed sometimes, sure. What couple doesn't?"

"Some people I've talked to overheard the two of you arguing at Shane Duran's press conference."

"Who?"

"Did you argue with him there?"

I lowered my eyes and nodded.

"What was it about?"

I explained about the scheduling mix-up and how I had to do the audition live, but then couldn't find Jason afterward. "I felt as if he'd abandoned me and I told him so. I was also upset with him because I thought he'd stolen my Landscam story."

"Were you able to resolve your differences?"

I shrugged. "It just wasn't a big deal anymore. We got on with our lives."

"So, he didn't apologize? Didn't admit he'd done you wrong?"

"No."

"At the time of his death, did you feel he'd done nothing wrong in reporting that story?" Carl's tone was low and his questioning was slow and deliberate, but I could feel him gently shoving me like the strong flow of a river, inexorably pushing me along against my will toward an unknown destination.

"I can get…" I stopped.

"Go on."

"Nothing."

"You were going to say something else."

"Just that sometimes I can get impulsive and jump to conclusions about things. But eventually, I settle down."

"Had you settled down about feeling he'd stolen your story?"

I drilled Carl Olson with my eyes. "Yes."

He took a sip of water.

My lips were dry. My mouth felt like cotton. I took the first sip from my glass, but put it down as quickly as I could so that Carl wouldn't see my trembling. I laid my hands in my lap out of his sight.

"I know you've told me this before, but describe for me again the events leading up to Jason's fall," he said.

I told Carl of being with Kirk at the Korner Café when Jason called to let me know he'd be in the area.

"What was your reaction when you learned he'd be talking privately with Shane Duran?"

"I was concerned for Jason's safety."

"Did you voice that concern?"

"Yes I did. Quite strongly, as a matter of fact."

"Did you feel any competitive jealousy?"

"A tinge, perhaps."

"A tinge?"

"I was more concerned about Jason."

"But a part of you was also concerned that you were getting scooped?"

"Surprisingly, no, not really."

"Surprisingly?"

I laughed. "Don't tell Lionel. His first instinct would have been to sneak out there and talk to Shane, too."

"But that wasn't yours?"

"No."

"Why not?"

"Because I respected Jason. I knew that if I showed up it could undermine his confidential relationship with a source, not to mention our relationship, too, so I backed off."

"Then what happened?"

"Kirk and I went our separate ways. He went to the courthouse in Madison, I went back to the office."

"Did Kirk know where Jason was going to meet with Duran?"

"No. He asked, but I ducked his question. I didn't want to violate Jason's confidence."

"Can Lionel and Muriel Stone confirm that you were at the newspaper office?"

I shook my head. "Lionel was out of the office and Muriel left to run errands shortly after I arrived. I was there alone."

"Then what?"

"I went back to the Korner Café where Jason and I had agreed to meet. When he didn't show up, I got worried. Just as I was going to go up to the bluff to look for him, Kirk came back and together we went looking for Jason."

"Tell me more about Kirk."

"What do you want to know?"

"Describe your relationship with him."

"Collegial. We work together."

"Anything romantic?"

"No."

"You sure?"

I bristled. "What are you getting at?"

"I'm just trying to understand the situation," Carl said, calmly.

"Meaning possible love triangle?"

"To put it tabloid-style, yeah."

"There was nothing like that."

"You sure?"

"Carl, I told you: I'm a prude."

"Let me ask it this way," Carl said. "Were you in any way conflicted about the way you felt about Jason and Kirk?"

I blushed. "In some ways, yes."

"What do you mean?"

"I liked them both." With my finger, I wrote imaginary doodles on the tabletop to keep from looking Carl in the eye.

"Romantically?"

"I guess. Things were already romantic with Jason."

"But then Kirk came along."

I nodded.

"And he's a good looking guy…"

"Yeah."

"And Kirk likes you more than just a friend…"

"Objection. Leading the witness."

"Sustained." He paused. "But true?"

"Yeah."

"And you liked him more than a friend?"

"I wouldn't go that far. But even if I did, that's hardly a motive for murder."

"I didn't say it was. I'm just trying to explore all possible angles here, Lark."

"But what about the cigar?" I asked.

"What about it?"

"You did find one at the scene, didn't you?"

"Yes. That's no secret anymore," he scowled.

"And it was a Koenigshaven, Shane's brand, right?"

"Uh huh."

"Was it Shane's?"

"Don't know."

"Why not?"

"No prints. None. Wiped clean."

"That's weird."

"Since you brought up the cigar," Carl said, "let me ask you this: how did you learn the brand Shane smokes?"

"He told me."

Carl raised his eyebrows. "When?"

"The day he tried to cheat me when I almost sold him my grampa's farm." I felt my anger building. "He offered me a cigar. It reeked, but he bragged about how great it was—and told me the name of the brand."

Carl pushed himself back from the table and stood. "Thanks very much for the water, Lark, and for answering my questions. It made my job a lot easier."

Relieved, I stood, too. "No problem. I hope I was able to help."

"Oh, you helped a lot." He unclipped his handcuffs from his belt.

I froze.

"I'm placing you under arrest for the murder of Jason Jordan."

Gently, but firmly, he turned me around and, before I could react, he clasped the cuffs tightly to my wrists.

"Is this some kind of sick joke?"

"I wish it were. Believe me, I take no pleasure in doing this."

"But why? What about Shane Duran?"

"At the time Jason was murdered, Shane was in a meeting with twelve other people at a bank in Madison. His alibi is airtight. Let's go, Lark."

Chapter Forty

The sun was just setting as Carl Olson led me out my front door, down the steps and toward his police car, the words *Bluff County Sheriff* stenciled in gold and black on the side of the white Crown Victoria.

Jonathan Anderson stood off to one side, busily snapping pictures of me.

"Did you tip off that little weasel?" I hissed.

"I wouldn't do that to you, Lark." Carl said softly. "He must've figured it out for himself."

I lowered my head and twisted awkwardly so that Jon wouldn't be able to see my face, but he darted to the other side of the walkway and continued snapping.

"Just doing my job," he explained between shots.

"Go to hell," I snarled.

Carl opened the back door for me. "Watch your head, Lark." He placed his hand gently against my head to keep it from bumping against the car's doorframe as I maneuvered myself into the back seat. The cuffs pinched my wrists.

Once seated, I bowed my head and turned away from the window, through which Jonathan peered with his ever-snapping camera.

My lower lip trembled in a mixture of rage and shame.

After we pulled away from the curb, I lifted my head. A metal mesh separated me from Carl. I became aware of every detail: the cold of the vinyl seat, the crackle of the police radio.

This can't be happening. I'm innocent.

I sat in stunned, silent, humiliation as we drove the few blocks to the sheriff's department.

In my mind I turned over all the things that I knew were totally innocent, but which were now being so horribly misconstrued. Appearances do matter, I concluded. How things look and sound can be twisted into something grotesque.

For the first time, I tried to see things from Carl's perspective. I was a logical suspect, but I hadn't seen it that way before. Only now was I beginning to realize that all my actions and statements were being looked at through a lens of suspicion. And, by some sort of sick, cosmic trick photography, the image of my guilt was now almost fully developed.

I thought about praying, but felt like a hypocrite. God would see right through me and would know that I only turn to Him when I'm angry at Him or in a jam. But I prayed anyway.

"I'm sorry," I whispered.

In no time, we had pulled into the parking lot behind the sheriff's department at the rear of the courthouse and jail. Carl turned off the ignition, got out, and came around to open my door.

Just that little prayer had calmed me down enough so that I could make a self-deprecating joke. "You're such a gentleman, Carl. Where's my corsage?"

But Carl interpreted it as bitterness. "Don't make this any worse on yourself than it already is."

Inside, he took me down a narrow hall that smelled of cigarettes and sweat. We stopped outside a heavy door and Carl waved at a guard sitting on the other side of a thick glass window. Carl led me through the door after it buzzed. It shut behind us with a loud thud.

Carl removed the cuffs and I rubbed my chafed wrists.

"Come this way, Lark." Carl led me into a small room off the entrance. At the far end on a tripod stood a camera pointing at a dark blue wall. But this was no passport or driver's license photo shoot. I was about to get my mug shot taken.

"Stand over there." He pointed to the blue backdrop. Superimposed onto it was a ladder of hash marks to measure height.

Standing with my back to the wall, I put a hand flat against the top of my head and against the wall, then ducked and looked back to see the place where my hand touched. Five-foot-two.

An ample-tummied deputy came into the room and stood behind the camera. "Look this way," he said.

"At least you didn't say 'smile.'" I didn't.

The camera flashed.

"Now turn to your right." His voice was a bored monotone.

I did.

Flash.

"Now your other side."

I turned.

Flash.

"What happens next?" I asked Carl.

"Fingerprints. Edgar will do the honors." Carl nodded at the man taking my picture.

"What about my one phone call?" I asked.

"That's next," Carl said, finishing up some paperwork.

The fingerprinting process was slow and deliberate. Talk about feeling like a criminal. I tried to detach myself from the situation and merely observe.

Edgar was probably in his mid-fifties with wispy salt-and-pepper hair. He wheezed quietly as, one by one, he took each of my fingers, rolled them on an inkpad, then rolled them again onto a postcard-sized piece of paper. The paper was divided into ten squares, marked left thumb, right thumb, left index finger etc.

After each print, Edgar did his best to wipe the ink off my fingertip with a rag.

Next, Edgar took me to a small room no bigger than a closet and handed me a plastic bag, a pair of flip-flops and a gaudy-orange jumpsuit.

"Put this on and put all your personal clothing and effects in the plastic bag. Knock on the door when you're done," he instructed.

As I did as I was told, I felt my personal dignity ebbing away.

Finally, when I was allowed to use the phone, I called the Stone's home number. Muriel answered.

"It's me," I choked.

"L-Lark?"

"Uh huh."

"What's the matter? Are you hurt?"

"I'm in jail, Muriel. They think I killed Jason." I began to cry.

Chapter Forty-One

After talking with Muriel, she turned me over to Lionel whose first words to me were, and I quote, "What the hell?"

I started to tell him about my pre-arrest conversation with Carl Olson, but Lionel stopped me.

"Don't say another thing. They record all phone calls. They really mean it when they say anything can be used against you. Where's Carl now?"

"He's standing right next to me."

"Lemme talk to him," Lionel barked.

"Lionel wants to say 'hi,'" I smiled, handing the phone to Carl. I kept smiling as I tried to imagine what Lionel was saying. I could hear his raised voice seeping through the phone at Carl's ear, but couldn't make out any words.

Carl tried to talk, but Lionel kept cutting him off, so the side of the conversation I heard consisted of the Sheriff of Bluff County, Wisconsin saying such clever things as, "but" and "wait" and "no, actually..."

Eventually, Carl rolled his eyes, took a deep, exasperated breath and just listened until Lionel's fury was spent. Finally, Carl spoke his first sentence. "No need to come down tonight, Lionel. Visiting hours are over and a judge has to set bail. She'll be spending the night here. You can see her in the morning." He paused. "Yes. I promise to take good care of her. See you then."

Carl held the phone out to me, "He wants to talk to you again."

I took the phone. "Hi," I said weakly.

"You hang in there, kid. I'm gonna get you the best lawyer I can. I'll see you in the morning."

"Thanks, Lionel."

"You stay strong, Lark. We're gonna beat this thing."

I didn't feel strong, but it was comforting to know that Lionel was already fighting for me.

After I got off the phone, Edgar led me down a hallway where we were buzzed through another door and into a large caged room. A middle-aged woman with wild eyes paced back and forth, muttering to herself. The analogy of a zoo was not lost on me at that moment.

Edgar unlocked the cage door and opened it for me.

I stepped across the threshold.

The woman cackled demonically as the door clanged shut. I scurried across the room to be as far away from Demon Woman as possible, sank to the floor, and huddled in a corner.

"Hey, Edgar," I called as he was walking away.

"Yeah?" He stopped and turned to look at me.

"Could you please bring me a blanket?"

"Sure." He turned to go.

"And a Bible?" I added, impulsively.

He didn't say anything, but returned a few minutes later carrying the items. He slid them to me between the bars.

He'd brought me a King James Version. I leafed through it, looking for some inspiration and comfort. Parts I found virtually unreadable because of its stiff, archaic language, but as I turned the pages, I settled on the 23rd Psalm. It helped a little.

After lights-out, I curled in the fetal position on a hard bunk clutching the threadbare blanket. Demon Woman stayed away from me, but late that night, some loud, drunken women were deposited in the cell. One of them barfed near me. The stench was awful.

I tried to sleep, but couldn't. I also tried to pray. Silently. To myself. Alone. Which, unfortunately, is pretty much how I felt. I don't think I ever really "connected" to the Big Guy in the Sky. But I tried. And I cried. At least a little, and as quietly as I could.

Chapter Forty-Two

I must have been able to sleep a little bit because a loud *clang* startled me. I looked up to see Edgar standing at the open cage door with Muriel, Lionel, and another man I didn't know. Daylight streamed through the small slits that passed as windows near the ceiling. I'd spent the night in jail.

"You've got visitors, Miss Chadwick," Edgar said. "One of 'em's your lawyer. We've got a room where you can talk."

As I stood, Muriel rushed to my side and hugged me.

"How you doin', kid?" Lionel asked.

I shrugged. "Not great."

"Lark," Muriel said, "this is Leighton Meadows. He'll be your attorney, if you want him."

Leighton Meadows was no country bumpkin. He was about sixty, had a high forehead, thinning white hair, rimless glasses, and delicate features. His eyes were wide and intelligent. He wore a three-piece, dark blue, pinstripe suit and held a thin, black leather briefcase at his side with his left hand.

"Hi, Mr. Meadows." We shook hands. "Thanks for coming."

Edgar led the four of us to a room nearby where we could talk. As we walked, Muriel asked, "Is there anything we can get for you to make you more comfortable, Lark?"

"Just get me outta here."

"We're workin' on it," Lionel said.

When we got to the door, Leighton Meadows said to Lionel and Muriel, "I'll have to ask you two to wait outside. Lark and I must meet alone, or anything she says won't fall under the attorney-client privilege."

"Yeah. Sure. Whatever," Lionel grumped.

Meadows entered the room after me and shut the door behind him. The room was Spartan, just a table and two chairs. We sat across from each other.

I spoke first. "I'm not guilty, Mr. Meadows."

"You don't need to convince me of that, Ms. Chadwick. The burden of proof is on the government."

"So what happens next?"

"You'll be arraigned in an hour."

"What does that mean."

"You'll be formally charged." He gestured precisely with both hands. "You'll be asked how you plead. I want you to say 'not guilty.' No speeches, just a simple 'not guilty, Your Honor.'" He looked at me sternly.

I nodded my agreement.

"The government will have to tell a judge why you're in jail and why you should stay there. I'll argue that you have a clean record and won't run away if they let you out. The judge will set bail, Lionel will pay it, and you'll be free. At least that's what I hope."

"But how can Lionel afford it?"

"Bail will probably be fairly high because it's first-degree murder, but Lionel will use the value of his home to secure your bail. If you bolt, he loses his house."

"That won't happen."

"Agreed."

"Then what?"

"You'll have to maintain a low profile while we prepare for trial. The less you say or do in public, the better."

"But I want to tell the world I'm innocent."

"I understand that. But the prosecution will take anything you say, twist it, and use it against you. That's how you ended up here in the first place."

I grimaced. He was right and I knew it.

"Any time some cop comes to 'just talk' about an on-going investigation, a person should get a lawyer immediately."

"But that just makes them look guilty."

"It can also keep them from getting arrested. Remember, the government has to prove you're guilty. You don't have to prove anything, not even your innocence."

"But everybody'll think—"

"Doesn't matter." He leaned forward to make his point. "Now that you're in the slammer, a lot more people are thinking—and talking—about whether or not you really did it, than if you'd not talked with the sheriff."

I did not like what I was hearing, but I knew he was right, and I appreciated his no-nonsense way of telling me the facts of life. I liked him. He reminded me of…me.

Leighton Meadows opened his briefcase and removed a yellow legal pad. From his shirt pocket, he extracted a fountain pen and uncapped it.

"Now then," he said, businesslike, "let's try to find some ways to poke holes in the prosecution's case—at least what little of it we know at this point. First of all, talk me through your conversation with the sheriff and what it is that leads him to believe you killed Mister, um," he looked at some papers, "Jordan."

As best I could, I described my conversation with Carl Olson, including Shane's threat at the press conference, the spat Jason and I had gotten into just before it started, and the call I got from Jason in which he told me of his appointment to meet Shane on the bluff.

"It all sounds reasonable," Meadows said. "Why didn't the sheriff buy it?"

"He says Shane has an airtight alibi because he was in a meeting at the time he's supposed to have killed Jason."

Mr. Meadows began to write on his legal pad. "So," he began, "we need to find out just how airtight that alibi is. I'll try to find out when he had that meeting, where, who was in it, and try to talk with those people."

I began to relax. For the first time, it felt like someone with clout was in my corner. Someone with the skills necessary to derail the legal locomotive speeding toward me as I lay tied to the tracks.

"Of course," Mr. Meadows continued, "I'd be less than honest if I didn't tell you that this will take time."

"And money?"

"Yes." He pushed his glasses off his nose.

"But I can't afford to pay you," I said.

"That's no concern of yours. The Stones have paid my retainer. Cases like this can become a diabolical game to the prosecution. They can stall until the last minute. That can be frustrating because it postpones whatever effective investigating I can do on your behalf. So, Ms. Chadwick, I urge you to be patient, which is something I've heard you have trouble being."

"Who told you that?" I demanded.

"Just about everyone who knows you." He smiled.

I didn't.

"Oh, one more thing," Meadows said, reaching into his brief case. He pulled out a newspaper. "Here's some reading material."

It was the latest edition of the *MadCity News*. The front-page headline blared:

STUNNER!
CHADWICK CHARGED WITH JORDAN'S
MURDER AFTER LOVERS' QUARREL
By Jonathan Anderson

Chapter Forty-Three

Beneath the banner headline was a picture of Carl Olson escorting me from my home in handcuffs.

I sputtered with rage as I read Jonathan's article.

Local celebrity Lark Chadwick, who just weeks ago was profiled in this newspaper as a "fresh face on Madison television," has been charged with murder in the death of her WMTV colleague Jason Jordan.

Bluff County Sheriff Carl Olson arrested Chadwick at her Pine Bluff home yesterday.

Prior to her arrest, Chadwick had implied that Madison real estate developer Shane Duran murdered Jordan after luring him to Granddad's Bluff under the pretense of reconciling their differences.

Those differences first surfaced at a tense news conference in which Duran appeared to threaten Jordan for a report alleging that Duran was behind some fraudulent business dealings now widely known as "Landscam." But the case took a stunning turn with Chadwick's arrest.

It's widely believed that Chadwick and Jordan were lovers, but neither of them ever talked publicly about their relationship other than to say they were "friends." But Chadwick and Jordan got into a hushed but heated argument as reporters were gathering in the conference room of Duran's Madison office for what became a confrontation between Duran and Jordan.

[See ARREST on page 2].

The story jumped to the next page. When I turned to it, I was stunned to see a candid picture taken of Jason and me as we argued in Duran's conference room before the start of his news conference. Jonathan's frizzy-haired photographer probably took the picture before I even knew of Jonathan's interest in writing a profile piece on me.

In the shot, my teeth are bared while Jason looks down meekly. It was a damning image. Alongside it were head-and-shoulder shots of Jason and Shane Duran.

Barely able to contain my anger, I continued to read.

> Bluff County authorities are extremely tight-lipped about the case, but Chadwick herself, in an exclusive pre-arrest conversation with this reporter, provided possible clues as to why she's now charged with murder.
>
> According to Chadwick, the argument she had with Jordan in Duran's conference room was because she was "irked" and "angry" with Jordan for "stealing" her Landscam story and then "abandoning" her when she auditioned as a weekend anchor at WMTV.

"What the hell?" I yelled. "All that was supposed to be off the record."

"It's not anymore," Meadows said, sadly.

"He lied to me," I seethed. "He must've turned on the tape recorder as he put it into his backpack."

Meadows shook his head sadly, but said nothing.

"That bastard," I muttered, as I continued to read.

Chadwick alleges she and Jordan later made peace, but when pressed, she could not say when.

"I honestly can't remember," she told me.

Nor can she account for her whereabouts at the time of Jordan's death.

Duran, however, was in a meeting in Madison at that time and several people who attended the meeting with Duran confirmed to this reporter that Duran was present.

Chadwick, 26, of Pine Bluff, first gained fame in the area six months ago when she solved the mystery of the car-train collision that orphaned her as an infant. She has been working under the tutelage of famed newspaper editor Lionel Stone at *The Pine Bluff Standard*.

When contacted for a comment by *The MadCity News*, Stone hung up on this reporter.

Chadwick will be arraigned in Bluff County Court this morning.

I mashed the paper into a ball and threw it as hard as I could against the wall.

Chapter Forty-Four

After my meeting with Leighton Meadows, Edgar escorted me back to the holding cage where I was to wait until my ten o'clock arraignment.

About fifteen minutes before court was to convene, Meadows returned. Once again, Edgar shuffled me to the interrogation room.

"They want to make a deal," Meadows said when we were alone.

"Yeah?"

"If you agree to manslaughter, it's all over."

"What's manslaughter?"

"You did it, but you didn't mean to. Essentially, Jason tripped and fell. His death was accidental, not intentional."

"And you said?"

"I said I'd talk to you."

"And I say you tell them to go to hell."

"That's what I thought you'd say."

"Use those exact words."

"Okay," he smiled. "It'll be fun."

The next time I saw my lawyer was in court. The room was full of people, cameras, and reporters. I shouldn't have been surprised, but I was. I don't think of myself as a celebrity, but since I'd so publicly solved the mystery surrounding the spectacular deaths of my parents, been interviewed for an hour on CNN, gotten the weekend anchor gig, and all of Jonathan Anderson's stories about me, I was definitely a person of interest to the public. And always would be, it seemed, like it or not.

Speaking of Jonathan, the weasel sat in the front row next to Kirk, taking more pictures as I was led into the courtroom in handcuffs, my hair a mess. I wore a bright orange jumpsuit and flip-flops. The room was hushed. All I could hear were the shutter-clicks of still cameras. Several

TV cameras at the back of the room tracked me as I trudged to the table where Leighton Meadows stood to greet me.

The Stones sat behind the defense table. Muriel smiled at me bravely, but I could see her clutching a hanky, her eyes red-rimmed and moist.

Mr. Meadows pulled the chair back for me and I sat with my hands in my lap.

"Your Honor," Mr. Meadows was on his feet, his voice strong and urgent. His face was flushed.

The judge, a small, balding man well into his sixties, peered over his half-moon glasses from his perch on the bench. "Mister Meadows? Do you have something to say already?"

"I do, Your Honor. Sir, I insist that the handcuffs be removed immediately from my client. Having her appear in shackles, in front of all this press coverage, is extremely prejudicial. And, I would submit, Your Honor, that the prosecution not only knows this, but is exploiting the perception that my client is guilty, even though they have yet to prove anything."

"Ms. Landis?" the judge said, turning his attention to the prosecution.

A plain-looking, tight-faced, humorless woman wearing a brown pantsuit stood. "We object, Your Honor. Miss Chadwick is charged with the murder of another human being. Our interest is not in humiliating Miss Chadwick, but in guarding the safety of the community in case she should try to escape."

"Very well," the judge said. "Since the court has armed guards, I think the community will be adequately protected, even if Ms. Chadwick sheds her shackles. Bailiff, have the guards remove the handcuffs from the defendant."

A chorus of shutter-clicks erupted as a sheriff's deputy came toward me with a key, but whether he intended to or not, he stood in front of the photographers, blocking their view of me being unshackled. The pictures that the rest of the community would see of me would be the ones of me being led into the courtroom in cuffs.

"Your Honor?"

"Yes, Mr. Meadows."

"Would you please order the state to refrain from having handcuffs on my client during any future court appearances?"

"So ordered. Bailiff?"

"Yes, sir?"

"No more handcuffs for Ms. Chadwick when she's in court. Is that clear?"

"Yes, sir."

"Thank you, Your Honor," Meadows said. He sat and whispered into my ear, "Score one for the defense."

"Anything else, Mr. Meadows?" the judge asked.

"Yes, judge," Meadows said, springing back to his feet. "We also ask that Ms. Chadwick be allowed to wear street clothes in subsequent court appearances and not prejudicial orange jumpsuits."

"Nice try, Mr. Meadows, but I'm not going to go that far. I'll let her wear civvies during her trial in front of the jury, but for routine motions and such, she's going to be stuck with the admittedly unfashionable jailhouse garb, assuming she's not released on bail. I haven't decided that one, yet. Anything else?"

Meadows and Landis shook their heads.

"The defendant will rise," the judge glowered at me over his half-moons.

I stood. More shutter-clicks from behind me.

"Ms. Chadwick, you are charged with first degree murder in the death of Jason Jordan. How do you plead?"

"Not guilty," I said as loudly as possible. "Absolutely, positively *not* guilty."

"Very well. Ms. Landis? Do you have anything to say about bail?"

Landis stood. "Your honor, because of the nature of the case, and the danger faced by the community if the defendant flees, we argue that she be held without bail until trial."

"Mr. Meadows?"

My lawyer stood. "Your Honor, my client not only strongly and indignantly asserts her innocence, she has a totally clean record. Furthermore, her employer, Lionel Stone, a world-renowned Pulitzer Prize-winning former *New York Times* journalist, has consented to post her bail, has agreed to let her live with him and his wife, and assures me that Ms. Chadwick will remain in the community and be available to this court."

"Very well. Thank you, Mister Meadows and Ms. Landis. Here's what I'm going to do. I'm setting bail at a steep, but not excessive $250,000. Furthermore, if the defendant is able to make bail, she will be required to forfeit her passport and wear an ankle bracelet that monitors her whereabouts. The court is restricting her movements so that she can only be at the residence of Lionel and Muriel Stone, the offices of *The Pine Bluff Standard,* and Channel 15 in Madison on the weekends. She will only be allowed to travel to and from those locations. She can only go outside those bounds if Mr. or Mrs. Stone accompanies her.

"In addition, I'm imposing a gag order on both sides. I want this case tried in a court of law, not the court of public opinion. That means," he looked sternly at the prosecution, "no more leaks, and..." he glared at Lionel, "...no journalistic crusades. I can't keep *The Pine Bluff Standard* from covering the news, but I will consider any editorials proclaiming Ms. Chadwick's innocence a breach of my order."

The judge looked at my lawyer. "Mister Meadows, if your client and her supporters in the media violate the terms of my order, bail will be revoked immediately, and she'll be a guest in my iron-bar lodgings until and throughout her trial. And, Ms. Landis," the judge glowered at the prosecutor, "if there are any more leaks, you and Sheriff Olson will personally be held in contempt of court. Is that clear to everyone?"

Before anyone could respond, the judge banged his gavel. "Court's adjourned."

We all stood, as the judge bounded from the bench.

"Now what?" I asked Meadows.

"Once Lionel signs the paperwork, you're free—relatively speaking."

"What do you want for dinner tonight, Lark?" Muriel called.

"How about spaghetti?"

"Spaghetti it is."

"Spaghetti is ambrosia," I said to Mr. Meadows as the guard led me away.

Chapter Forty-Five

Dinner at the Stone's was festive. Mr. Meadows was there; so was Kirk. Muriel insured that the mood was light. Lionel enthralled us with stories from his career. There was plenty of wine, too.

At one point, we had been talking about mistaken identity. "That reminds me of a story," Lionel said. He turned to Kirk and me. "You two will get a kick out of this. Muriel's already heard it a million times."

"Is this the one about Naomi Nover?" Muriel asked.

"Right," Lionel said.

"Yes. I've heard it," Muriel said, getting up. "It is amusing," she said to me as she picked up my plate and a few others and took them to the kitchen.

Lionel took a sip of wine and began his story. "Naomi's husband founded the Nover News Service back in the early '70s. Naomi took over when he died in about '73, but she never did much reporting, just showed up at briefings and went on as many overseas trips with the president as possible. When I knew her, she was already pretty old. Always carried a big canvas bag stuffed with, well, stuff."

Kirk and I chuckled.

"Naomi had white hair," Lionel continued, "and wore it in a style that looked like the wigs worn by the early colonists and founding fathers. She was on the trip when Reagan went to China. At one stop, Reagan and his wife were getting a personal tour of some museum, but the event was closed to everyone except the small press pool."

"The press pool?" Kirk asked.

Lionel nodded. "The pool usually consists of a wire reporter, someone from one of the TV networks, and a camera crew. They share their stuff with all the other members of the press corps who had to be left out because they wouldn't all fit into the room."

"I see. Sorry to interrupt," Kirk said.

Lionel continued, "Anyway, Naomi tried to get into the event, too, but an armed Chinese guard blocked her entrance. I think Gary Schuster of CBS was the pool reporter that day. He had a great sense of humor. He told the guard that Naomi is a very important person in the United States, but the guard didn't speak any English. So Gary pulled a dollar bill out of his wallet, showed the guard the picture of George Washington on it, then gestured back and forth between Naomi and George Washington. The guard's eyes got real wide as he saw the obvious resemblance and waved her right in."

By now we were all laughing.

"True story," Lionel chuckled.

Mr. Meadows excused himself immediately following dessert.

"I feel my life and freedom are in good hands with Leighton Meadows," I said after he left. "Thanks for finding him for me, Lionel."

"No problem, Lark. It's the least I can do," Lionel said, jauntily. His face was flushed and he seemed a little tipsy.

"You've both done so much—as usual. And you know I'm going to pay you back for your legal fees, don't you?" I said.

Lionel brushed aside my comment with a wave of his hand. "We'll talk business later. Tonight we celebrate your release from jail."

"Lionel," Muriel said, "would you please help me with the dishes?"

Kirk stood and picked up his dinner plate. "I'll give you a hand."

"Nonsense," Muriel said, reaching for the plate. "You stay here and keep Lark company."

Kirk sat down at his place next to me. When Lionel and Muriel had retired to the kitchen, Kirk said, "If it weren't for that damn ankle bracelet—which is very stylish, by the way—I'd invite you to go out for an after dinner drink, or something."

"That's sweet. Thanks."

"How are you holding up?"

"Better now. It's all pretty overwhelming. It never occurred to me that I could be considered a suspect."

"I know."

"Will you be checking out Shane's alibi?"

"Probably. We'll see where Lionel wants to go with this. My hunch is that with that gag order, we may not be able to get very far on our own. The stakes are higher for everybody now if either side begins to do any leaking."

I sighed.

"Let's change the subject," he said. "You're beginning to obsess."

I laughed. "That's my middle name."

"Pick a subject. Any subject."

I chewed my lower lip as I thought. "How about you?"

He blushed. "What about me?"

"Looks like you and journalism are a good fit."

"I love it. And the extra bonus has been working with you." He paused, uncomfortable. "I could say more, but now's probably not the time."

"What do you mean?"

He put his hand on top of mine. "I like you, Lark. I like being with you. I like talking with you."

My hand—involuntarily, it seemed—slid out from beneath Kirk's. "Oh, Ja—, I mean…" Tears welled in my eyes. "It's too soon," I croaked.

"I know. You're right, but I had to say it, anyway."

Just then, Muriel and Lionel returned to the room and scooped up more dirty dishes from the table.

Chapter Forty-Six

Later, after Kirk went home, I insisted on helping Lionel and Muriel with the dishes. We quickly fell into a routine: Muriel put away leftovers, Lionel brought me dishes from the dining room, I rinsed, and then Lionel loaded the dishwasher. Once it was loaded, Lionel poured in the dishwashing powder, set the dials and revved it up.

"Lionel, I'd like you to wash the pots and pans that didn't fit in the dishwasher," Muriel said.

Lionel rolled his eyes, but said nothing.

Immediately, Muriel turned combative, an edge to her voice. "I cooked. The least you can do is some scrubbing."

I intervened, trying to head off what I feared might be the beginning of another argument. "I don't mind doing the pots and pans," I said.

"That's okay," Lionel said, slipping on a green apron with *Kiss the Cook* stenciled across the chest. "I'll wash and you can dry, Lark."

"Thank you, Lark," Muriel said to me, ignoring Lionel. "I'm heading to bed."

"Thanks so much for the party, Muriel. It's just what I needed."

"We're glad you're free, sweetheart. I'll see you tomorrow."

"G'night," I called as she left the room.

Lionel had already begun filling the sink with soapy water.

"I must say, Lionel: that apron looks very becoming on you," I teased.

He turned off the water and glared at me over his glasses. "Very funny," he sneered and stuffed a dirty saucepan into the sink.

We worked in silence for a few minutes before I said, "I think I'm gonna read more of Holly's diary tonight."

"How's it going so far?" he asked, scrubbing dried tomato sauce off the pan.

"You're right: Holly's being very hard on you."

"Finding any hope?" Sweat glistened on his brow.

I thought a minute.

"Your silence is thunderous," he said.

"No, I was just thinking. There is some hope in there. It's obvious to me that Holly cared about you, but the two of you were so much alike that she was having a hard time finding her own way—or figuring out how to articulate it so that it didn't always end up in an argument with you."

Lionel nodded grimly and scrubbed harder causing some soapy water to splash onto the rolled-up sleeve of his white shirt.

"I think eventually the two of you would have worked out your differences," I added.

"Or not."

"You don't know that, Lionel."

"Neither do you."

I sighed. "True. But I'm trying to be the optimist here."

"And I'm being the realist." He placed the saucepan on the drain board.

"So," I said, picking up the pan and wiping it with a towel, "what else happened when you went to Peru to reclaim Holly's body? Were you able to learn any more about how the accident happened?"

"I did a preliminary investigation of my own," he replied. "With Mike Sutherland's help from the U.S. Embassy, I was able to interview the chief investigating officer and Holl's tour guide."

I held up the now-dry pan. "Where does this go?"

"Down there," he said, nodding at a cupboard below the counter next to the sink.

I opened the cupboard door and placed the pot in a clear space next to some neatly stacked Tupperware containers.

"I also read the police report," Lionel said.

"What did it say?"

"It said Holly was part of a group of sixteen people: a couple from Australia, a Swede, three Irishmen, a German, two Canadian women, and six other Americans—three men and three women—from various parts of the country. A Peruvian guide named Alejandro headed the group."

Lionel was, once again, in his just-the-facts, ma'am Reporter Mode. I leaned against a counter, dishtowel draped over my shoulder, patiently listening as Lionel stood telling his story at the sink filled with soapy-greasy water.

"Hey, you want some wine?" he asked.

"Sure."

He dried his hands on his apron, found two glasses and a half-full bottle of Merlot and poured us each a generous portion.

"To your health," he said, handing it to me and holding up his class for me to clink.

"And to yours," I said, the lip of my glass clicking against his. We each took a swig. "As Winnie the Pooh says, doing the dishes is much friendlier with two," I said.

Lionel chuckled as he placed his glass on the counter to his left. "Right. As if Pooh ever had to wash pots and pans."

"Yes, well, I took some liberties with the context, but it's the principle of the thing."

Lionel resumed his scouring—and his story. "The police report contained interviews with everyone."

"How many men, how many women?"

"About half and half, as I remember," Lionel replied. "I can't remember their names." He handed me a big stainless steel pot.

237

"What did they say?" I asked, wiping the outside of the pot first, then the inside.

"According to their statements, no one had a firm recollection of seeing Holly that morning. Alejandro told police that he didn't realize Holly was missing until about 7:00 a.m., which was two hours after the group began hiking."

"Geez. They started hiking at five in the morning?" I groaned. "What's up with that?"

"I'm getting to that. Patience." Lionel placed a plastic colander on the drain board.

"So, you say you interviewed the chief investigator?" I picked up the colander and began swiping at it with my towel after putting away the pot.

Lionel nodded. "Sutherland lined it up, drove me there, and was my translator. He was great. Just great. Our first stop was the police station in Urubamba. It's a forty-mile drive from Cusco. We were literally in the clouds, about eight-thousand feet above sea level."

"Wow," I said.

"Our driver took us through spectacular mountain passes, down into the valley on winding switch-backs, and then along the rushing Urubamba River."

"Was it pretty?" I asked.

He rolled his eyes. "Breathtaking. Mesmerizing. The paved, two-lane road was in good condition and was filled with tour buses. At various scenic lookout points, clusters of wrinkled old women wearing brightly-colored peasant clothing squatted next to piles of alpaca sweaters, shawls, and blankets. The goods were laid out in elaborate displays. At each place, a tour bus or two had stopped to disgorge people who were picking through the piles of stuff. But there was a lot of poverty, Lark. Many of the homes we passed were mud-brick shacks with tiny, grassless, junk-strewn yards."

As Lionel painted his word picture of Peru, I made a mental note to go there someday. I could see myself wrapped in a red alpaca shawl.

"The Urubamba police station is located just off the main drag in a massive adobe structure with three-foot-thick beige walls," Lionel continued. "We were directed to an office on the second floor, up a curving staircase made of immense granite fieldstones. Then we walked down a creaking, wood-planked floor to an office illuminated by three-foot long, garish neon bars mounted horizontally along each wall just above eye level." He gestured with his hands.

I was glad Lionel was taking the time to paint the picture for me. Not only could I see and feel what he was experiencing, but I also sensed that getting him to talk about it was somehow therapeutic for him, even if he eschewed anything that smacked of therapy.

Lionel handed me the stainless steel spaghetti tongs he'd just washed and I managed to dry them before any more than a few drops of water dripped onto the kitchen floor.

"I'll never forget the chief investigating officer," Lionel smiled. "Julio Martinez. He was tall, thin, about thirty-five, with black hair and earnest eyes that didn't seem to miss much. He wore an olive drab uniform over a white shirt with two chevron insignia on the collar. Sutherland and I sat in rickety chairs in front of the cop's scuffed, wooden desk. Martinez seemed nervous. Probably wasn't used to being grilled by some Gringo.

"I asked Martinez if fatal falls from the Inca Trail are common. He only spoke a little English, so Sutherland translated. Martinez told me fatal falls are not common. He said that every now and then someone falls and breaks a leg, but it's rare that someone dies in a fall.

"'What about murder along the trail?" I asked Martinez. 'Has that ever happened?'" Lionel dropped his sponge and let it float in the dishwater, bringing himself to attention. He took on an officious, indignant tone, imitating Officer Martinez.

"'Murder?' Martinez said in English, raising his eyebrows. 'No. Never.'"

Lionel turned to look at me. "It was as if even the suggestion of murder was a personal affront."

"What made you ask about murder? Were you suspicious?" I asked.

"Not at all. I was just trying to explore the different possibilities, same as a cop would do." Lionel paused, then continued. "I finally cut to the chase and asked Martinez if his investigation assumed from the outset that Holly's death was an accident."

"What did he say?"

"He stiffened. Got real indignant. Said he resented the inference of my question. Insisted he's a professional police officer and makes no assumptions about any case he investigates. Let the facts speak for themselves. He sat glowering at me, hands folded tightly in front of him. His dark brown skin had turned a shade darker and his eyes flashed. While he was staring me down, I heard the rasp of a dot matrix printer on a desk behind me."

Lionel turned to look at me. "Can you believe it, Lark? They still have dot matrix printers down there."

I laughed. "And all along, I thought you were the last person to join the twenty-first century."

He scowled at me and continued his story. "I tried a new tack with Martinez. I asked him what specifically led him to conclude that Holly's death was an accident. Martinez listened to Sutherland's translation, then faced me and replied in rapid-fire Spanish, looking me squarely in the eye. He talked for two minutes, punctuating his comments with elaborate gestures."

Lionel waved his arms, windmill-style, like sportscaster John Madden describing an amazing touchdown run. "Martinez didn't even bother to pause for Sutherland's benefit. When he finally finished speaking, he flashed an angry glance at Sutherland and stabbed a finger at me. 'Tell him!' Martinez ordered Sutherland in English.

"Sutherland summarized for me. He said the trail is fairly narrow at the point where Holly fell and makes a sharp curve to the right. In the early morning, misty cloudbanks shroud the trail, meaning that if Holly was hiking rapidly, or not paying attention, she might not have noticed the curve in the trail in time. And, Sutherland translated, there were no witnesses or anything that made Martinez seem suspicious of either murder or suicide. He told Sutherland that a tragic accident was the most logical conclusion."

"Did you have a follow-up?" I asked.

Lionel shook his head. "When Sutherland finished translating, Martinez said in English, his tone softening, 'I'm extremely sorry for your loss, Señor Stone. I, too, have a daughter—a little girl. Please accept my sorrow.' I did."

Finished with his story and the dishes, Lionel pulled the plug and the dirty-brown dishwater gurgled down the drain.

"And you met with the tour guide. I forget his name."

"Alejandro."

"Right."

Lionel smiled. "He was another memorable character—a real Lothario." He put away the drain board, then sponged off the counters and rinsed the sink. "Let's take our wine into the other room," he said as he refreshed each of our drinks.

Chapter Forty-Seven

Lionel turned out the kitchen light and led me into the living room carrying his glass in one hand and the nearly-empty wine bottle in the other, hooked at the neck by two fingers. He sagged into a wingback chair, placed the bottle on the coffee table, and put his feet up on the ottoman.

I sat at the end of the sofa closest to Lionel's easy chair.

"Sutherland and I met later that evening with Alejandro at a dimly-lit bar on what's known as 'Gringo Alley.' It's around the corner and up the hill from the office of the travel agency that employed him. Classic rock—Hendrix, Beatles, Stones—provided the background soundtrack. We sat on two couches that faced each other on opposite sides of a low coffee table with a candle in the middle. In fact, that gives me an idea."

Lionel got up from his chair, went to the fireplace, picked up a massive cylindrical candle from the mantel and placed it in the center of the coffee table next to the wine bottle. He fished a packet of matches from his trousers, lit the candle, then went to the rheostat by the front door and dialed down the lights.

"There," he said proudly, "a little after-dinner mood lighting." He walked quickly across the room and sat back down in his chair. "Promise me, Lark, that you won't fall asleep on me."

"Don't worry, Lionel. I really want to hear what the tour guide told you."

Lionel picked up his wine glass and held it between the fingertips of his two hands. "Alejandro sat across from Sutherland and me, his arms draped casually on the back of the couch. One booted foot rested on the edge of the coffee table. He wore jeans and an 'I Survived the Inca Trail'

T-shirt. He had short-cropped black hair. His English, though broken, was good. We were all drinking *Cusqueña,* the local brew."

"How old was he?" I asked.

Lionel shrugged. "Young guy. Probably thirty, if that. Young and cocky. He had dark skin, so when he smiled, it made his teeth gleam."

"Cheshire cat?"

"Exactly. He told me he'd been a tour guide for four years. Before that, he said he was in the Army fighting the Shining Path guerillas in the jungle. He had a scar on his left forearm. I pointed to it and asked if it was a war wound.

"Alejandro nodded, took his right arm off the back of the couch and rubbed the scar. 'Shrapnel,' he said. He told me that seven of his friends died that day...and he almost joined them."

Lionel turned silent for a moment, remembering. When his reverie seemed a bit extended, I asked, "What are you thinking, Lionel?"

He gazed sadly at the candle flickering on the coffee table. "The reporting stint I did in Vietnam. A mortar attack pinned down the unit I was with. The gore was awful. A nineteen-year-old pimply-faced Marine PFC died in my arms...screaming for his mother." Lionel bit his lip, then brushed the memory aside with a wave of his hand. "I'll never forget that kid. What a waste."

I sat patiently, my eyes glued on Lionel. The soft candlelight gave his face an amber tint; shadows seemed to intensify the deep lines on his forehead and at the edges of his eyes. He looked distinguished, wizened. I could only imagine all the experiences he'd had and wondered how I might have handled what he'd been through. Ever since I'd met Lionel, I made a pact with myself to soak up every last bit of wisdom I could from him.

"Anyway, back to Alejandro," Lionel said, taking a swig of wine. "He told me that he loved being outside—'at one with nature' is the way he put it—so, when he left the Army, he became a tour guide. He said the pay is good and he meets many interesting—and beautiful—people.

"Alejandro chortled when he said 'beautiful,' making it clear to me that he probably got laid plenty, considering all the young college girls who hike the trail. It made me begin to wonder if maybe he and Holly had a thing going."

"Did you ask him?" I leaned toward Lionel.

He shook his head. "Not directly. I didn't want to scare him off, so I just asked him to tell me what he remembered about her. He said she was definitely one of the beautiful ones. Described her as 'statuesque.' He even said, 'I have to tell you, I fell in love.' I smiled ruefully at him and said, 'You wouldn't have been the first.'

"Alejandro laughed and admitted he had 'competition'—his word—adding that there were several men on the trip and many of them were trying to get Holly's attention."

"Did any succeed?" I asked Lionel.

"Apparently."

"Oh?" I asked, intrigued.

"Alejandro told me that at various times, he saw Holly talking intently with all of the guys."

"Did he see anything romantic?" I asked.

"He claims he didn't."

"Do you believe him?"

"No."

"Why not?"

"He just has this supremely confident way about him that I know women dig."

"How do you know?"

Lionel looked at me over his glasses. "Because he reminds me of me when I was his age."

"Wild oats?"

"Acres and acres."

"Is that why you were so protective of Holly?"

He winced and then nodded. "Uh huh. I know what guys are like 'cuz I happen to be one."

I thought of my lusty friend Heather. "But maybe Holly didn't want to be protected," I said gently.

Lionel nodded slowly, a distant, thoughtful expression on his face.

"You see the double standard, don't you, Lionel?"

My question brought him suddenly to the present. He turned to focus on me, a quizzical look on his face.

"Every one of those wild oats you, um, sowed, was someone's little girl." My voice was soft. I wasn't trying to score any rhetorical points. I just wanted him to see his daughter—and himself—differently.

He pursed his lips and nodded grimly. "So all my good intentions of trying to protect Holly had the opposite effect of her wanting the forbidden fruit all the more?"

"Yes. I think so."

Lionel was quiet for a moment, then nodded slowly. "I see what you mean."

"Did Alejandro say if Holly seemed interested in any of the guys on the hike?" I asked.

"He said he thought she was 'receptive, but choosey.' That's a quote."

"Did she hook up with any of them?"

"Hook up?"

"Think oats."

He laughed. "Kids these days." He shook his head. "I dunno. I was getting too pissed at Alejandro to think straight, so I let it drop. Around this point in our conversation, Alejandro's eyes strayed to the couch next to us where four attractive college-age young women were laughing and drinking. One of them, a gorgeous girl with straight blonde hair, even looked a little like Holly. "Light My Fire" by The Doors was playing on the sound system. I put two and two together and assumed the worst— about Alejandro AND Holly– and moved on with my interview to the next subject."

"How Holly died." I said.

"Right. You're good," he smiled. "Remind me to give you a raise."

"Gimme a raise."

"In your dreams."

I chuckled.

Lionel cleared his throat and continued his story. "I asked Alejandro to explain to me why he didn't realize Holly was missing until 7:00 a.m. when they all began hiking at five."

"I want to know why they started hiking so early," I said.

Lionel held up his hand like a traffic cop to stop me. "As soon as I asked him the question, Alejandro did a curious thing: He slid his watch off his wrist and began turning the flexible wristband inside out, then back again."

"Hmmm. What do you make of that?"

"Not sure. It was as if he was fingering worry beads. Alejandro got real serious and leaned forward, resting his elbows on his thighs. I noticed that when he nervously clenched and unclenched his hands, the muscles in his forearms bulged, sort of like Popeye."

"Strong guy?"

"Very."

"What did he say?"

"He seemed almost forlorn. Said he was extremely sorry about what happened to Holly. He said no one had ever been seriously injured or died on any of his tours before. He told me that he makes it a point to be sure everyone is okay throughout the trek. He said he is especially alert for stragglers, people who may be having a hard time hiking in the high altitude. The expression on his face, Lark, was almost pleading as he continued to play with his watchband. He went on to say that he often hiked behind everyone else so that he can closely accompany someone who may be out of breath and hiking slowly. Said he even carries an oxygen canister in his backpack, just in case."

"With this particular group, were there any stragglers?" I asked.

"Alejandro said just one. A short, slightly overweight American. Alejandro said the guy wasn't in good shape because he smoked."

"Did he lag behind that morning?"

"Alejandro said he wasn't sure."

"And why hike before dawn?"

"Alejandro said that on the last day of the hike, he gets everyone up at four o'clock in the morning to get in line at the last checkpoint on the trail before Machu Picchu. It's a two-and-a-half hour walk from the checkpoint to a place called *Inti Punku*, the Sun Gate. He said he tries to time it so that the group arrives there just as the first rays of the rising sun strike Machu Picchu. He said the view is unforgettable."

"I'll bet it is."

"Alejandro made it sound as if he personally supplied the sun for the tour group," Lionel laughed.

"Did Alejandro notice if Holly lagged behind that morning?"

"That's where Alejandro's memory got hazy. He said Holly was fast. She was in very good shape and she was often near the front. But he said he has no distinct memory of where she was that morning."

"Did he lag behind?"

"He was vague about that, too. He said the last time he saw her was at the checkpoint as the entire group waited in the dark for it to open at five."

"What finally made him aware that Holly was missing?"

Lionel smiled. When I asked him that, I chose my words very carefully. I asked, 'When did you realize you had a problem?'"

"How did he react?"

"He almost broke the wristband on his watch he was twisting it so much. He said the group arrived at *Inti Punku* at seven. He gathered everyone around to give them a brief explanation of what they were seeing. It was then, he said, that he realized Holly was missing."

"Was everyone else there?"

Lionel nodded. "Only Holly was missing."

"Who realized it first?"

"He said he didn't remember, but he said he thought it was one of the men in the group because he said they always seemed to be keeping an eye on her. He said he simply remembers that someone asked, 'Where's Holly?'"

"Then what happened?"

"He said he immediately tried to determine who had seen her last and where."

"And?"

"No one could remember."

"Then what?"

"Alejandro said he sent someone ahead to look for her, while he retraced the group's path."

"How did he know to go back?"

"He said he didn't. It was just a guess. He said it took about thirty minutes, maybe more, to find her. He told me he's hiked the trail at least 200 times, so he knows it well. He said he expected to see her at any moment. When he didn't, he began to run. Eventually, he said he saw a hiking stick lying on the ground at the edge of the trail. When he looked over the side, he saw her body lying on the rocks at least a hundred meters below."

"Do you believe his story?"

Lionel shrugged. "Lots of memory lapses at key times, but his remorse seemed genuine. After he told me his story, Alejandro looked at me with anguish in his eyes. 'I'm so, so sorry, señor,' he said sadly, shaking his head, 'So sorry.'

"The next day I returned to the United States with Holly's body lying in a casket in the plane's cargo hold." Lionel drained his wine, then, holding the glass by the stem, he slowly rotated it absentmindedly and looked dejectedly at the dregs in the bottom of his empty glass. There was nothing more to say.

Chapter Forty-Eight

By the time Lionel had finished telling me about his interviews with Officer Martinez and Alejandro, the tour guide, it was after midnight, so I went to bed, and was far too tired to tackle any more of Holly's diary. It would have to wait.

The next day, Saturday morning, I had to get out of the house, and the only place the court would allow me to go was the newspaper office, so that's where I went. It felt as freeing as when I'd gotten out of jail. True, my ankle bracelet pretty much tethered me to the office, but it was good to be in a new location, doing something.

I checked my email. Here's a sampling:

Lark. I'm writing to let you know I'm praying for you. This must be an awful time for you. Hang in there. Jesus loves you.
—Unsigned

That was nice, but it was pretty much downhill from there:

You murdering bitch.
—Unsigned

Lark. You were my hero. (Emphasis on "were"). How could you DO such a thing?
—Unsigned

All you media types are the same: self-centered. Get over yourself, honey. So what if he took your story? Is it really worth killing him over?
—Unsigned

About ten o'clock I was still slogging through the depressing emails when I got a call from Ron Bourne, the news director at Channel 15.

"Lark," he said. "I'll get right to the point. I don't think it would be a good idea for you to be doing the news while this, um, legal matter of yours is pending." His voice was distant and echoed, as if he were on a speakerphone.

"Why not? The judge said there's no reason I can't." I felt myself becoming petulant and defensive.

"I know, sweetie. But I don't think it would be good P.R."

"What do you mean?" I pictured him sitting at an ornate desk, feet up, the company's lawyer sitting across from him, taking notes, waiting for me to fly into a tizzy and make accusations or threats.

"It would be as if we're taking sides."

"Seems to me that by cutting me loose, you've already chosen a side." I tried to keep my voice even.

"I'm not cutting you loose at all, Lark." His voice sounded wounded, misunderstood. "Let's just say you're being put on hold until all of this is resolved."

"I was kind of looking forward to coming in tonight," I sighed, weakly.

"And I'm looking forward to the time when you can again," his tone a patronizing pat on the head. An instant later, his voice became strong and upbeat. "You hang in there, okay, sweetie?"

"I'll try, but this won't make it any easier. And stop calling me sweetie."

He'd already hung up.

Chapter Forty-Nine

Even though Ron Bourne hadn't actually fired me, that's how it felt. He was rejecting me, casting me aside, refusing to allow me to do something I found myself liking. The irony made me smile. Almost throughout our entire relationship, Jason had been goading me to do the anchor audition. When I finally gave in, did the audition, and got the job, I found myself looking forward to the weekends. The anchoring was a nice change of pace and I apparently was good at it—or so people seemed to think. But now, to have it yanked away, stung.

At 6:00 p.m., out of morbid curiosity, I turned on the TV, just to see who'd be sitting in my place at the anchor desk—as if it had ever really belonged to me. Ginger and Grant were co-anchoring. Grant read his scripts with what looked like an annoyed scowl, but I couldn't tell if it was because he was peeved at having to do more than his sports-only gig, or if he felt uncomfortable taking on a new role for which he was clearly out of his league, so to speak.

Ginger, on the other hand, seemed thrilled to be doing more than just the weather—and the camera loved her. My heart sank a little when I realized that it wouldn't be long before Grant would be allowed to go back to doing just sports, allowing Ginger to shine solo in the spotlight.

I turned off the set and began to read more of Holly's diary. Soon I was enthralled by her account of her trip to Peru.

She described the view from 30-thousand feet above the Andes between Lima and Cusco as "spectacular: wispy white clouds blended with snowcapped peaks against a bright blue sky." To Holly, the undulating mountain range looked like a "creased and crumpled brown blanket stretching to the horizon."

Holly wrote that as soon as she got off the plane in Cusco, she immediately sensed the crisp, cool air—"such a relief from the heat gripping Washington." She wrote that she felt "fit and fine" as she bounced down the stairway to the tarmac, but, moments later, when carrying her light, two-pound backpack up a flight of stairs inside the terminal, she felt the first effects of being eleven thousand feet above sea level.

"My heart was racing; I had to stop at the top of the landing to catch my breath," she wrote.

Holly said that the travel agency had advised her to arrive two days before the hike in order to get acclimated to the thin air at the high altitude. In her diary, she described how she stood in the airport terminal "panting, and beginning to wonder—and worry—if two days would be time enough to adjust."

She took what she described as "a ten-minute, bone-grinding taxi ride on cobblestone streets to the $20-a-night hotel I'd booked online." It was on Centenario Avenue, five blocks from the center of town. Even though she'd been traveling for nearly eighteen hours and had slept very little, Holly wrote that she couldn't wait to begin exploring. She stashed her backpack in her room, grabbed a crude street map of the central city at the front desk, and set out on foot toward the main square.

She wrote, "I fell in love with Peru—and its people—instantly."

As she strolled Cusco's streets, the sights, sounds, and smells of the city of 300,000 people "overwhelmed" her senses. Mountains encircled the city, giving Holly the sense of "walking inside a giant, earthen punch bowl."

Holly portrayed the poverty she saw as "depressing." She relayed an anecdote about being "accosted" barely a block from her hotel by a steady stream of children, each no more than ten years old, peddling everything from postcards to trinkets:

At first, I was friendly. Taking advantage of this, one persistent kid walked alongside me for a block, showing me one postcard after another, undaunted each time I said, "no, gracias."

Finally, he tried a new tack:

"Maybe later?"

"Yes. Maybe later," I quickly echoed, trying to get the kid to leave me alone.

"Remember me," he smiled impishly. "My name is Tom."

"Tom?"

"Si," he said, eyebrows raised. "Tom Cruise." He broke into a big smile.

I laughed out loud. "Hi, Tom." I shook his hand. "I'm Katie. Katie Holmes."

But no sooner had "Tom Cruise" faded away, when another street urchin was at my side, this time peddling a stack of some surprisingly good watercolors.

"Did you paint these?" I asked, incredulous.

"Si," the boy said, rapidly thumbing through them for me. "I'm Pablo."

"Don't tell me. Pablo Picasso, right?"

"Exactamente!" he beamed.

"No thanks, Pablo," I laughed. "Maybe later."

But this time I meant it.

After leaving "Tom" and "Pablo," Holly wrote that she walked down "a narrow street paved with uneven, rough bricks." It emerged onto Cusco's main square—the *Plaza de Armas*. "Two massive stone churches dominated adjacent sides of the plaza," she wrote.

"Dodging an onslaught of attacking taxis, their tinny horns beeping incessantly," Holly wrote that she bounded across the street to the park at the center of the square where six wide marble sidewalks converged on a large fountain in the middle.

"Suddenly," she wrote, "my head ached dully and I felt a bit dizzy—all symptoms of altitude sickness. But it was to be expected. I hadn't been sure how my body would adjust to the thin air, but I was relieved that the expected dizziness, headache, and lethargy weren't acute. But they were noticeable, and definitely slowed me down."

As I read, I began to wonder if dizziness due to the high altitude might have been a contributing factor in Holly's fatal fall.

Her Peru travelogue continued.

A bit winded, Holly said she collapsed onto one of the green, metal benches that encircled the fountain.

As I sat by the spitting fountain, I remembered from my reading that it was on this site that the last Incan Emperor, Tupac Amaru, was beheaded, executed by the Spanish.

I let my mind wander as I imagined what it must have been like to be alive on that day, September 24, 1572. I'd read that the square was filled with as many as 20,000 people whose thunderous wails filled the city in anguished protest at the death of their leader—and the end of their empire.

Holly clearly had a love for ancient civilizations. As I continued to read her diary, written neatly in ink, I could easily see her as a teacher or perhaps a writer of historical fiction. She no longer struck me as a self-absorbed diva.

In her diary, she wrote a gripping account of the forty-year-conquest of the Incas that began when Francisco Pizarro and his "relatively paltry" band of 180 Spanish *conquistadors* arrived in Peru in 1531.

Desperately outnumbered, Pizarro hatched a breathtakingly audacious scheme. Rather than show weakness and retreat, he successfully lured the Inca Emperor, Atahualpa, and his retinue to the Cajamarca town plaza for a little talk. As a show of good will, Atahualpa and his men came unarmed.

When Atahualpa refused to convert to Christianity, Pizarro had the legal justification to declare Atahualpa an enemy of Spain and the Catholic Church. Pizarro gave the signal and his troops, who had been hiding in buildings just off the plaza, ambushed and massacred some 2,000 of Atahualpa's forces and captured the emperor.

Pizarro then used the captured God Emperor to control the demoralized Incas. Atahualpa, hoping to buy time—and his freedom—ordered his people to bring Pizarro vast amounts of gold and silver. But it was never enough. Pizarro always wanted more.

Finally, the Incas revolted. The battles were awful and bloody, but the formidably superior weaponry of the Spanish eventually overwhelmed the Incas.

After the fall of the empire, the Spanish systematically destroyed much of the Incan influences. I can only describe it as the rape of a culture.

Disgusting.

After she'd finished resting at the fountain in the *Plaza de Armas*, Holly said she spent the next hour wandering up Cusco's side streets, "marveling at ancient walls made of gigantic, perfectly fitted stones."

She was intrigued by how the granite blocks had been cut precisely to fit so tightly together that no mortar was needed. She noted that over the centuries, earthquakes had caused the more "modern" Spanish architecture to crumble, yet the ancient Inca walls continued to stand.

Holly wrote that as she walked farther away from the main square, "the exotic smells of cooking food drifted out to the street from various homes and restaurants, but when I turned onto an even narrower street, the overwhelming eye-stinging stench of urine made the thought of a meal—or even a snack—unappealing."

Holly's descriptions of Cusco street scenes went on, but she really got my attention when she wrote, "I'd become so immersed in exploring that I suddenly realized that I was about to be late for my first face-to-face meeting with the enticing Mystery Man I'd met online. More on that later."

Chapter Fifty

There was no way I was going to turn out the light with Holly enticing me into reading about her meeting with "Mystery Man," as she so tantalizingly referred to him. I found myself becoming more deeply connected with Lionel and Muriel's daughter.

I felt sorry that Muriel didn't seem to want to share in what Holly was learning and experiencing in Peru. And, the more I read, the more I felt Lionel might come to see that, for all of her ranting against him and journalism, deep down Holly possessed some true journalistic instincts that Lionel could admire.

Holly's next entry was written the following day as she sat in the second-floor window of a restaurant overlooking the main square. She picked up her narrative right where she'd left off, writing that she was so worried that she would be late for her meeting with her Mystery Man that she began to trot, but she quickly had to lean against a wall in frustration, trying to catch her breath, her head throbbing.

She described her thoughts as she proceeded, slower this time, toward her rendezvous. Holly revealed that in the weeks leading up to her trek, his emails gradually reeled her in—and she loved it. She said she often daydreamed about the relationship they had forged because "he was so unlike most of the guys I knew."

> Most guys are either so intimidated by my looks that they don't even bother to approach me. The confident ones who do, usually turn out to be bad boys who—deep down—are mean and controlling, or they quickly turn into emotionally needy little boys who pour out their feelings for me—on the second date!

Bluff

Meredith and I talk about this a lot and we feel the same way: a "real man" is hard to find. And just what is a "real man"? Meredith and I came to the conclusion that a real man has:

1. Confidence
2. A sense of humor
3. Great looks
4. Sensitivity.

But in our experience, the confident guys are arrogant; the lookers are narcissistic; the funny ones are ugly; and the sensitive ones lack confidence. But Mystery Man seemed to embody the whole Real Man package.

How did I know? Because I'd tested him.

First, I sent him my picture. Usually, that flushed out the wussies pretty fast, because as soon as they see my picture, they seem to fall all over themselves to win my approval by trying to impress me with the size of their bank accounts, the car they drive, the high-powered job they have, or heap excessive compliments on me about my beauty.

Blah, blah, blah. How boring.

But MM was different. If anything, his emails became more playful after he'd seen my picture. Even though I wore a bikini, his response was, "Wow. You're the first blonde I've ever seen who does such a good job dyeing her roots black."

I'd burst out laughing when I read that because it was so unexpected and so...well...confident. He wasn't intimidated. He wasn't trying to win my approval.

More tests followed. He easily passed the looker test. His picture was eye-popping. And it took a lot of coaxing to get it. Most guys,

259

especially the good-looking ones, are quick to cough up a studly photo. MM played hard to get.

At first, I feared he had something to hide—like blimp tendencies—because he kept putting me off: "I want to be loved for myself," he'd pretended to pout. "I don't want to be treated like a piece of meat."

Again, I'd laughed out loud.

When I finally saw his picture—dark hair, strong chin, massive chest, and big guns flaring from his short-sleeved dark polo shirt—it was all I could do to keep from becoming the wuss I despised in others. The closest I came to that was inviting him on the hiking trip to Peru.

Normally, I'm not that forward, but at the time, I thought Meredith would be on the trip, too, so I figured it would be safe if he turned out to be some kind of psycho stalker.

Holly wrote that as she got closer to the *Plaza de Armas*, she felt the butterflies begin to circle in her stomach. She was about fifteen minutes late.

"What if he got fed up and left? What if he doesn't like me?" she worried, then scolded herself for letting her emotions get the best of her.

I paused at the curb, looked both ways, and scampered across the busy street, dodging traffic. On the other side, I quickly scanned the crowd for his familiar face. Just as I began to fear that he had indeed abandoned me, someone stepped toward me with a look of recognition on his face.

"Um, Holly?" he asked, tentatively.

Bluff

Finally, I focused on him. "Thor?" I asked.

Thor. Thor. I knew I'd heard that name before. Of course! I'd met him and his new wife in Riverside Park the day Shane Duran tried to cheat me on the sale of Grampa's farm. In fact, I remembered, Thor met his wife when they were hiking the Inca Trail with Holly.

I kept reading, trying to keep my eyes from rushing so fast that I might miss critical details.

We stood facing each other not speaking for what seemed like an eternity. Around us swirled the bustle of Cusco, Peru. Cars honked, the breeze blew, a flock of pigeons suddenly took flight.

My jaw dropped.

He smiled sheepishly. "The screen name's Thor, but you can call me William." He held out his hand.

"I-I don't know what to say," I stammered.

"'Nice to meet you' would be the normal way to start." He still held out his bony hand.

I took it automatically, but let it go almost immediately. "N-nice to meet you...I guess."

"Look, I know you were expecting some stud," he began.

"Uh huh. I was." I looked behind him hopefully. "Where is he?

"He couldn't be here, so he sent me," he smiled, gamely.

I furrowed my brow, confused. "You mean you're not the guy I've been talking with online for all this time?"

"Oh I'm him. Same guy." He was still smiling, but he looked like a stand-up comic whose best joke had just bombed.

"Yeah. Right." I scowled.

His face fell. "Are you angry?"

261

"Wouldn't you be?" I felt my face get hot.

"No. Not really." He couldn't look me in the eye.

"You totally misrepresented yourself." My teeth were clenched and my voice rose an octave.

He raised his head, took a step toward me, and then lasered me with his eyes. "Yeah, but you yourself wrote, 'Looks don't matter.'"

"But telling the truth does matter. You didn't." I punctuated the last two words by giving him two staccato pokes on his concave chest with my index finger.

He took a step back and spread out his arms. "I can explain—"

But before he could, I'd turned and staggered to the curb.

"Holly!" he called.

I was already dashing across the street—away from him.

Chapter Fifty-One

I couldn't stop reading. The green digits on the bedside table clock gleamed 2:08 a.m. I plunged ahead.

In her next diary entry, written in an unsteady hand as her tour bus lurched toward Cusco at the end of a day trip to the Sacred Valley, Holly reflected on her meeting with Thor, reporting that she was "so stunned and bummed that I couldn't even fake it." She said she realized it was "dumb" to have rejected Thor so decisively, but she chalked it up to a number of factors: "the debilitating effects caused by the confluence of altitude sickness, stunned surprise that Thor had misrepresented himself so blatantly, and because I was so wiped out after my trip from D.C. that I had absolutely no room left on my emotional buffer for politeness."

Subsequent entries, written at various times during the day before the beginning of her hike, contained mostly routine references to the places she saw and some of the people she met on her sightseeing jaunts.

Thor didn't return to her narrative again until the night before Holly began her Inca Trail trek. She wrote the entry while in her hotel room after having attended an evening orientation meeting at the office of the travel agency in charge of the hike.

After getting a briefing from Alejandro, our cute Peruvian tour guide, we all lingered for crackers, wine, and cheese and a chance to get acquainted with the others who would be on the hike. I apologized to Thor for dissing him the way I did. Supposedly he accepted it, but then he kept hovering around me like a stalker.

It was my first chance to size up the people who I'd be spending the next four days with. I flirted with all the guys, but kept it light and shallow—no point getting attached to anyone too soon. I was just playing the field.

I'm used to guys coming on to me, so I've learned to decide pretty quickly which ones are interesting. There was a cute guy from somewhere in the Upper Midwest who got my attention, but when he started cracking jokes that just weren't funny, I knew it was time to move on. He was attractive enough, but his needy, hangdog desperation was a real turnoff.

Holly's next entry was during a noon siesta after lunch on day one of the hike. The trek had begun, she wrote, before sunrise in Cusco's tiny *Regocijo Plaza* where the rest of her group—and the porters who would carry the gear—gathered for the three-hour bus ride to the trailhead at kilometer 82 along the Urubamba River. Much to her chagrin, Thor was her seatmate.

"We need to talk," he said as he slid into the seat next to me.

"Not now," I told him, "I'm exhausted." For the next two hours, I pretended to sleep, but I let my head loll to the side so that I could still peek out the window without him noticing.

At about eight o'clock the bus stopped by the side of the river at a two-story, cinderblock house/restaurant where everyone sat down to a hearty breakfast of omelets and toast.

Thor sat next to me, but I managed to strike up a conversation with a stout, pleasant young woman named Laura from Door County, Wisconsin. Laura referred to Door County as "the Cape Cod of the Midwest."

The two of us chitchatted while Thor steamed. So far, I have managed to avoid having a showdown with him, but I know that eventually I have to deal with him because the other more interesting guys will leave me alone if they think I'm with Thor. I've got to shake him because he keeps circling me like a shark.

Holly wrote that after breakfast, they all got back on the bus and drove for about an hour until they came to the drop-off point, a clearing next to a narrow-gauge railroad track that snaked alongside the boulder-strewn rapids of the Urubamba. The day, she reported, was sunny, clear, and a pleasant seventy degrees.

When we got to the drop-off point, the porters—more than a dozen of them—swarmed around the bus, unloading the camping gear—tents, sleeping bags, cooking utensils, the works.

The porters are mostly short, copper-skinned young men in their early twenties with high cheekbones, prominent noses, dark eyes and thick, black hair. I'm surprised that most of them wear either sneakers or sandals, not hiking boots.

Working quickly and skillfully, the porters divvied up the equipment so that each man carried on his back a bulging pack wrapped in a bright blue canvas tarpaulin weighing sixty pounds, a load so heavy they have to stoop when they walk.

One porter, in addition to carrying the bulky backpack, also carried in his hand a wire mesh cage containing several cartons of eggs. I made a mental note to tip these guys generously at the end of the four days.

Holly's next entry was written later that night.

We took a half-hour siesta after lunch, then Alejandro got us going for the afternoon trek, during which the trail turned left, away from the Urubamba River and weaved along the Kusichaca, one of the Urubamba's many tributaries. The wooded area reminded me of Rock Creek Park where I like to jog in D.C.

I tried to walk with Laura and her college roommate, Paula, but Thor continued to hover. At one point, I finally just had to stop, take him aside and give him a piece of my mind, making sure Laura and Paula were watching and listening.

"Look," I told him sternly. "I don't want you following me."

He spread his arms, innocently. "I'm not following you."

"You are. You won't let me alone."

"I'm not bothering you."

"Actually, you are. You're making me extremely uncomfortable with all your unwelcome attention. I'm telling you politely, in front of witnesses," I gestured to Laura and Paula, "that I would like you to back off and leave me alone."

He stuck his chin out belligerently.

"And if I don't?"

"Then I will report you to Alejandro."

"Ooooo. I'm really scared."

"I'm not trying to scare you. I'm just making it crystal clear to you that your attention is unwelcome and I find it disconcerting if not downright menacing."

I turned and walked away from him, not waiting for a response. After that, he kept his distance, but he kept shooting me killer looks the rest of the day.

The trail became rockier and steeper, forcing Holly and the others to stop frequently to catch their breath. They arrived at the first night's campsite "just as the setting sun began to cast long shadows."

The porters had already assembled eight small, rounded, nylon tents. The tents, Holly reported, stood next to each other in a long, even row on a flat, earthen terrace. Dinner in the dining tent "was even more sumptuous than lunch"—soup, chicken, rice, and a variety of fruits and vegetables. "The conversation around the table was festive, but Thor sat glowering at me from a corner of the table at the far end of where I sat. At least he's keeping his distance," Holly wrote.

Chapter Fifty-Two

It was now after 2:30 in the morning, but I still wasn't tired. I got up and tiptoed to the bathroom, but came right back to cuddle up with Holly's diary.

Her next entry was written in the predawn hours before the beginning of the trek's second day. Holly wrote that she'd been paired with "a tall, friendly blonde" from Vancouver named Sabrina. After dinner, they talked and giggled in their tent until they fell asleep.

I awoke somewhere around 1:30 with a strong urge to pee. Throwing a fleece jacket over the nylon running suit I'd worn to bed, I quietly unzipped the tent and made a dash through the cold night air to the nearby latrine. (It's disgustingly Spartan, but that's a story for another time.)

On the way back to my tent, I stopped to gaze at the full moon as it began to emerge from behind the mountains on the other side of the Kusichaca River valley. I could hear soft snoring coming from several of the two-person tents about fifty feet behind me.

The view was mesmerizing.

Suddenly, I felt a light tap on my shoulder.

"Oh my God!" I gasped, bringing my hands to my mouth.

"It's only me," someone said softly.

I turned, expecting to see Thor, but instead I saw Alejandro smiling at me, his hands on his hips. He wore a black fleece jacket. A cloth band around his head covered his ears.

"Alejandro," I laughed, exhaling the breath I'd been holding. "You scared the hell out of me."

"I'm so sorry," he chuckled. "I only wanted to say hello."

Alejandro is one of the cute ones. He's short, outgoing with an infectious smile and laugh, and he carries himself with a lot of confidence—totally unlike Thor.

During the day, Alejandro had been busy shepherding the entire group, so I was grateful for this bit of secret, one-on-one face time.

Apparently, he was, too.

"What do you think of the hike so far?" he asked, his Cheshire cat smile gleaming in the moonlight.

"I love it." I stepped beside him and turned around so we were both looking at the moon.

He lowered his voice. "Did you know this camp is haunted?"

"It is?" Involuntarily, I hugged myself.

"Yes," Alejandro said, pressing his shoulder lightly against me. "It's haunted by the ghost of a porter." He spoke slowly, his voice nearly a whisper.

I looked at him and could tell by the slight smirk on his face that he was teasing, but I played along.

"Really?" I drew the word out long and dramatically.

"I'm serious." He leaned closer, conspiratorially. "Do you want to know what happened?"

"Tell me," I whispered eagerly.

"Long ago, maybe twenty years, a porter was carrying an even bigger and bulkier load than they're allowed to carry now. He was near this very spot, trying to go as fast as he could, but he tripped, staggered, lost his balance, and fell off the side of the trail and down, down into the valley hundreds of meters below."

"That's terrible," I whispered, taking a step back, away from the precipice.

"Yes. His body wasn't found for months and his spirit couldn't get to the Other Side. Every so often, someone sees him in the middle of the night running along the trail, a huge pack on his back."

"Have you ever seen him?" I asked, my eyes wide.

Alejandro backed up slowly so that I had to turn slightly to look at him.

"Yes. I have seen him," Alejandro said softly, reverently.

Suddenly, he focused on something just behind me. His eyes widened and a look of terror came across his face.

On one level, I knew he was teasing me and I'd been playing along, but in the bright moonlight the look of horror on his face was truly terrifying.

I felt my flesh tingle and crawl. Without thinking, I turned to see what he was looking at.

As I turned, Alejandro grabbed me by both shoulders.

"There he is!" he hissed in my ear.

With his two strong hands still cupped firmly on the side of my shoulders, he swiftly extended his arms as if pushing me, but he didn't let go.

I squealed with terror—and delight.

Just as quickly, Alejandro pulled me close to him and encircled me from behind with his arms, resting his chin gently on my left shoulder, his lips inches away from my ear.

I giggled softly and nuzzled the side of my face against his.

We stood this way for nearly a minute looking at the moon, then slowly, gently, he turned me around so I was facing him.

Bluff

My breath was shallow and fast. I started to say something, but he put his finger against my lips, then replaced his finger with his lips.

I moaned, threw my arms around his neck, and kissed him hungrily.

Chapter Fifty-Three

Holly Stone chronicled day two of her Inca Trail trek in entries that she made during several rest stops along the way. She wrote that the day started out easily enough with a walk through a forested area alongside a rushing mountain stream. Holly said that most of the time she could only hear the brook because the thick tangle of gnarled trees hid the rushing water from view.

As the morning wore on, the hiking became increasingly strenuous. At various points, the gradual incline was interrupted by steep stone stairways that, she wrote, "required dexterity and concentration to ascend."

Barely an hour out of camp, the extra exertion caused Holly to begin to feel hot, even though the day was pleasant and cool. Before she'd begun to work up a sweat, she took off her fleece jacket and the bottom part of her zip-off hiking pants to make them into shorts.

I prefer to be by myself on the trail because at the altitude of 12,000 feet and climbing, it's no longer possible to carry on any kind of meaningful conversation before quickly running out of breath. It didn't take long to discover that huffing and wheezing conversations are no fun. They merely tire me out more quickly and slow me up.

It's amazing to watch Alejandro at work. One minute he's at the head of the pack, keeping pace with the three Irish guys from Belfast, then he drops all the way back to keep an eye on the straggling real estate tycoon who smokes those disgusting cigars, then

Alejandro dashes—and I literally mean dashes—to the front, pausing briefly as he passes me to say something funny.

He wanted to do more last night, but I wouldn't put out.

"Not yet," I told him. "I'm not ready."

Actually, I was MORE than ready, but he didn't push it. It gives us both something to look forward to.

Holly described the vistas as "awe-inspiring." She said she stopped often to unscrew the cap from a liter water bottle and take a swig, catch her breath, and snap a picture.

I took pictures of the misty clouds clinging to the mountains on the other side of the valley. I took pictures of the various hikers in the group. I took pictures of the porters as one by one they passed me at nearly a trot, straining and sweating under the heavy loads they carried on their backs. (Those guys are truly amazing!) I even took pictures of the trail itself—smooth, irregularly shaped stones that could easily have been in place for centuries.

But, when I moved too quickly trying to snap a shot of a hummingbird, the camera slipped out of my hand, bounced crazily off a granite trail rock and disappeared over the side, into a dense, inaccessible thicket of trees and brush at least 90 feet below where I stood. I cursed my clumsiness and sullenly resumed my hike.

By late morning, the forest had given way to thick, dry, brown grass—the thatch, Holly observed, that people who lived in the area still used to make the roofs of their homes. The trail continued "relentlessly" higher.

Holly said she realized it was less daunting if she didn't look too far ahead because doing so—"seeing the trail stretching into the distance with seemingly no end in sight"—was discouraging.

The day's midpoint was at Dead Woman's Pass, the saddle that linked two tall mountain peaks. The higher she hiked, the colder and cloudier it got.

I stopped to put on my poncho because I was literally in the middle of a damp cloudbank. As I neared the summit, I could see more clouds, pushed by a stiff wind, shoot up and over the pass and into the valley to my right. It looked like a train made of steam, highballing over the pass.

I felt a strong sense of elation when I finally reached the top of Dead Woman's Pass—an elevation of more than 14,000 feet. Everyone in the group paused to rest, relax, and savor what we had accomplished.

"Why is this place called 'Dead Woman's Pass?'" someone asked Alejandro. "Did a woman fall off?"

"Actually," Alejandro explained, a sly grin forming at the side of his mouth, "it doesn't have anything to do with that. Take a look," he continued, pointing down the trail as it descended the other side of the pass where we'd be hiking for the rest of the afternoon. "Imagine that we are at the head of a woman who is lying on her back. On either side of us are mountaintops. You see? They are her breasts pointing at the sky," he laughed.

A few of the men chortled, but the guy who likes cigars laughed the loudest. I heard his guffaw ricochet off the side of the "dead woman's" left "breast."

Bluff

Alejandro collected everyone's camera and took a series of group shots as everyone yipped and yelled with glee, raising our hiking sticks in a brazen salute.

Much to my annoyance, however, the cigar-smoking tycoon managed to wangle himself next to me for the group shot. His breath stank of stale cigar as he draped an arm possessively around my shoulder.

Each time I shrugged it off, he put it back in place. I'm sure that in at least one picture, my nose is turned up as I react to his stench.

After resting at the top of Dead Woman's Pass, the hike continued downhill for the next couple hours, before rising and going over another, much lower pass.

It was near the end of the second day of hiking that I realized one of the guy's on the trek had been keeping up with me, yet keeping his distance. I was intrigued—and thrilled. I'd met him at the travel office briefing the night before the hike began and had flirted with him at various times during the past two days. I guessed he was a couple years older than I am. I thought he was cute, probably the best looking guy in the group, but I didn't want to appear to be too eager, so I'd been aloof, but careful not to be too reserved.

That night, after dinner, he made his move.

"Let's go for a walk," he said, touching me gently on the arm. (No names. Sorry, Daddy.)

"That's all we've been doing for the past two days," I laughed, but I felt my heart beat a little faster. This guy is confident and knows what he's doing, I said to myself. I wanted to be with him.

"C'mon," he said, ignoring my halfhearted objection and taking me by the hand. "The moon's full. I'll bet the view of the valley from that spot over there is spectacular."

He led me away from the camp down the trail in the direction we'd be hiking the next day. The moon was so bright we didn't need to use our flashlights.

We stopped at a grassy spot sheltered by trees and rocks about 200 yards from the camp and at an elevation about 100 feet higher. From there, we could see the campground—and hear a raucous card game that was going on in the dining tent—and we could see the moon and the shadowy mountains and valleys all around us.

He was unlike any man I'd known before. Yes, he was good looking, but for me, that's nothing new. What set him apart—and what I found mesmerizing—was his quiet, self-confident ability to empathize. He listened attentively when I talked and seemed to really care about what I had to say. He even listened sympathetically as I poured out to him my frustrations about growing up as the daughter of a famous—but oppressive—father.

We spent the next two hours at our secluded perch talking, then kissing, then making love.

Chapter Fifty-Four

Day three along the Inca Trail was the last full day of Holly Stone's life. I felt my heart beat faster as I got to Holly's final entry.

It was written exactly two years to the day earlier—just hours before her life came to an end:

June 6—

What an experience! There's been virtually no time to write. Lots of hiking. I'm pooped.

Saw some spectacular sights. In places, the trail gets very narrow. One slip and it's curtains, because the drop offs are sheer. Good thing I got new hiking boots before I came. I feel as sure-footed as a mountain goat—and, until the shower I took today, I probably smelled like one, too.

The sun is setting. I'm sitting in the middle of an ancient set of Inca ruins known as Winawayna, which, in English means "Forever Young." The name of the place, its pastoral setting, and the personal turmoil going on right now in my life, have put me in a philosophical frame of mind.

She described the giddiness she felt as she sat next to her lover at breakfast, careful not to let anyone else notice how she felt because, she wrote, she'd already managed to alienate some of the men on the trip— she didn't want to aggravate them even more.

But it was hard to avoid letting at least some of my joy show. Secretly, I squeezed his hand as it rested on his thigh below the ta-

ble. Later, on the trail, he (or I) would stop, look around to see if anyone was watching, then steal a kiss.

Not only was I almost literally on the top of the world—I felt like it, too.

The day's trek began with a gradual incline past the place where they'd spent time just hours before locked in each other's arms. The higher they walked, the cloudier it got.

"The trail was shrouded in mist," she wrote. In several places, before making an abrupt turn, the trail looked to Holly like it was heading "straight into the sky."

She wrote, "At times, I felt like I was gazing into infinity." The trail passed through a subtropical jungle filled with bamboo trees, orchids, and hummingbirds. Sometimes, the two of them stopped to listen to the melodious call of some exotic bird.

"I was thankful for the cool weather—and for his company," Holly wrote.

About two in the afternoon, they stopped for a snack. As they munched on power bars, she got out her cell phone and was amazed to find that she had a signal. She phoned home. And that, Holly wrote, is when her day turned sour.

Calling you and Mom was a big mistake, Daddy. Why can't you let me grow up without injecting all your biases? Yes! Biases! You cultivate this reputation of being the avuncular, trustworthy, above-the-fray, OBJECTIVE journalist, yet you have biases coming out of your ears, especially when it comes to me. You're a hypocrite, Daddy; no better than the politicians you loathe. Can't you see it? Mom gets it. She understands me. Why don't you?

Geez. Listen to me. I'm letting my twisted relationship with my father spoil my vacation. I can't even write in my own journal without it turning into a diatribe at Dad. As much as I want to break free of his clutches, deep down I know he means well. He really does.

Mom has tried to help me see that he really does care for me, and wants the best for me. She told me once that he loves me so much that he just doesn't want to see me get hurt. I guess I'm beginning to understand that.

I tried to tell the guy I slept with last night that I need some time to think, but now he's pissed and blames my father for trying to break us up.

Geez!

I made a mental note to ask Lionel and/or Muriel to give me a better idea of what was said in that final telephone conversation.

Holly described herself after she hung up on her folks as "emotionally numb" for the rest of the afternoon, barely noticing the Inca ruins she passed, or even the steep and treacherous stone stairways she had to navigate. She kept turning the conversation with her father over and over in her head.

"I had certainly left the impression with Daddy that I'm in a really serious relationship, when, in reality, I'm merely infatuated," she wrote.

"Love is too strong a word to describe my feelings. Lust is more like it."

Hiking came to the end for the day about 3:30 at a hostel where the facilities were "marginally better" than they had been on the trail. The porters had erected the tents on a terrace about fifty yards from the hostel.

Holly described it as "a big, echoey, adobe building" with tall ceilings, a bar and several common areas where many hiking groups could eat at once. Most importantly, she wrote, there were showers.

They weren't great, but that was okay. For a couple dollars, I was able to rent a towel, some soap, and a few minutes' worth of lukewarm water.

As I washed three days of grime from my body, I realized I was right to want more space—and time—to think, to assess my relationships. The shower was a metaphor for cleaning my "boy" slate and starting over.

After her shower, but before dinner, Alejandro took the group to the nearby Inca ruin where Holly sat making the final diary entry of her life.

She noted that *Winawayna* had only been discovered in 1941. It was built into a steep mountainside. Terraces made it feel to her like a "giant amphitheater with a vast valley stretching out below us as the stage."

After Alejandro's brief lecture, everyone was free to roam the place until dinnertime. Holly decided to sit and write in her journal.

The hike itself has been exhausting, exhilarating and inspiring, yet I've managed to piss off at least three men on this trip—maybe four, perhaps even five. I'm now sitting here trying to figure out what I did to bring it on and what, if anything, I can do to set things right.

Even though I apologized to "Thor" for dissing him the way I did, I still had to firmly tell him to back off. He did, but yesterday, after we all had our pictures taken at the top of Dead Woman's Pass, he sidled up to me and said, "I notice the rocks on the trail are wet. Be careful that you don't slip and fall. I wouldn't want to see you hurt yourself."

He didn't say it in a mean or threatening way, but I've been trying to do my best to stay aloof because he creeps me out.

The cute "comedian" from somewhere in the Upper Midwest who got my attention at the pre-hike mixer may feel I moved on from him too abruptly because he's been kinda snarky to me all week.

I keep wondering about Alejandro, too. We really clicked that night under the moon when he told me the ghost story. We both felt a strong attraction—and we both acted on it instinctively. But then I suddenly backed off. If he's bothered by what he might see as my sudden change of heart, he doesn't show it. That has me a little spooked because, in my experience, most guys get angry if I shut them down.

And then there's Cigar Man. Every chance he gets, he tries to impress me with how rich he is. He doesn't realize how NOT into money I am. Frankly, money—or the excessive love of it—is one of the things seriously wrong with the U.S. It seems like trying to aggravate me has become his obsession.

Holly wrote that earlier she'd heard members of another hiking group at the hostel talking about having a card game. "I think I'll join them," she wrote, "and maybe get drunk."

Her diary came to an end with these words:

I don't want anyone near me on the trail tomorrow. Was just dozing now and had a weird dream. I dreamed I was on the trail. It wound higher and higher into the sky. The moon was full. Some-

one was chasing me. I couldn't tell who it was, but he kept getting closer and closer. I smelled the stench of a cigar. Kept turning around to see if Cigar Man was chasing me, but I couldn't see his face.

Suddenly, I was pushed from behind, tripped, and went falling over the side of the cliff. I woke up before I hit, so I suppose that means I won't die any time soon.

That was the last entry in Holly Stone's diary. My heart was galloping by the time I came to the end. I had so many questions:

The dream was obviously a premonition of her death, but was it a self-fulfilling prophecy?

Did she become so obsessed with the possibility of falling that she accidentally tripped and fell to her death?

Was she drunk or hung over after staying up late drinking?

Or was Holly pushed? And, if she was pushed, who did it?

For the past year, Lionel and Muriel had firmly believed that Holly's death was a simple accident. But they'd never read all of what she'd written in her diary. I had a gnawing feeling that Holly Stone was murdered.

I was more than a little spooked that I'd already met "Thor." Was he capable of murder? Holly thought so.

And just who was the "comedian" from the Midwest? Jonathan Anderson did standup. And he'd hiked the Inca Trail. But was it just too neat of a coincidence for him to have been on the same hiking trek as Holly?

Plus—and this really freaked me out—the parallels between Cigar Man and Shane Duran had me wondering if Holly's killer also murdered Jason.

Chapter Fifty-Five

I couldn't sleep. About six I quit trying. I crept into the kitchen and brewed a pot of coffee. Muriel, wearing a powder blue bathrobe, shuffled in about 6:30.

"Lark. What are you doing up so early?"

"I couldn't sleep. I read the rest of Holly's diary."

Muriel didn't react. She took a mug from the cupboard and poured herself some coffee. "Mmmmm. This is good. I should have you make the coffee around here all the time."

"You really think reading Holly's diary is waste of time, don't you?"

She nodded. "For me it would be. I have my memories and those remain vivid. I just think it would be too painful to read her inner thoughts. And it's a boundary thing. That's Holly's private domain."

I hesitated before I said what had been playing on my mind, but I had to let it out. "Muriel?" I asked, tentatively.

She put down her mug and looked at me.

"I don't know exactly how to say this, so I'll just say it."

"Oh, dear. It's too early for all this drama," Muriel laughed, but her smile was tight, tense.

"I don't think Holly's death was an accident."

Muriel looked stunned as if struck by lightning. "Y-you don't?"

"No. I think she was pushed."

Muriel shut her eyes tightly. "What makes you think that?" she whispered.

Quickly, I summarized what Holly had written about Thor, Cigar Man, The Comedian, and the other men she may have alienated. "And," I concluded, "the last entry is about a dream she had a few hours before she died that Cigar Man may have been chasing her when she fell off the mountain. It was the last entry of her diary, Muriel."

Muriel, whose eyes remained tightly closed as I talked, suddenly put her hands to her face and sobbed, "Oh, my baby!" She doubled over and her body bucked spasmodically as wave after wave of grief poured from her.

I scooted to her side and put my arm around her.

Lionel rushed into the room wearing a dark brown bathrobe.

"Muriel! Are you all right?" He stopped and his eyes took in the tableaux. "What happened?" he demanded.

"I just told her I think Holly was murdered."

He moved to his wife and put his arms around her as I withdrew.

Muriel continued to sob silently into her hands. Her head was bent and she bobbed up and down.

I said nothing, waiting for Muriel to calm down. Finally I said, "I feel awful for dropping such a bombshell."

Lionel looked at me—glowered is a better word. "Why do you think she was murdered?"

For the second time that morning, I quickly summarized what I'd read. "And," I added, "Cigar Man bears a creepy resemblance to Shane Duran."

"Oh, come on, Lark. That's quite a stretch, don't you think?" Lionel said.

"Maybe," I allowed.

Lionel relaxed and turned his attention back to Muriel, whose sobs had turned to sniffles. She accepted the tissue he offered, blew her nose, and sagged into a kitchen chair.

"Holly mentioned calling you from the Inca Trail," I said, "but she didn't go into much detail. Can you fill me in on that?"

"I can do even better than that," Muriel said, getting up. "I still have a recording of her phone call."

"You do?" Lionel and I asked simultaneously.

"Uh huh." She stood by the phone, fiddling with the controls. "When Holly called, Lionel and I were out, so she started to leave a message on the answering machine as we were coming in the door. The answering machine was still recording when we picked up."

"You never told me that," Lionel said, his tone an accusation.

Muriel shrugged. "It's been there all along. I listen to it sometimes, just to hear her voice." Muriel finished what she was doing with the answering machine and turned to look at Lionel and me.

"Anybody want to give a listen?"

"Sure," I said, and looked at Lionel.

"Might as well," he shrugged.

Muriel pushed a button.

"Greetings from the Inca Trail," Holly's voice filled the kitchen, sounding strong and jubilant. "Sorry I missed you guys. It's the third day of the hike, I'm taking—"

Muriel's voice interrupted. "Hi, Holly."

"Hi, Mom."

"Your father and I just walked in the door."

The connection was surprisingly good.

"Daddy's there too?"

"He's on his way upstairs to get on the extension."

There was a clunk, followed by Lionel's voice. "Hi, Holl! How's it goin'?"

He sounded jovial, upbeat.

"I'm doing great. It's the third day of the hike and I finally have cell phone service again. We're just taking a breather, so I thought I'd check in."

"Are you having a good time?" her mother asked.

"I am. It's wonderful!"

"How's the weather?" Lionel asked.

"Really great. Not too hot, and no rain. We've been lucky."

"That's just grand," her mother said.

"I just wanted to tell you guys that I met someone special on the hike."

For a moment there was silence, then Lionel spoke, "'Special' as in you're thinkin' of getting married?"

"Well, actually…"

"Dammit, Holly," Lionel exploded, "you're too young to even think about getting married."

"Dad—"

He barreled on. "This was just supposed to be a fun getaway after graduation. Nothing serious."

"Dad—"

"I didn't spend all this money so that you could go out and get yourself tied down with some guy." He was ranting.

"But he's really sweet," Holly tried.

"I don't care. You're too young."

"Mom, can you talk some sense into him?"

"I'll try, dear."

Lionel kept going. "So, promise me you'll reconsider. Give yourself some space to think about him objectively. Calmly. Rationally."

"I'm promising nothing," Holly yelled into the phone. "You can't tell me what to do."

"The hell I can't."

"This conversation is over."

The line went dead.

Lionel's face was flushed, his face contorted in what looked to me to be a mixture of grief and rage.

"Anyone want to hear it again," Muriel asked, dabbing at her eyes with a handkerchief.

"No," Lionel said, softly.

"I hope you're proud of yourself, Lionel," Muriel whispered hoarsely.

"Wait just a goddam minute," he bellowed.

"No. You wait, Lionel," I said, stepping between them.

He looked at me, stunned.

"After she hung up, Holly wrote in her journal that she realized that she didn't love the guy and had decided to back off. She actually took your advice."

Lionel stood looking at me, astonished, his mouth agape.

"Well, my dear," Muriel said to Lionel, "I think it's time the two of us read Miss Holly's diary for ourselves. Seems both of us have been living in denial for too long."

"I'll go get it," I said.

I brought Holly's diary into the kitchen and set it on the table in front of where Muriel had taken a seat. She flopped it open. Lionel stood behind her chair, looking over her shoulder.

"Where do you want to begin, dear?" Muriel said to Lionel.

"Lark, what do you suggest?" He looked at me and for the first time I had the uncomfortable feeling that the tables had turned: I was the mentor and he was the mentee.

"It'll be painful, but I'd say start at the beginning. Take your time. But promise me you won't blame each other. That won't bring Holly back. It will only embitter you toward each other. I love you both very, very much," my voice broke. "Don't hurt each other. Help each other."

At first there was silence, then Lionel said, "Sounds like a plan." He pulled a chair next to his wife. "What do you think, sweetheart?"

"I think Lark's right," Muriel said.

When I left them, they were sitting next to each other, Holly's diary splayed open on the kitchen table in front of them, Lionel resting a hand on Muriel's shoulder.

And, I realized, it was time for me to do some digging, too.

Chapter Fifty-Six

What kept gnawing around my subconscious was Holly's ominous dream. Building inside me was the determination to check out my hunches. But how?

I called my friend Heather.

"Hey," she said, "I've been meaning to call you. You've been all over the news. How are you?"

"I'm okay," I said. "It's been tough, but I'm holding up."

"I'll bet you could use a drink. Wanna go out tonight?"

"I'm under house arrest."

"You are? What does that mean?"

I explained to my sometimes dense friend the limits on my life placed on me by the judge.

"Well that sucks," Heather said. "So, did you do it?" she chuckled.

"Heather!" I laughed.

"I know. I know. You can't talk about the case."

"Yes, I can. In fact, that's why I called."

"Really? What's up?"

"I just need to think out loud about a bunch of stuff."

"I'm all ears."

I brought her completely up to speed, telling her about Landscam, Shane Duran, and ending with the cryptic references in Holly's diary that led me to suspect that the same person who killed Holly might have killed Jason. I concluded, "I need to find out who was on the trip with Holly."

"How are you going to do that?"

"I'll see if Lionel or Muriel can put me in touch with the travel agency that handled the trek, then I'll go from there."

"Uh huh. That sounds like a good start," Heather said.

"And there's something that maybe you could look into as well."

"Sure. Anything."

"Remember that night when we were at the Nitty Gritty?"

"Comedy night. Right."

"Remember the guy named Jonathan who did all those impersonations?"

"The cute blond guy. What about him?"

"He's Jonathan Anderson."

"You mean the guy who's been writing about you in the *MadCity News?*"

"Right."

"Whoa. What's he got to do with this?"

"I dunno. Maybe nothing. Maybe everything."

She laughed. "That's helpful."

"Here's what I know about him: He's a hiker."

"Yeah…"

"He told me he hiked the Inca Trail last year."

"Yeah…"

"He had a crush on me, or at least I think he did."

"Lucky you."

"He might have been jealous of my relationship with Jason."

"That makes sense."

"And you and I both know he does impersonations."

"So?"

"So, I think it's possible that he lured Jason to Granddad's Bluff by pretending to be Shane Duran."

"Hey, you're right. In fact, didn't he do a Shane Duran impersonation that night?"

"Right. But here's what I don't know: I don't know if he was on the hiking trip with Holly Stone."

"Why don't you ask him?"

"He and I aren't on speaking terms right now."

"Why not?"

"He tricked me into going off the record, then used my words to make it sound like I might have been angry enough with Jason to murder him."

"What a bastard. Okay. What do you want me to do?"

"Since Jonathan doesn't know you and I are friends, I'm thinking you could meet with him and get him talking about hiking. I need to find out when he hiked the Inca Trail and the company he used when he made his arrangements."

"I could pretend to be planning a hiking trip," Heather said, starting to get excited. "Sure. I could do that. Gimme a couple days, okay?"

"That would be great."

"It's sort of like being Mata Hari," she continued, warming up to her new role. "Maybe I'll even get laid."

I laughed. "No need to get carried away."

"Ooooo. That sounds like fun, too," she squealed. "Talk to you soon."

"Thanks, Heather."

Lionel and Muriel came into the room as I hung up. They were holding hands.

"We're taking a break," she said. She looked drawn and tired.

"Gonna shower and get dressed," Lionel reported. They were still wearing their bathrobes.

"How's it going?" I asked.

"It's very hard, Lark." Muriel's eyes were red and she looked drained. "I think it's good that we're reading Holly's diary together, but it's slow going. Seems like each entry prompts a long, painful discussion. It's like therapy, only in this case, it's the blind leading the blind."

"Is there anything I can do to help?"

"Just be patient," she said.

"That's the hardest part."

She chuckled.

I looked at Lionel. He, too, seemed haggard and distracted, his gray hair disheveled.

"Lionel?" I asked. "Do you still have the police report of Holly's accident?"

He scowled and shook his head. "I thought I did, but I was looking for it the other day and can't find it. I think I lost it when we moved here from D.C."

"Didn't you tell me it had the names of the people who were on Holly's trek?"

His eyes came alive. I could tell he was thinking along the same lines as I was. "Yeah. I can call Mike Sutherland at the embassy in Lima. Maybe he can track it down for me."

"Do either of you happen to know the name of the organization that sponsored Holly's hiking trip?" I asked.

"Sure. I have it in a file upstairs," Muriel said. "I'll get the name and number of the place for you." She started up the stairs with Lionel right behind her.

"Also," I called after them, "do you know how I can contact the two people who were just in town who met Holly on the trip. I forget their last name."

"Oh, yes," Muriel said. "That would be Laura and, um, William Benedict. I've got that upstairs, too."

In less than five minutes, Muriel came back downstairs with all the raw information I needed to get started on my quest.

Chapter Fifty-Seven

I placed a call to Laura Benedict's cell phone. A woman answered on the second ring.

"Is this Laura Benedict?" I asked.

"It is," she said. "Who's this?"

"Hi, Laura. It's Lark Chadwick." I tried to sound cheerful, enthusiastic, but my heart was pounding. "I work with Lionel Stone. We met in Riverside Park in Pine Bluff a couple weeks ago when you and William were passing through."

"Oh. Yes. I remember. You took our picture. How are you?"

"I'm fine. How was your honeymoon?"

"We had a great time."

All I could think of was how Thor had seriously spooked Holly by his creepy stalker behavior and his ominous comment about not wanting to see her slip and fall on the trail. I wondered what Laura might know. I had so many questions, but lacked a coherent plan.

"Where are you now?" I asked, stalling for time, my mind racing.

"We live up in Door County."

"Cool. It's pretty there," I said, faking it—I'd never set foot in Door County, Wisconsin. I only knew that it was in the northeastern part of the state beyond Green Bay.

"It is," Laura said simply. She didn't sound suspicious, but I couldn't be sure.

My turn to talk, but I didn't know what to say. After an uncomfortable silence, I pressed on, making it up as I went along.

"Um, I was wondering, Laura, if you or Thor have ever hiked Granddad's Bluff here."

"In Pine Bluff?"

"Uh huh."

"No, we haven't, but we saw it when we were in town."

"Well, I love to hike and I was wondering if you and, um, Thor wouldn't mind stopping by sometime soon and go for a hike up there. I know Lionel and Muriel would like to see you both again."

"Let me talk it over with Thor," Laura said. "Can I call you right back?"

"Sure." I didn't want to lose her, but I didn't think I had any choice. I didn't want Thor to think that I suspected anything. If he got spooked, Laura either wouldn't call back, or if she did, she'd have some lame excuse about why they couldn't stop by.

But, in the time it took to worry about all the reasons why I might not get a chance to confront Thor, Laura called back.

"Lark, we'd love to go hiking on Granddad's Bluff. We can be there Saturday. Is that okay?"

"That's great, Laura. See you then. Oh, and would you mind bringing the pictures of your Inca Trail hike? Holly's camera was never recovered and I know Lionel and Muriel would like to see them."

"No problem."

On Monday, I gave the hiking company a call.

I got the runaround at first, but was finally connected to someone in reservations.

"Hello," I began, sweetly, "I'm trying to find out the name of some-one who was on one of your trips to Peru recently."

"I'm sorry," the person explained. "That information is confidential."

"Do you still have the records?"

"Oh yes. We keep all records."

"Well, instead of giving me all the names, can I give you a name and you can confirm if that person was on the trip?"

The person on the other end hesitated. "Can you tell me a little more? What's this about?"

"The daughter of my boss was on one of those trips and died in an accidental fall from one of the mountains." I wasn't sure how much information would be helpful and nonthreatening to the obviously paranoid secretary. I certainly didn't want to get into the possibility that Holly may have been murdered. "I want to talk with people who were on the trip to get a better idea of how the accident may have happened."

"I see," the person said. "But you just said you already have a name and you just want to know if that person was on the trip. If you already have the name, why not just ask that person directly? Are you with an insurance company?"

Damn! This was not getting me anywhere.

"No. I'm definitely not with an insurance company. But I'm getting the impression that you're not very willing to help me."

"It's not personal, it's just that we need to protect the privacy of our clients. How do I know you're not a jilted lover checking to see if your significant other may have been on a secret rendezvous with your best friend?"

I grunted. "It's not that."

"But you can see my position, can't you? Client confidentiality is very important to us."

"Yeah. I guess. Thanks anyway." I hung up, disgusted with myself for not being successful, and even more disgusted that the company indeed had the records of the other people who were with Holly that week, but they wouldn't reveal anything. I wanted to know NOW if Shane Duran or Jonathan Anderson was in a position where one of them could have killed Holly. My brain was still trying to come up with a way to check out my hunch. It was excruciating to have so much pent-up curiosity with no place for it to roam.

I called my lawyer, Leighton Meadows.

"Hi, Mr. Meadows. It's Lark Chadwick."

"Hello, Ms. Chadwick. Are you staying out of trouble?"

"Yes, sir. What have you been finding out?"

"So far, it appears that Mr. Duran does, indeed, have himself a fairly solid alibi. I've spoken with several people who were in a meeting with him during the time Jason would have been killed, so that angle is not looking very good, I'm afraid."

"I've come across some information that might be helpful."

"What have you learned?"

"It's just a hunch, but I think the person who killed Jason may also have killed Lionel Stone's daughter."

"I thought her death was some sort of hiking accident in South America," Mr. Meadows said.

"Right. But there may be a Pine Bluff connection."

"I'm listening."

I told him about what I'd read in Holly's diary.

"That's intriguing," he said.

I explained the problem I was having trying to confirm my hunch that Shane and possibly Jonathan were on the same trip with Holly. "Is there some way you as a lawyer might be able to get access to those records?"

"Yes. Of course. It'll take some time. I'll probably have to get a court order, but it can be done—eventually. Do you have the contact information of the company and the dates of the trip?"

I gave him the information.

"I'll look into it. Thanks, Lark."

Chapter Fifty-Eight

By Thursday, I was getting impatient. I had yet to hear back from Leighton Meadows, plus Lionel was running into roadblocks. Mike Sutherland, his friend in Peru, had been reassigned making it harder for Lionel to extricate the police report from the decrepit Peruvian bureaucracy.

But then I got a call from Heather. She was ready to give me an update on what she learned about Jonathan Anderson's possible connection to Holly. By this time, I was getting claustrophobic. I craved companionship and had a deep need to get out of Pine Bluff. We agreed to meet that evening at a shopping mall on Madison's east side.

The terms of my release from jail required either Lionel or Muriel to be with me, so Muriel tagged along, but, because she said she didn't want to intrude, she kept her distance while Heather and I "shopped."

"Look at these shoes, Lark. Aren't they just to die for?" Heather held up a black clodhopper that looked like something Dorothy's Auntie Em wore in *The Wizard of Oz*.

"Um, it's hideous, Heather," I scowled. "I thought you had better taste than that."

She pouted and put it down. I swear it clunked.

"So, what did you find out from Jonathan?" I asked as we ambled out of the store. The mall was busy, but not crowded.

Heather put a hand to her mouth and began to laugh. She wore a sleeveless pink sheath.

"Okay, what's so funny?" I asked. We stood just outside the door of the shoe store, waiting as a throng of giggling middle school girls passed by.

"Guys are such losers," Heather said.

"Breaking news. What do you mean?"

"All you have to do is crook your finger and they come hither." Her dangling gold bracelets clinked against each other as she demonstrated.

"What did you do?" I asked, alarmed. I was beginning to have second thoughts about the wisdom of dispatching Heather to question Jonathan.

"I called him up at work. Told him I was a hiker and had heard that he's quite the expert."

"What'd he say?"

"He was suspicious at first. Wanted to know where I'd heard that. I made up something."

"Like what?"

"Before calling, I Googled him and saw that he'd written a column about hiking, so I read it in the *MadCity News* archive, then blathered deliriously about it to him."

"Good move. So, then what?" I waited as a young woman passed us holding the hand of her obviously bored boyfriend, then I led Heather across the walkway and took a seat on a bench. Heather sat next to me.

Muriel hovered nearby, window-shopping.

"I figured that I might get more information from him if we met in person," Heather explained, crossing her shapely legs primly, "plus I wanted to be able to better gauge his honesty if I could see his expressions, so I suggested we meet for a drink." She turned to look at me. "I think I purred a lot. Guys get off on that." Subtext: *You should try it sometime, Lark.*

I smiled, wishing I could have seen her in action. "Did you meet?"

"Uh huh. At the Nitty Gritty."

I shot her a worried glance. "He didn't recognize you, did he?"

"I was afraid he might, but I don't think he did. I wore my hair up and wore my glasses instead of contacts."

"And you left my name out of it, right?"

She gave me a look. "Of course."

"So, what happened?

"It's funny. He's shy at first, but I made it seem like I'm a total ditz."

"I'll bet that was some acting job," I laughed.

"Uh huh," she deadpanned, not getting my teasing dig. "Anyway, all I had to do was ask him to tell me about some of the coolest hikes he's been on and he began opening up like a flower. He went on and on. At one point, I think I might have dozed off." She gave me a worried frown.

"Did he talk about the Inca Trail?"

"He raved about it. Said it was so cool. He gave me all kinds of history about how the Spanish basically raped the Inca culture."

"Charming analogy," I grimaced, remembering Holly's diary entry and my own near-rape experience. "Did Jonathan say when he hiked it?"

Heather's ringlets quivered as she nodded. "I'm getting to that. I didn't want to make him suspicious by zeroing in on Holly's trip, so I just let him pontificate for a while. You'd kind of freaked me out when you told me he might have killed Jason, so I have to tell ya, Lark, it was all I could do not to jump out of my skin, but thank God, he did most of the talking."

"Did he talk about any of the people who were on the trip? Did he meet Holly?" I leaned toward her, elbows on the thighs of my jeans.

"He did talk about the people on the trip. Said it was a lot of fun and that he met some interesting people, but he didn't mention Holly by name. He did say, though, that there were some girls on the trip who had just graduated from college. He said they were stuck up and didn't want to have anything to do with him, which, he said, ticked him off royally."

"Did he try to come on to you?"

"Of course! Duh!" She looked offended.

"And?"

"He's cute, Lark, but you had me so spooked."

"How'd you deal with his come on?"

"He asked for my email address."

"Did you give it to him?"

"Let's just say I gave him *an* email address," she giggled. "By now he probably knows that it's bogus."

"But doesn't he already have your phone number from when you called him?"

Heather gave me a coy smile. "I called him from a pay phone."

"Oooo. You're good," I laughed. "So, what's the bottom line on his Inca Trail hike?"

Heather opened the zipper of her straw clutch purse, dug out a slip of paper and handed it to me. "Here are the dates he went on the trip and the name of the travel agency that sponsored the trek."

The dates didn't match Holly's trip. Neither did the company. A dry hole.

"Damn," I said, pounding the bench with my fist.

"What's the matter?" Heather asked.

"Looks like I've hit a dead end. Jonathan Anderson might well be a weasel, but it doesn't look like he killed Holly Stone."

"But did he kill Jason?" Heather asked.

"Good question. I don't know." I chewed on a fingernail and turned to look at Heather. "What do you think?"

She shrugged and used her fingers to tick off her main observations. "He's definitely got jealousy issues...he's got extremely cold blue eyes...and he was really upset with the girls who dissed him."

"What if he got upset with someone who he felt was his rival?" I wondered aloud.

"What do you mean?" Heather asked.

"Do you think his jealousy would lead him to kill Jason?"

"That's hard to say. He doesn't seem like the violent type."

"Neither did Ted Bundy," I frowned.

Chapter Fifty-Nine

Laura and William (a.k.a. "Thor") arrived in Pine Bluff about mid-morning on Saturday. By this time, both Lionel and Muriel had read Holly's references to Thor in her diary, so they, too, were anxious to talk with the Benedicts.

Muriel packed a picnic lunch. As we hiked, I was thankful that the judge's order had allowed me at least some leeway so that a foray to Granddad's Bluff, supervised by Lionel and Muriel, would put me in the middle of nature.

I took deep breaths of the cool, fragrant, spring air, relishing the beauty of my surroundings—and my freedom.

Before the Benedicts arrived, Muriel, Lionel and I had huddled. We decided that more important than the hike—which we all agreed would be good for my mental health—would be the conversation with Thor. (Muriel got Lionel and me to scuttle the word "confrontation" which we'd been using to describe our plan.)

Instead of parking at the foot of the bluff and hiking to the top, we drove to the top and hiked along the trails near Table Rock because it would be less of a strain on Lionel. He'd already had two heart attacks in the past two years, so Muriel didn't want Lionel to get overstressed.

It was a pleasant walk. That is, until we came to the rocky plateau where Jason died. I pointed it out to Lionel and Muriel as we walked past it on our way up to Table Rock. Muriel walked next to me for a bit and hugged me close.

We got to Table Rock about one.

"Wow. The view is spectacular," Laura cried, a cool breeze tousling her wavy dark hair. "Take a look, Thor." She shrugged off her backpack.

"Uh huh." He grunted as he sat down and leaned against a rock to rest.

His long-sleeved T-shirt fit loosely on his lanky frame.

"This is great. Thanks for suggesting it, Lark," Laura said. She was big and brassy, reminding me of Rosie O'Donnell.

Lionel, flushed and breathless, mopped his brow with a red-checked bandana, while Muriel spread out a blanket and began taking sandwiches out of the backpack I'd carried.

"I'll bet there's no comparison between this and the sights you saw along the Inca Trail," I said to Thor, but it was Laura who answered.

"Yes, that's true," she gushed. "It's so beautiful there." She loosened the fleece jacket that had been around her waist and put it on over her dark blue T-shirt.

"Maybe Lionel and Muriel have heard the story of how you met," I said, "but I haven't. Would you two mind giving me the Cliff's Notes version?"

Laura laughed. "Not at all. I love to tell the story."

Thor leaned back against the rock and closed his eyes.

"I was on the Inca Trail hike with my college roommate," she began. "We'd just graduated, like Holly, and thought this would be a fun summer getaway."

"Did you know Holly before the trip?" Muriel asked.

"No. My roommate and I met her the first day. My roommate was the only one I knew before the trip."

"So, did you and Thor hit it off right away?" I wanted to know.

"No. In fact, I thought at first that he and Holly were together."

"Why'd you think that?" I asked.

"Because on the first day of the hike, I saw Thor get into an animated conversation with Holly," Laura replied.

"Do you remember what you and Holly were talking about, Thor?" I asked.

"I forget." He kept his eyes closed and sucked on a piece of grass, his cheeks cadaverous.

"I guess you can chalk it up to my own insecurities, but I thought they were boyfriend-girlfriend," Laura continued.

"Just because they were talking with each other?" I asked.

"No," Laura said. "It was because of the way they were talking with each other. All the pretense and niceties were gone. At first, I couldn't hear what they were saying, but when I got closer it was clear they were having a spat."

"Is that true, son?" Lionel asked Thor.

Thor, his eyes still closed, shrugged.

"Answer me!" Lionel said, sharply.

Thor's eyes snapped wide open in surprise and alarm.

"Lionel..." Muriel admonished.

He ignored her and took a step toward Thor. "What you were arguing about with my daughter?"

"I wouldn't call it an argument." Thor drew out the last word, as if getting ready to quibble about its meaning.

"What would you call it, then?" Lionel pressed.

"Mr. Stone, excuse me, but I don't like your tone," Laura said, her voice brittle.

I spoke up. "Laura, I think Lionel's just very sensitive right now. After all, his daughter died on that trip."

"I know. And I'm sorry about that. But," Laura said, looking back and forth between Lionel and me, "I don't understand why he thought it necessary to speak so sharply to William."

"I'm just trying to learn more about the events leading up to Holly's fall," Lionel said turning to Laura, his voice softening. "It's extremely important to me."

"But we talked about that the last time we were here," Laura said, impatiently. "I'm not sure there's much more we can tell you. Neither of us saw what happened. Holly was alone at the time."

"Was she?" Lionel countered. "Are you sure? Isn't it possible someone saw what happened?"

"As far as we know, she was alone," Laura sighed.

"Are you suggesting I had something to do with Holly's death?" Thor stood up.

"I'm not suggesting anything. I'm asking," Lionel said evenly.

"Is that what you're asking?" Thor challenged belligerently.

"Yeah," Lionel said, his face reddening. "Did you push my daughter off a cliff?" He took two menacing steps closer to Thor. "Did you kill my daughter?" His fists were clenched at his side and he was breathing heavily, nostrils flaring.

Thor stuck out his chin and gritted his teeth. "No. I did not kill your daughter," he snarled, then, more softly, Thor added, "But I wanted to."

"Thor! What are you saying?" Laura turned to her husband, alarmed. "Why would you say such a thing?"

"Because Holly Stone was a slut."

"How dare you—" Lionel put up his fists and lunged at Thor who thrust out his hands protectively and jumped back.

"No!" Laura threw herself in front of her husband, while Muriel and I grabbed Lionel to keep him from hitting Thor.

"Lionel, don't!" I shouted.

He stopped, but his body was tense and ready to spring once more at the slightest provocation. He was trembling with rage.

Thor had an insolent expression on his face, but I could see in his eyes that he was frightened.

Muriel was crying softly. "Lionel. Dear. We need to go about this calmly."

"What's going on here?" Laura demanded.

"Here's the deal," I said. "Since you were here last month, Lionel, Muriel, and I have been reading the diary Holly kept during her trip to Peru."

Thor shifted uncomfortably.

"You're named in it, Thor," I said.

He turned and walked away.

"You are?" Laura glowered at her husband. When he didn't say anything, she turned back to me and asked, icily, "What does she say about him?"

"She says they met in an Internet chat room."

Laura turned and looked at Thor. "What were you doing in a chat room?"

"Chatting." He sat down and leaned against a rock.

"Don't get lippy, kid," Lionel said, "I can still knock your block off."

Thor ignored Lionel and spoke to Laura and me. "It was a hiking chat room. We hit it off. What's so bad about that?" He pulled a long blade of grass out of the ground and began sucking on the end.

"Nothing," Laura answered, "But why didn't you tell me?"

"Why didn't you ask?" he snapped, glaring at her.

"Well, excuse me, but it's not the first question that comes to mind when you meet someone," she said indignantly. "You need to get rid of your attitude, mister, and start telling us what was going on between you and their daughter."

Thor sighed. "Nothing was going on. And that's the problem."

"What do you mean?" Laura asked, her eyes narrowing.

"We hit it off in the chat room. We exchanged emails. She was fun, so we arranged to meet on the hiking trip. But it didn't work out."

"What happened?" I asked.

"She unceremoniously dumped me."

"Is that what you were arguing about?" I asked.

Thor nodded. "I wanted her to give me a second chance, but she wouldn't."

"So, you killed her?" Lionel bellowed.

"No. I told you—I didn't kill her," Thor said, annoyed.

"But you stalked her," I said. It wasn't a question.

He bit his lip.

"Did you stalk her?" Laura demanded.

"Maybe a little."

"A little? What's that supposed to mean?" Lionel challenged.

"I was angry at her because she was mean to me. And rude."

"Not our Holly. She wasn't that way," Muriel said.

Thor gave Muriel a look. "Actually, Ma'am, she was."

"Then she must have had a good reason," Muriel said, her voice steel.

"What reason did she give for dropping you?" I asked.

"She said I misled her."

Me again. "Why did she think that?"

"Because the picture I emailed her wasn't of me. Something like that."

"Well, you can understand why she'd be a little miffed at that, can't you?" Laura asked.

He nodded. "Yeah. I guess. But she hurt my feelings."

"Oh, you poor little baby," Lionel taunted.

"Lionel! Hush now," Muriel said, lightly touching the sleeve of his jacket.

"So anyway," Thor continued, "I just wanted her to know that even though she didn't want to have anything to do with me, I was still going to, shall we say, assert my presence."

"Meaning?" I asked.

"It means that I would make sure that she knew I was around."

"By doing what?" Muriel asked.

"I watched her. And I made sure she knew I was watching her. She'd pushed me aside, but I wasn't going to go away."

"If that's true, then by your own admission, you would have been keeping an eye on her when she fell," I said.

The silence was deafening.

Thor shook his head. "That's when Laura came along."

"What do you mean?" I glanced at Laura who continued to drill Thor with her eyes.

"It means," Thor said, turning to me, "Laura diverted my attention."

Laura smiled sheepishly and shrugged. "When I saw that the relationship between Thor and Holly was over, I saw my chance and so I moved in."

"And she was good at it. I never saw it coming." Thor smiled for the first time.

"What did you do?" I prompted.

"I saw he was hurting, so I, um, comforted him," Laura said, blushing. "And we talked."

"By the time Holly died, I was focused on Laura," Thor said.

"Where were you on the trail when she died?" Lionel asked, looking back and forth between them.

"Thor and I had hiked ahead," Laura answered. "Holly must have lagged behind."

Thor added, "And by this time, other guys were showing interest in Holly, so it was hard to keep track of who she was with and who she wasn't."

"That raises another important question," I said, "who else was on the trip? Can you tell us about them?"

"I can do better than that," Laura said. "I brought the pictures from the trip like you asked, Lark. They're on my laptop." She opened up her backpack and rummaged through it. "Here it is." She pulled it out, opened the lid, and fired it up. She found the file quickly and opened it.

All of us except Thor gathered around.

"Here we go," Laura said. "I'll skip the panoramas and find a good group shot."

"Wait! Stop right there," I said.

Her cursor came to rest on a distinctive rock outcropping.

"Click on that to make it larger," I directed.

She did.

"I've seen that rock some place before," I said.

"I'm sure you have. It's very famous," Laura said. "But it's not just a rock. It's *Huayana Picchu*, the huge mountain that towers over Machu Picchu, the so-called 'lost city of the Incas.' It was the destination of our trek."

Laura babbled on like a tour guide about "high priests" and "virgins," but I wasn't listening. I was trying to remember why the picture had caught my eye and why I had thought of the mountain as merely a rock.

Suddenly, I remembered Shane Duran striking a match on a massive granite paperweight sitting on the desk of his office. The wide base and tapered top of the mountain in the picture looked just like the dark, granite rock on Shane's desk.

When Laura paused to take a breath, I cut in. "Let's find that group shot you were looking for," I said eagerly.

309

Skillfully, she moved her cursor and clicked on a picture. It filled the screen.

The shot showed about a dozen people grouped along a stone trail with steep mountains in the background. Holly stood out from the crowd. She had lustrous yellow hair and a deep tan that made her teeth seem exceptionally white. Thor and Laura stood together on the left side of the group.

I lasered in on the two people flanking Holly.

"Oh my God," I gasped.

Muriel saw it too. I know because she fainted.

Chapter Sixty

Laura and William Benedict returned to their home in Door County later on Saturday. I spent the rest of the weekend huddling with Lionel and Muriel, discussing what should—and could—be done about the damning images we saw on Laura's laptop. She emailed the pictures to me and I forwarded them to my attorney, Leighton Meadows, with instructions that he should share them with Sheriff Olson and the District Attorney's office.

Early Monday morning, Kirk arrived at the newspaper office as I was checking my email.

"Hey there," he called.

"What's up?"

"I brought you something."

I turned to look at him. He stood smiling at my desk holding a paper bag and a covered Styrofoam cup. He held them out to me.

"What's this?" I asked, reaching for them.

"I just realized you can't even go to the Korner Café, so I brought you something to help get your day off to a good start."

"Thanks." I put down the cup, opened the bag and peered inside. "A bagel. How did you know?" I laughed.

"Because you have one every day," he smiled. "And the coffee's got cream, no sugar, just the way you like it."

"You're sweet. Thank you."

He plopped down at the desk next to me and opened his own take-out. "What've you been doing?" He peered over at my computer screen.

"Just going through email."

"Anything special?"

"Mostly hategrams."

"Oh?" He seemed interested. "Anything of a sexual nature?" he leered.

"Stop it. You're beginning to sound like Shane Duran."

He chuckled. "He's definitely a bad influence. What a sleaze ball. I wish we could pin Jason's murder on him."

Before I could answer, Lionel stood up at his desk and loudly cleared his throat. "Gather 'round, everyone. I have something important to announce."

Kirk and I exchanged quizzical looks.

Lionel moved to the center of the room. Muriel pulled up a chair, while Kirk and I remained at our desks.

Lionel coughed again. He seemed more nervous and uncertain of himself than I'd ever seen him before.

Kirk must have noticed, too, because he threw me a questioning what's-up-with-him? look.

I responded with a beats-me shrug.

"The reason I've called you all together is to let you know that I'm getting older," Lionel began.

Muriel chimed in, "Breaking news."

Kirk and I laughed.

"I'm just getting started, hon. Stay with me." Lionel took a hanky out of his back pocket, mopped his brow, and began to pace. "As my age advances, I'm even more acutely aware that my days in journalism are numbered. I always thought I'd live forever."

Was Lionel about to have another heart attack? I shot a worried glance at Muriel. Muriel looked puzzled.

"Anyway," Lionel went on, "I've been doing a lot of thinking about this newspaper and I believe the time has come to officially name an assistant editor. Someone who will carry the torch after I'm gone."

We all shifted in uncomfortable anticipation.

Lionel walked over to his wife and smiled down at her. "Now, I suppose the logical choice is Muriel, my love and soul mate. She and I have discussed this and she agrees that she doesn't know enough about journalism to continue the paper. If I die, God forbid, Muriel says she'll simply sell the paper and write the great American novel."

We laughed.

"However, she made one concession. She says she'd hold on to the paper if I named the right person to carry on after me." He continued pacing.

"Now, who should that be, you ask?" Lionel came to a stop in front of Kirk. Kirk sat forward eagerly.

"Young Kirk here is a logical choice. He's been a great catch and my star reporter. He's done marvelous work on both Landscam and the investigation into Jason Jordan's death. There are many reasons you'd make a good assistant editor, Young Kirk."

"Thank you, sir. It would be a privilege to serve so close to someone I've idolized for such a long time."

Lionel winced. "That's what I was afraid you'd say. You see," Lionel said, moving over to my desk, "I've decided to name Lark as my assistant editor."

Kirk's face fell, then reddened.

Lionel went on. "Lark is…she's like a daughter to me." His voice cracked. "She's the daughter I don't have anymore. She's smart, she's got spunk and, well, I love her."

My ears buzzed. I glanced at Muriel. Tears glistened in her eyes.

"So," Lionel concluded, "Lark is my choice for assistant editor. Congratulations."

He stepped toward me. I stood and he embraced me in a gargantuan bear hug.

Muriel clapped politely. So did Kirk, but his face was slightly contorted, as if the noise of the applause hurt his ears.

"I don't know what to say, Lionel," I said. "I'm overwhelmed."

"Okay. Speech over," Lionel laughed. "Everyone get back to work."

Muriel drifted back to her spot behind the counter.

Lionel put on his trench coat. "I've got to run an errand," he said to Muriel. "I'll be back in a few."

"Okay," she said.

He kissed her on the forehead and left.

I walked over to Kirk who was logging in on his computer. Standing behind him, I put my hands on his broad shoulders.

He stiffened, but continued to type.

"You okay?" I asked. "This is just as much of a surprise to me as it is to you."

He pounded the keys.

"Look. I know you're upset."

He shrugged.

"Let me make it up to you."

Kirk stopped typing. "What do you mean?" He looked at his computer screen, not at me.

I leaned down and whispered into his ear. "Let's run away together."

He turned to look at me. "What?"

"You heard me," I said, my voice low and seductive.

He smiled lecherously. "What do you have in mind?"

"Follow me." I took him by the hand and led him outside. "Get in," I said, pointing at Pearlie.

Chapter Sixty-One

Kirk remained planted on the curb looking dumbly at Pearlie. "Are you sure?"

"Positive." I walked around to the driver's side. "Get in," I repeated.

He opened the door and got in.

I fired up Pearlie and did a U-turn in the middle of the street.

"Where are we going?"

"You'll see." I licked my lips, threw him an alluring glance, and unbuttoned my top button.

"Wh-what about your monitoring bracelet?"

"Do you really think they have someone keeping track of my every move? Get real. They only check that thing if I don't show up for court and they need to find me. We'll be done and back at work before they ever know it."

He leaned back comfortably and touched my arm. "I love it when you're rebellious."

I shot down Main Street and in no time we were winding our way up Granddad's Bluff. I was grateful for the warm, sunny weather.

Kirk squirmed in his seat.

I parked in the lot near Table Rock. "Here we are. Let's go."

"Did you bring a blanket?" he asked.

"Uh huh." I opened the trunk, pulled out a blanket, then grabbed his hand and pulled him eagerly down the trail toward Table Rock. The view was magnificent as we burst through the woods and onto the rock.

"I have to get on with my life, Kirk. This is the best place to do it."

I spread the blanket on the rock and beamed at him triumphantly. "God, it feels good to have some freedom. And illicit freedom is even sweeter than I expected."

"Come here," he said. He opened his arms in a wide embrace.

I hesitated. "Let's savor the moment."

"Let's savor it in each other's arms." He took a step toward me.

I stepped back. "Let's go slowly. Don't you understand that a woman likes to take her time?"

"I've been taking my time. I'm ready. I'm more than ready."

"And you'll still be ready when I am."

"I thought you already were. It was your idea to come racing up here, remember?"

"And now that we're here, what's the hurry?" I laughed. "Do you think I'm eager to get back to being under virtual house arrest? No way. I want to savor this time with you."

I sat down on the blanket.

Kirk dropped his arms awkwardly to his side and sat down cross-legged facing me on the blanket, his forearms resting on his knees.

"Now what?" he asked.

"Let's talk."

Kirk's face fell. "Um, okay… About what?"

"About Holly."

"Who?"

"Lionel's daughter," I said softly.

His eyebrows pinched together. "What about her?"

"You never told me that you knew her."

He laughed. "I didn't know her. That's probably why I never told you."

"And what about Shane Duran?"

"What about him?"

"You never told me you knew him, either."

"What's this all about, Lark? You're getting spooky."

316

"I must say, Kirk, some things are coming together nicely for me, but others are still a mystery."

"What's with you?" He frowned.

"Remember that day when we were both going to confront Shane on the street outside the Korner Cafe?"

"Yeah…"

"All of a sudden you ditched me. Gave me some lame excuse about how you were going to gauge his expression from a distance."

"It wasn't lame, but go on."

"The next thing I know, you're across the street."

"Yeah? So?"

"And then at the press conference…"

"Uh huh…" Kirk stood. So did I.

"You were in the back of the room with your head down," I said.

"Go on." His face was angry, his hands clenched.

"You and Shane had met before, hadn't you?"

"Go on." He flexed his fingers, but stood where he was. We were about ten feet apart.

"As soon as you saw Shane coming toward us on the street, you recognized him, but you didn't want him to see and recognize you. How'm I doing so far?"

"Just fine. Go on." He took a step toward me. The edge of the cliff was a few yards behind me. I stood my ground.

"So, you admit you knew Shane from someplace else," I said.

"I admit nothing, but go on. This is fascinating, even if it is more than a little annoying."

"Annoying in what way?"

"Go on, Lark. I want to hear how this ends."

"Let me connect the dots for you. You met Shane Duran and Holly Stone on a hiking vacation in Peru two years ago."

317

"What makes you think so?"

"I saw the pictures. They were of Holly, but you and Shane were in them, standing on either side of her."

"Go on."

"Shane was coming on to Holly, but his stinky cigars—among other things—turned her off."

"Koenigshavens, uh huh," Kirk grinned.

"How do you know Shane's brand?" I asked.

"Duran bragged about how great they are. You're right. They're awful."

Kirk took another step toward me. I kept my feet firmly planted, but my heart pounded.

"Then you swept Holly off her feet," I said.

"Go on." Eyes gleaming, he took another step.

"But then she cooled toward you."

Kirk started to take another step, but stopped. "It was her dad. He made her drop me," he pouted.

"So you wanted to get back at her dad the same way you got back at your brother so long ago by killing his dog."

"You're good. How'd you know that?"

"I didn't. I guessed. You just confirmed it."

"Go on." He took another step. One more and he'd be able to grab me.

I spoke rapidly. "You killed your brother's dog as a way to make your brother suffer for the favored place he had with your parents, just like you killed Holly to make Lionel hurt. But there's one thing I don't understand."

"What's that?"

"Why did you push Jason over this ledge after luring him up here with your dead-on Shane Duran impression?"

"For all the same reasons," Kirk said, in a how-could-you-be-so-dumb voice.

"What do you mean?"

"I transferred to U.W. Madison so that I could see Lionel's pain after losing his daughter. I never really expected to get a job working for him, so that made it even better. I could watch him hurt up close. And then I fell for you, but you chose Jason over me. So getting rid of Jason was a way to make you hurt."

"You sick sadist," I hissed, a lump forming in my throat.

"And now, by killing you, I can make Lionel hurt some more."

He was about to lunge at me when Carl Olson and Lionel broke through the tree line behind Kirk.

"Police! Hold it right there!" Carl yelled.

Kirk glanced over his shoulder.

Carl's arms were fully extended. He held his service revolver with both hands and pointed it directly at Kirk's head.

Kirk swiped at me, but I dropped onto my back, entwined my feet in his legs and twisted him around and off balance. Kirk toppled backward over me, tumbled onto his stomach, and slid feet first toward the edge of the cliff. Somehow, he managed to grab my ankle.

Desperately, I tried to scramble backward away from the ledge by digging my elbows into the rock, but I couldn't get any traction.

Kirk came to a stop face down, his legs jutting beyond the ledge. He clutched my ankle in a vise-like grip as he leaned his weight onto his left elbow to anchor himself and keep from sliding over the edge.

"Let her go!" Carl commanded. He was next to me now, crouched just to my right, both arms outstretched, his revolver just inches from Kirk's head.

Kirk was breathing hard. He took his eyes off my ankle, looked at Carl's gun, then at Lionel panting directly behind me.

"Don't do this, Kirk," I pleaded, my voice a panicked rasp. "You can get help. You still have a future."

Kirk lowered his eyes and looked into mine. "Things could've been so great between us," he said, his eyes sad.

"You're scum, kid." Lionel spat.

Kirk's face darkened. He shot an angry look at Lionel. "I've made you hurt once, old man. Now I'm gonna do it again." Kirk looked at me. "Let's go, Lark."

With his left hand, Kirk grabbed my other ankle. I felt myself being dragged toward the precipice.

Just then, Carl Olson's gun roared. The top of Kirk's head blew off.

Lionel grabbed me by the arm, but it wasn't necessary—Kirk's hands relaxed as he was blown backward. A few seconds later we heard the thud as Kirk's body hit the rocky plateau 300 feet below us.

Chapter Sixty-Two

Lionel pulled me to my feet and smothered me in a bear hug, while Carl holstered his weapon and walked to the edge to see where Kirk landed. After a moment, Carl shook his head, backed away from the drop off, and came to where Lionel and I stood hugging.

"Lionel explained everything to me on the way over here," Carl said to me, "including how Kirk planted the cigar up here to throw suspicion onto Shane for Jason's murder."

"Right," Lionel said. "He even weaseled that cigar clue into one of his stories just so he could publicly name Duran as a suspect. He lied to me, Carl. He said you and the D.A. were his sources, and I believed him. Geez."

Carl put his hand on Lionel's shoulder. "That's okay, Lionel." Then Carl turned to me, "I've gotta tell ya, Lark, luring Kirk up here was a pretty nervy thing to do. You could have been killed."

I shrugged. "It was a chance I was willing to take. I had to know why he killed Holly and Jason, and I knew I'd never find out unless he told me. And I knew he wouldn't tell me unless he was about to kill me."

I pulled my tape recorder out of the pocket of my jacket. The red light was still on and the tape was still rolling. "And I got him on tape confessing, so I guess that gets me off the hook. You got here just in time. Thanks, Carl."

"I tried to talk her out of it, Carl," Lionel explained, "but you know how stubborn she is."

Carl smiled. "I'm beginning to. I'm just glad that you're innocent of Jason's death, Lark. No hard feelings, I hope."

I shook my head. "You were just doing your job, Carl." I looked up at Lionel. His eyes were damp. "Oh, and Lionel?"

John DeDakis

"Yeah?"

"I've been thinking. I'm gonna call that news director and tell him I'm done being a TV news anchor. Newspapering with you is much more fun."

Lionel let out a deep sigh and pulled me to him. "I love you, kid."

322

Epilogue

Lemme tie up loose ends:

Shane Duran was stripped of his real estate license. Even though what he did was not illegal, the state real estate board considered it unethical. Later, Shane went to prison for bribing a state official.

That state official, Insurance Commissioner John Callahan, was removed from office in a recall election. He, too, went to prison for accepting bribes.

Jonathan Anderson got a job at the *Wisconsin State Journal.* I've heard he doesn't like it, though, because his editors there don't let him get away with the kind of stuff he pulled while at the *MadCity News.* I avoid him.

Lionel agreed to go with Muriel to marriage counseling. I notice they hold hands a lot more these days.

The evening after that little episode between Kirk and me on Table Rock, Lionel and I sat side by side in the studios of WMTV in Madison waiting to be interviewed. A technician clipped a mic to the lapel of Lionel's suit coat. Lionel fiddled with his IFB.

"Here, let me help you," I said, reaching for it. "You nervous?" I asked.

"Nah. I've done this a gazillion times. You?"

"Not really."

"I'm gonna make some news tonight." He smiled at me knowingly.

"Oh?"

"Muriel and I had a long talk last night. Tonight I'm going to announce that I'm giving a million dollars to the University of Wisconsin in Holly's name to endow a chair for archaeology."

"Oh, Lionel. What a wonderful gesture."

"I know," he beamed.

I laughed.

"But it feels good, y'know?"

"I'm sure it does. Hard decision?"

"Giving the money? Nope. I think the hardest part was coming to grips with the fact that Holly just didn't want to go into journalism. I'll always regret the way I pushed her. But maybe this is the way I can make up for that by tangibly acknowledging her passion and giving it a chance to live on through others."

I reached over and squeezed Lionel's arm. "I love you, Lionel."

"Yeah. Sure. Whatever," he sniffed, swiping at his misting eyes.

In our earpieces, we each heard the opening theme music, then that familiar voice:

"Happening Now! She's done it again. First she dramatically solves the mystery surrounding the deaths of her parents. Now, she solves the murder of her boyfriend and her boss's daughter. Lark Chadwick and Pulitzer-Prize winning journalist Lionel Stone are my guests. I'm Wolf Blitzer and you're in 'The Situation Room.' This story is a cliffhanger!"

THE END

About the Author

Journalist, novelist, manuscript editor, and writing coach John De-
Dakis is a former Senior Copy Editor on CNN's "The Situation Room
with Wolf Blitzer." DeDakis, a former White House correspondent,
regularly teaches novel writing online and at literary centers, writers'
conferences, and bookstores around the country and abroad. A native of
La Crosse, Wisconsin, DeDakis now lives in Baltimore, Maryland.
Website: www.johndedakis.com

Excerpt from **Troubled Water** by John DeDakis
A Lark Chadwick Mystery

CHAPTER 1

The lilac sprig I clutched in my right hand had long since lost most of
its spring-fresh scent. Three days earlier, as I began driving from Wisconsin to Georgia, I'd cut it from a lush lilac bush that shaded the graves
of my parents.

I never knew them. They died in a car accident a quarter century ago
when I was an infant. Annie, my father's younger sister, raised me. We
were like sisters. Now, she's buried next to them—and that lilac bush.

Every few miles, I'd take another deep whiff so that spring in Wisconsin would stay with me— and in me—as I drove farther and farther
into the Deep South.

I'd never been to that part of the country before, so I had all kinds of
preconceived notions of what life would be like living "down there."
Actually, I'm ashamed to say I haven't traveled very much at all. So,
after a long heart-to-heart with my friend and mentor, Lionel Stone,
publisher of the *Pine Bluff Standard*, we agreed it was time for me to
leave my reporting job at his paper and spread my wings.

Through Lionel's contacts, I landed a job as a cops and courts reporter at the *Columbia Sun-Gazette*—a daily paper in west central Georgia
about a hundred miles southwest of Atlanta and just across the river from
Alabama. Lionel told me the paper had a reputation for scrappy investigative journalism that led to Pulitzer Prizes for reporters who then went
on to prestigious publications like the *New York Times* where Lionel
recently retired as the paper's National Editor.

"It'll be a good place for you to park for a while, kid, until you're ready to go on to the big time," Lionel had said to me a couple weeks earlier when I was weighing the paper's offer.

Lionel won his Pulitzer in the early 1970s when he was the White House Correspondent for the *Times* during Nixon's presidency. Lionel had also covered the Civil Rights Movement, so he insisted that I stop in Memphis on my way south and tour the National Civil Rights Museum located in the old Lorraine Motel where Martin Luther King, Jr. was assassinated in 1968.

On my drive south, I also made a detour to the King Center in Atlanta to see MLK's tomb, tour the neighborhood where he grew up, and visit Ebenezer Baptist Church where he and his father preached.

About nine-thirty on this Saturday night, I was cruising down I-185 closing in on Columbia, but still in the boonies and having a heck of a time staying awake. I'd had so much caffeine that I was facing the law of diminishing returns—it seemed like the more coffee I drank, the sleepier I got.

To entertain myself, I kept hitting the scan button on my radio to see what kind of nonsense could be strung together by the brief bursts of audio snippets. One particularly amusing string sounded like this:

"Governor Gannon's presidential campaign got a boost today when he won the endorsement of—*[fffftttt]*—JAY-zuss. Thank you, Lord. Thank you, Lord for your—*[fffftttt]*—Dodge Charger. It comes fully-equipped with—*[fffftttt]*— your own personal banker. That's right. I'm here to—*[fffftttt]*—got a line on you, babe, yeah—*[fffftttt]*—I can't get noooo . . . sat-is-FACK-shun. No, no, no—*[fffftttt]*— are you SAVED by the blood of the LAMB?"

After awhile, that got boring, so I called Lionel because I can always count on him to keep my mind energized. We'd been yakking for a few minutes when my bladder began competing for my attention.

"Lionel, if I don't stop this car right now, I'm gonna wet my pants."

"You should've worn a diaper, Lark," he chuckled.

"What are you talking about?"

"Don't you remember the story about the former astronaut who drove cross-country wearing a diaper?"

"That must've been before my time."

"She was in such a hurry to confront the 'other woman'—her romantic rival—that she didn't want to take rest stops, so she—"

"Lionel!" I barked.

"Whuh?"

"I can't talk any longer. I've gotta pull over. Now!"

"Oh, all right," he sighed.

"I'll call you right back."

"Okay."

I hit *end call* on my iPhone and peeled off the interstate at the very next exit—exit 252—Skunk Run Road. On impulse, I turned right at the bottom of the ramp, the hyper-caffeinated urine in my bladder pressing urgently for release.

There were no gas stations or fast food joints. Traffic was sporadic. I needed to find someplace more private. I turned right again at the first road that came along. It was narrow and had no shoulder. Trees and shrubs crowded the pavement. There was no place to pull over.

I pressed on the accelerator and Pearlie, seeming to understand my plight, lurched forward. Pearlie is my yellow VW Beetle. We've been through a lot together.

"I've gotta go, Pearl. Help me out here."

We rounded a curve. Down the road, I saw four pairs of headlights. At first, it looked as though one car was passing another. Quickly, however, I realized the lights weren't moving toward me at all. The four lights looked like two small cars parked side by side on a narrow bridge.

"What the hell, Pearl. Are they about to drag race right at me?" I eased back on the accelerator.

Suddenly, the car lights darted forward, swerving in tandem into my lane.

I hit the brakes and screamed.

For more information visit: JohnDeDakis.com and wherever books are sold.

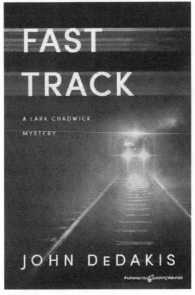

Made in the USA
Middletown, DE
02 July 2022